KILL
THE
HEROES

ALSO BY DAVID AND AIMÉE THURLO

KILL
THE
HEROES

A CHARLIE HENRY MYSTERY

DAVID THURLO

MINOTAUR BOOKS

NEW YORK

This is a work of fiction. All of the characters, organizations, and events portrayed in this novel are either products of the author's imagination or are used fictitiously.

KILL THE HEROES. Copyright © 2017 by David Thurlo. All rights reserved. Printed in the United States of America. For information, address St. Martin's Press, 175 Fifth Avenue, New York, N.Y. 10010.

www.minotaurbooks.com

Designed by Omar Chapa

Library of Congress Cataloging-in-Publication Data

Names: Thurlo, David, author.
Title: Kill the heroes / David Thurlo.
Description: First edition. | New York : Minotaur Books, 2017. | Series:
    A Charlie Henry mystery ; 4
Identifiers: LCCN 2017010854| ISBN 9781250119667 (hardcover) |
    ISBN 9781250119674 (e-book)
Subjects: LCSH: Retired military personnel—United States—Fiction. |
    Iraq War, 2003–2011—Veterans—Fiction. | Veterans—Crimes against—
    Fiction. | Mass shootings—Fiction. | GSAFD: Suspense fiction. |
    Mystery fiction.
Classification: LCC PS3570.H825 K55 2017 | DDC 813/.54—dc23
LC record available at https://lccn.loc.gov/2017010854

Our books may be purchased in bulk for promotional, educational, or business use. Please contact your local bookseller or the Macmillan Corporate and Premium Sales Department at 1-800-221-7945, extension 5442, or by email at MacmillanSpecialMarkets@macmillan.com.

First Edition: August 2017

10 9 8 7 6 5 4 3 2 1

For Marilyn, the light of my life

Acknowledgments

I want to acknowledge the support and guidance given to me by Peter Rubie, my agent. You are greatly appreciated, Peter.

Thanks again to Hannah Braaten, my editor, for all your help in bringing these stories to life.

KILL
THE
HEROES

Chapter One

Charlie Henry felt a gentle squeeze from Ruth's hand and realized he'd zoned out. They were seated in generic metal folding chairs with the other guests facing the newly completed monument being dedicated at Recognition Park. He was half listening as the widely unpopular Albuquerque mayor gave a "brief" speech to the crowd gathered in the small park. Unfortunately the talk had been anything but brief. The smarmy politician had droned on for ten minutes already.

At least it was comfortable out here on the grass, and the sun had set a half hour ago. The event was being held to dedicate the new public park, complete with a large, polished granite monument that honored the local heroes of the community. The mayor needed to pick up the pace, because darkness was approaching and the citizens were getting restless. The event was scheduled to conclude with the "heroes" mingling with the crowd for handshakes and hugs. Charlie felt uncomfortable with the label of hero, or being hugged by strangers—a Navajo taboo—but couldn't find a good excuse for not attending. Besides, it was the perfect opportunity for him to invite Ruth to accompany him on what was phase one of their first date.

The single mother worked at his and Gordon's shop, FOB Pawn, and he'd finally decided the time was right to ask her out. They had plans for dinner once the event concluded, and he was looking forward to having her all to himself.

Charlie hated ceremonies, suit jackets, and ties, but he was in good company, and not just because of the woman beside him. He was in the front row, Ruth at his right, and beside her was Nathan Whitaker, a decorated former army helicopter pilot who now ran a local company dedicated to helping vets find jobs. Behind them, in two more rows, were other honored vets and first responders, including police officers and fire department personnel. They'd all gone above and beyond their job descriptions in serving the citizens of the community. Each of them was with a family member or their personal guest.

The recently established neighborhood here on Albuquerque's west mesa, just south of the city of Rio Rancho, was named Freedom Heights by the opportunistic developers. Freedom Heights had decided to create the park and Charlie had been roped in as one of those being recognized.

His name had been one of the first announced to the gathering, and he'd done the mandatory stand and nod, which was still quite embarrassing. Charlie had been raised as a modern Navajo, with professional parents, but culturally he knew that showing pride and immodesty was contrary to the Navajo Way of his ancestors. Still, the park was a welcome addition to the community, with a field of grass, plenty of trees, and a playground for youngsters.

Finally the mayor concluded his speech, and turned once again to recognize the "heroes." Ruth turned to Charlie and whispered, "Smile, handsome, everyone is taking your picture."

Charlie tried to suppress a chuckle, turning to grin at the beautiful woman who was still holding his hand. Out of the corner of his eye he saw a sudden flash and heard a familiar boom. Realization jump-started his brain in an instant.

"Gun!" he yelled, as two more shots erupted. "Down!" He yanked Ruth toward him as he dove to the grass. "Shooter to the southeast!" he added, knowing there were armed cops among the crowd.

Looking around for a second gunman as he pulled Ruth beneath him, Charlie, unarmed, felt helpless as he heard two more shots whistling overhead. The shouting and screaming made communication impossible, but after a few more seconds the shooting seemed to have stopped.

Whitaker, the chopper pilot, had taken a hit in the chest, center mass, and was slumped back, sliding out of his metal folding chair. Charlie glanced down at Ruth at the same time he reached out to grab the wounded man.

"I'm okay, Charlie," she mouthed, or spoke. It was impossible to hear her.

"Stay flat and play dead!" he whispered, hoping she'd understand. The pause after five rounds suggested that the shooter had a weapon with an old school five-round magazine, and was either out of ammo or inserting another mag. If it was a terrorist attacker, these people rarely stopped shooting until their rage or ammunition was spent.

Hoping the armed officers at the ceremony were already

making a move to locate the gunman, he got to his knees and tried to steady the badly wounded pilot. The woman beside him, who'd been introduced a half hour ago as Whitaker's sister, Janice, was flat on the ground, curled in a fetal position and covering her head with her arms.

Charlie reached out and touched Janice on the shoulder to get her focused. Instead she screamed, inching even farther away. He was straddling Ruth's leg now, but needed to get closer to the wounded man. Maybe he could stop the bleeding. He looked down at Ruth, who nodded and rolled away, allowing him to get next to Whitaker.

The screaming and shouts had died down. "We need some help!" Ruth yelled, looking behind her, where another person was also on the grass, bleeding from a wound in the bicep.

Charlie inched over, still on his knees, and pulled Whitaker flat onto the grass, cradling his head and staring into the man's eyes, which were wide open. The man blinked. "Help," he managed, bloody foam slipping from his lips.

Charlie brought out his handkerchief and began pressing it against the chest wound, which was just a few inches from the victim's heart. He quickly surveyed the scene, noting that the crowd had scattered like baby quail fleeing from a Cooper's hawk.

At least two other people were down, bleeding from wounds or other injuries brought on by the chaos, but they were being tended by those who'd had the courage to stay behind. Purses, hats, and chairs were scattered everywhere, some upright and out of line, others folded, upside down, or sideways.

Suddenly Whitaker's sister came back to life. She sat up, turned around, and saw what had happened to her brother. "Nathan!" she yelled, inching over next to him. She looked up at Charlie, tears in her eyes. "Please, help him."

Charlie nodded, kept pressure on the wound, then caught the eye of an EMT running in his direction, sidestepping and dodging his way past the fallen chairs and personal items on the grass. The medic was carrying a medical kit retrieved from their unit, one of three parked along the street curb.

The EMT was a woman, Charlie realized as she approached, tall, slender, and barely twenty-one. He inched away to give her some room, but didn't take the pressure off the hole in Whitaker's chest.

"At least one bullet wound," he announced as the medic crouched to evaluate the situation. She looked back at the two other victims, one a cop in uniform, the other a fireman.

"This man goes first," she announced. "Keep pressure on the wound until I'm ready, Sergeant Henry," she added, remembering his Army rank.

"Copy," Charlie replied. He saw movement to his right and realized that Ruth had crawled back to the next row of overturned chairs. She was helping the wounded police officer, who'd managed to sit up.

"Okay, get ready to switch. I've got a trauma bandage ready," the EMT ordered, getting his full attention again.

The medic was joined by another on her team, and Charlie was able to stand up and step back. Ruth had also been relieved by a professional, and she wordlessly joined him, slipping her bloody hand into his own. She looked up at him, her face pale with grief.

"What happened? Who was shooting at us?" she whispered.

Charlie shook his head. "The shots came from over there, in

front of those houses." He glanced across the road, which was illuminated by the red and blue lights of at least a half dozen emergency units. "I saw the flash, but it was too dark to see the shooter."

"Maybe they caught whoever it was. I didn't hear anything after the four or five shots," she said. Ruth turned around in a slow circle. "Your friend Nancy must be out there, searching."

Charlie nodded. "She's a good cop, and there's plenty of law enforcement here. Whoever did this was willing to take the risk of getting their instant attention," he added, noting the arrival of several uniformed officers, along with a cop in street clothes, a man he recognized immediately.

"Here comes Detective DuPree," he announced.

"A familiar face, I'm sad to say." Ruth sighed, looking in that direction. "But a good officer."

Charlie nodded, then made room for an ambulance crew, who were pushing a gurney across the grass to where Nathan Whitaker was being tended. The EMTs had already attached an IV with fluids, and were getting ready to transport the man. Whitaker's sister was standing alone, still in shock.

Ruth let go of Charlie's hand and went to comfort the woman, who was shaking uncontrollably. Charlie had seen men struck by bullets more times than he'd like to admit, and in his experience, Nathan Whitaker's life was right on the edge at the moment. If the former captain survived the night, he'd at least have a chance.

Charlie turned and saw that the other two who were wounded appeared to be in much better shape. Both were conscious and sitting up as they were tended by medics. Out in the street, a crime scene van had arrived, and their team was setting up lighting equipment to illuminate what was now a crime scene. He caught the eye of Wayne Dupree as the cop approached, reading the man's grim expression. The experienced officer's tightly clenched jaw told Charlie they hadn't nailed the shooter—at least not yet.

Whatever happened next, Charlie knew it was going to be a long night for the cops—and the witnesses, especially for him and Ruth, who'd been within a dozen feet of all the victims. That dinner date he'd planned was definitely no longer on tonight's agenda.

"Charlie," DuPree greeted, stepping up and holding out his hand.

Charlie shook his head, holding out his bloody hand, palm up. "Better not this time, Detective."

"You get hit?" DuPree asked quickly, giving Charlie the once-over.

"No, this belongs to Captain Whitaker," Charlie explained, glancing toward the wounded man as he was lifted quickly onto the gurney. "I did what I could."

"Think he'll make it?" DuPree asked, his voice lowered now.

"I've seen worse," Charlie responded. "But . . ."

"Yeah," DuPree replied, then quickly turned to the uniformed cop beside him, a sergeant that Charlie didn't recognize. "Go with the EMTs, Kruger, and make sure nothing else happens to the wounded man. Call me immediately if there's any change in his condition."

"Yessir," the sergeant replied crisply, and quickly left to join the wounded and the medical team.

Charlie and DuPree watched silently as Ruth accompanied Whitaker's sister, Janice, to the rescue unit, then waited until the wounded man and the others climbed inside.

"You're with Ruth . . . Brooks now?" DuPree asked. "She's dropped the alias, right?"

"Yeah, she decided to keep Ruth but go back to her maiden name now that her ex is serving life. Makes it a lot easier, though the marshal's service still checks up on her and Rene once a month."

"She's the first person I've met who's actually been in the witness protection program," DuPree commented, watching along with Charlie as Ruth walked back to join them.

"I suppose you want to find out what I observed," Charlie asked, changing the subject.

"You were sitting next to Captain Whitaker?" DuPree asked.

"Actually, I was, Detective DuPree," Ruth volunteered as she came to Charlie's side. She looked up at both men. "And I'm doing okay, so don't worry about me. Not much gets me frightened anymore."

DuPree brought out a small digital recorder. "Okay, let's start by clarifying where everyone was seated, then move on to the moment that anything looked wrong or out of place. Either one of you jump in if you recall anything that might help track down the shooter."

The detective paused and looked around the cluttered park, switching off the recorder with his thumb. "Sweeney isn't here somewhere, is he?"

DuPree was referring to Charlie's Army buddy and business partner Gordon Sweeney, who was usually close by whenever anything dangerous went down. It was clear that the detective respected Gordon, though he found Gordon annoying at times. The two were like oil and water.

"Gordon is with my son Rene at the moment," Ruth said, managing the trace of a smile. "They're at FOB Pawn, supposedly messing around with the business computers. Or, if I know Gordon, more likely the game consoles."

"Hate to say this, but he might have been useful tonight," DuPree admitted. "Okay, let's get back to the facts. "Where was everyone positioned when the shooting started?"

Two hours later, Charlie was seated beside his Irish buddy Gordon, who was driving the two of them to the hospital to check up on the wounded. Charlie also wanted to see if Detective Medina—their friend Nancy—had learned anything about the incident that might provide some information.

Gordon and Charlie had worked on special ops during their four deployments in Iraq and Afghanistan, and though they were civilian shop owners now, they always seemed to end up in the midst of trouble, even here in Albuquerque, New Mexico. Once Charlie realized how close Ruth had come to being shot tonight, he had to know more about what was going on, and if the cops had any leads on the gunman.

"You think Ruth is going to be all right?" Charlie asked, checking his cell phone again to see what the local press was reporting about tonight's events.

"She's with Rene and Gina at her and Nancy's place, and they'll have plenty to talk about once they get the boy to sleep," Gordon reminded. "You know how Gina can make anyone relax."

Charlie nodded. He'd known Gina Sinclair since they'd dated back at Shiprock High School on the Rez, and though Gina had come out long ago and was with Nancy, they were still best friends.

"So Whitaker's sister, Janice, was his plus one, sitting to his right, and Ruth to his left. I think both women were lucky not to have been hit by one of the bullets. You say the shots came from a distance of more than a hundred yards?" Gordon asked.

"Maybe a little more than that. Cops found a fresh .223 shell casing pressed into the ground by a shoe print. It was to the right of a utility pole about that distance away. According to what I heard, that pole was in a direct line of sight to the front row of guests. DuPree thinks the shooter must have braced the rifle against the pole. For someone with skills, it wasn't a difficult shot," Charlie concluded.

"But five shots were fired?"

"DuPree thinks the shooter scooped up the other casings, but couldn't find the fifth before he decided to bail. I saw the muzzle flash from the first shot, and was able to narrow down the shooter's position."

"Makes sense. He was concentrating on getting the shots off before he was discovered. So they have shoe or boot prints?" Gordon asked.

"Yes, but just how clear they are, I have no idea. I'll see what Nancy knows, or at least what she's learned and can share."

"Think she's going to be assigned to the case?" Gordon asked. "She and DuPree make a good team. He's bad cop, she's really bad cop."

"We'll see." Charlie slipped the phone back into his jacket pocket as Gordon pulled his big pickup into the visitors' parking lot of Saint Mark's Hospital. Charlie had changed clothes, not wanting to go out again with his cuffs and sleeves stained with blood.

They were crossing the street, headed for the main entrance of the tall, old brick hospital, when Charlie spotted Janice, Captain Whitaker's sister, sitting with a man on one of the benches beside a flower garden. She was crying loudly, and her companion was cradling her in his arms.

"That's Whitaker's sister," Charlie observed, keeping his voice low.

"Just got bad news?" Gordon replied.

"That would be my guess," Charlie replied. "But she wasn't doing so great before."

"Whatever the case, let's pay our respects as best we can. There are two other victims in there that need some support too," Gordon reminded.

They quickly reached the emergency room counter and learned that Nathan Whitaker's status wasn't available to the public at the moment, but they could take a seat in the waiting room just ahead.

When they walked into the next room, Charlie spotted the APD sergeant that DuPree had instructed to accompany the wounded man and his sister during transport to the hospital. Kruger was on his cell phone, watching an attractive, distraught woman in her mid-thirties arguing with a blond-haired man about Charlie's size, wearing tight-fitting workout clothes.

The sergeant noted Charlie's arrival and shook his head, apparently conveying bad news. Charlie stepped back, waiting for the cop to complete his call, before getting the details.

Gordon, meanwhile, was watching the couple that were arguing, and Charlie tuned in to their low, harsh words.

"It's time to leave, Patricia," the man demanded, grabbing her by the arm. "Nothing you can do for the poor bastard now. His sister will take care of things. Let's go home!"

"Don't touch me, Steven, unless you want to end up in jail again. My business is my own now, and we're done until I see you in court. Leave me alone and let me grieve in peace."

"You ungrateful . . . you're still my wife, and you're coming with me. I've had enough of your—"

"Enough of what, tough guy?" Gordon interrupted, stepping forward within arm's reach of the bully, who was a little older than Gordon but still very fit.

Gordon's tone got everyone's attention, even the nurse behind the desk. Sergeant Kruger slipped the phone into his pocket and crossed his arms across his chest. "Let's calm down, people, before someone steps over the line."

"Then what, cop? You gonna Tase me or some bull like that?" Steven snarled, letting go of the woman and raising his fists.

In the blink of an eye Gordon reached out, grabbed the angry guy's right fist, and pressed down on a key nerve center on the back of his hand. Steven groaned, his legs sagged, and he drew back his other fist and threw a punch.

Gordon slide-slipped the punch, put on the pressure with his thumb, and Steven collapsed to his knees, yelling from the excruciating pain.

"Men who abuse a woman make me angry, you bastard. It's time for *you* to feel the pain," Gordon announced, his voice soft but full of emotion.

Steven groped with his free hand, trying to get hold of Gordon, but Charlie grabbed the man's wrist and twisted it high up behind his back. "Time for you to leave, Steve."

"Like the rhyme. Nod if you understand, asshole," Gordon added.

The man cursed, struggling for a moment, then yelled out again in pain. Finally, seeing two security guards standing by the cop, who now had his Taser out, Steven nodded.

Charlie and Gordon released their grip on the man, and he stood, shaky at first, then straightened up and strode stiffly to the exit. He walked out of the hospital, never looking back.

The woman Steven had called Patricia sat back down in a chair, her arms clinched tightly across her chest, trying to stop her shaking.

Charlie stepped forward, realized he had no idea what to say, but finally managed a question. "I'm sorry for all the trouble, ma'am. Are you related to Nathan Whitaker?"

The woman nodded. "Nathan was my first husband, but we had reconciled. We were planning on getting back together after my divorce. Now he's dead," she added, finally looking up at Charlie.

Charlie glanced over at Sergeant Kruger.

"Mr. Whitaker died several minutes ago," Kruger replied. "This lady and his sister Janice were called in as last rites were given."

"I'm Patricia Azok, at least until Steven signs the divorce papers. Nathan was the love of my life, and I wish I could have been with him tonight. I made a terrible mistake letting him go. You've seen who I ended up with."

"A pig," Gordon mumbled, then he looked over at Charlie, disgust turning to curiosity.

"Did Steven know you planned to get together again with your ex?" Charlie asked.

"Yes, but that was after I'd kicked him out of the apartment. Steven is cruel, possessive, controlling . . ." Patricia started to shake again, more angry than afraid now.

"Excuse me, I need to make a call," Sergeant Kruger said, stepping away and bringing out his phone.

"Where were you when you heard about the shooting, ma'am?" Gordon asked the woman.

"Were you with Steven?" Charlie added, following in the direction his pal was taking.

"I was at my apartment, and I heard about the shooting from a news bulletin on TV. I drove here, met up with Janice, and then waited with her. Both of us were praying for Nathan."

"And Steven? When did he show up?" Charlie asked.

"He was in the waiting room when Janice and I came back out. After . . ." She started with the tears and crying again, so Charlie and Gordon waited, exchanging glances.

Finally Patricia calmed down, looking up at them. "He followed me here, is that what you're thinking?"

Charlie nodded. "Was he with you anytime today?"

"No. Not unless he was watching my apartment. After he hit me and I had him put in jail, I got a restraining order against him. If he was anywhere near me that would be a violation," she pointed out.

"A piece of paper won't always be enough to keep an abusive husband or boyfriend away," Gordon interjected. "The guy knew about your plans to get together with Nathan again?"

Patricia nodded. "Steven blamed Nathan for our breakup."

Charlie thought about his next question for a moment, then saw that he now had Sergeant Kruger's undivided attention, so he decided to ask. "Does Steven Azok own any firearms? A rifle maybe?"

"Of course, and pistols too. He's a member of Firearms for Patriots and belongs to a local gun club. But, you don't think Steven killed Nathan, do you?"

Chapter Two

"I'm passing this new information along to Detective DuPree," Kruger announced. "Then I'm going to make sure Mrs. Azok gets home safely," he added. "Thanks, guys."

While Kruger was back on the phone, Gordon and Charlie introduced themselves to Patricia. Then they exchanged phone numbers and she thanked them for their support. When she and Sergeant Kruger left, Charlie asked the nurse at the counter for information on the two other victims. Even if they couldn't visit the wounded police officer and fireman, Charlie wanted to check on their condition and offer his support to the families.

A half hour later they were in Gordon's pickup, heading back to Gina and Nancy's home. Charlie was describing the brief meeting he'd had with the families of the two men while Gordon had been talking to other first responders who'd also come to express their support.

"None of the friends and relatives had been able to communicate with the wounded for more than a few minutes. They'd been sedated after treatment. The good news is that both men are expected to recover completely, the bad news is that neither of the guys, so far, have been able to add to what we already know. I'm sure that early tomorrow morning APD is going to be all over them with questions," Charlie explained.

"You think that the wounded just happened to be in the line of fire and were collateral damage? That whoever the shooter was—Steven Azok—came to take out his rival?" Gordon asked.

"Well, there was no attempt to take out as many people as possible—the usual terrorist tactic. All the shots were clearly directed toward a target around the center of the front row, which included Ruth and the dead man's sister."

"And you," Gordon reminded.

"Ruth and I were lucky, that's for sure."

"You aren't just lucky, you have skills and instincts. But I was really impressed with how you said Ruth handled herself. She's quite a woman."

"Sure is. As soon as the shooting stopped, she worked her way back to help the others, then took charge and worked to comfort the sister."

"You both are fighters. She just might be the woman you need in your life."

Charlie smiled. He should be so lucky.

It was seven thirty the next morning when Charlie stepped into the small office of FOB Pawn, "FOB" standing for "forward observation base" in military terms. Jake Salazar, their other employee, and Gordon were already seated, drinking coffee.

"Morning, other boss," Jake greeted. "Sounds like you and Ruth had a scary first date."

"In other words, it was just like another day at work," Gordon acknowledged.

"That would be funny if it wasn't so true," Charlie said, then groaned, recalling the situations in the past two years, when they'd all been in a world of hurt.

"Is Ruth coming in today?" Gordon asked.

"I suggested she take the day off when I drove her and Rene home last night, but she said that work was the kind of therapy she needed right now. She also didn't want to worry her son," Charlie said.

"There she is now," Jake announced, looking up at the section on the surveillance monitor that displayed the alley camera viewing field.

Charlie watched as Ruth hurriedly climbed out of her white Camry, grabbed her purse, and then nearly ran up the steps. As she came into the office, key still in hand, she waved to the three men.

"Turn on the news, boys, you won't believe this!" she exclaimed, nearly out of breath.

Gordon turned on the nineteen-inch television sitting on a shelf. He scrolled through channels until he found a "breaking news" report on a network morning show. They listened in silence as a local reporter, standing on the sidewalk outside the downtown Albuquerque federal building, began to read a prepared statement.

"This morning at around 7 AM an employee at Foraker Middle School in Albuquerque's north valley discovered a large envelope attached to the main gate of the facility. Printed on the outside of the envelope were the words 'Attention: Police Department.' Although the exact contents of this envelope have not been disclosed, law enforcement agencies have revealed that a message inside contained threats that may be connected to last night's deadly shooting at the Recognition Park dedication ceremony. It cannot be confirmed that yesterday's cowardly ambush is an act of terrorism, but authorities are asking that anyone who has information concerning this attack, or the placing of this envelope at Foraker Middle School, contact law enforcement agencies immediately."

When the bulletin ended, Gordon put the broadcast on mute.

"So they're calling this a terrorist attack? Here in Albuquerque?" Jake was the first to speak.

"Well, the targeting makes sense, I guess, shooting at those Americans who have been labeled heroes, and at a very public event," Charlie said. "This certainly gets everyone's attention."

"Whoever placed the envelope was smart, going low-tech and avoiding any chance of an electronic trace," Gordon pointed out. "I doubt any cameras at the school got any usable images that far from the buildings. But maybe someone driving by saw something . . ."

"Whatever was written must have sounded genuine, otherwise I don't think the authorities would have released this to the media so soon. Apparently there are no suspects yet, so it's possible there may be future attacks," Ruth said. "We're still in danger—"

"Hey, check this out," Gordon interrupted, turning the sound up on the TV as the image shifted to a breaking news header.

"We've got company, people," Jake announced, pointing to the surveillance monitor. An unmarked police car was pulling into one of the parking slots in the alley.

Gordon looked over, then turned the mute back on the TV. "That's Nancy. This can't be good."

Charlie stepped over and opened the door just as Nancy walked up the steps to the small platform, that served as a porch and loading dock. "Detective Medina. You're here on business, I'm guessing."

The thirty-year-old officer, dressed in civilian slacks and a matching jacket, had the looks and shape of a model, but the intelligent eyes of a smart cop—and a pistol at her hip. She held onto the open door and motioned Charlie back toward the office. "You and your staff are following the news, I see," she said, walking with Charlie over to the entrance to the office cubbyhole, now crowded.

"There's a lot more happening than what we've seen and heard, isn't there?" Gordon suggested.

"That's one of the reasons why I'm here, guys. Charlie, you're probably on the shooter's list—if this really was a terrorist attack. You too, Gordon. I know you weren't there, but your name was on the guest list that was published in the local newspapers," Nancy warned. "Homeland Security and the Bureau have come on board. All the major news networks already have their reporters hounding every law enforcement agency in the metro area."

"Sounds serious," Charlie replied. "Do the experts think this was a lone-wolf attack? One shooter?"

"And were any bombs or explosives found around the park?" Jake asked.

"No. The only real evidence we have at the time is the single .223 shell casing and two recovered slugs. One came from the deceased, and the other from the fireman's upper arm. The rounds are apparently surplus military issue, years old," Nancy said.

"That ammo could have been purchased almost anywhere. Not much help unless the weapon is found," Gordon said.

"In addition to the slugs, we have ejection marks on the casing. The FBI lab is working to determine the weapon used," Nancy confirmed.

"The news reports didn't indicate exactly what was said, only that there might be more attacks. Did you see the message itself?" Ruth asked. "What can you tell us?"

"I got permission to show you and Charlie the details, but it's being kept from the press for the moment. This afternoon, I've been told the content will be released, and I'm guessing that the entire country will go ballistic. So don't let anyone else know what I've shown you until it becomes public. You all willing to go along with that?" Nancy said, bringing out her smartphone.

They all nodded. Nancy swept an image into view, and turned it around so they could all see the display.

"'We will kill the American dogs you call heroes. Know that this is only the beginning,'" Gordon read. "Pretty clear photo of the ISIS black flag, but taken somewhere in the Middle East. Looks like the image was a screen grab."

"No slogans, except what's printed below the flag. Short and to the point. Is this it?" Charlie asked.

"Yes. Just two typed sentences and their banner, printed on a single piece of generic computer paper. The techs are working to determine what brand of printer was used. That won't help much either, not until we find the printer," Nancy said.

"If this was an actual terrorist attack and not a jealous

husband who decided to shoot his competition, does that mean Steven Azok is in the clear?" Charlie commented.

"I interviewed Azok late last night at his apartment, Charlie. He claims he was at his place, working out with his weights. No alibi that can be verified, unfortunately," Nancy said. "It turns out Azok has three registered firearms, a pistol and two rifles. None of them is a .223."

"Azok wouldn't use a weapon that could be traced to him. Not unless he's an idiot as well as a coward. The guy could have bought the murder weapon and ammo out of some guy's trunk at a gun show parking lot," Gordon said. "Or on the street. If he does have some shooting skills, this terrorist angle could be a smoke screen."

"Good point. From everything I've seen or heard about this kind of assault, they're usually carried out by suicidal maniacs who come out blasting, using large magazines that can spray twenty or more rounds at a time without reloading," Jake said. "They're ready to die, and are usually strapped with explosives to set themselves off when confronted."

"This does suggest a lone-wolf, do-it-yourself attack with no outside support or budget," Charlie said. "Until assault-type weapons became available everywhere in the country, almost all center-fire rifles, except for a couple of World War Two weapons, were limited to five rounds. That's all that were fired last night. Maybe the guy saw he scored some hits, but didn't have time to reload with armed cops already moving in his direction."

Nancy nodded. "Well, whoever the shooter was, radical or not, he wasn't suicidal. There were no religious epithets, war cries, or explosive vests. Those of us who were armed reacted quickly to what was clearly an active shooter situation. As soon as the first two shots were fired, I jumped out of my seat and moved in the direction Charlie indicated. I had to circle around some vehicles to get there, but I reached his likely position in less than thirty seconds. He got off five shots in about that many seconds, then split. Clearly this guy intended on making his escape."

"So he could do it again today, or tomorrow? Three people were shot, one killed. And he's still out there, waiting for the next opportunity. If this warning means anything, we already know who his next targets might be. What can we do about a sniper, Charlie?" Ruth asked, touching him gently on the arm.

"Avoid getting out in the open unless you're on the move, and stay away from windows and doorways," Nancy offered. "Charlie and Gordon are trained to watch for threats like this."

"So now what?" Charlie asked.

"I'm supposed to stay close to you guys until we get a better handle on what the situation is," Nancy answered.

"Then let's try a little investigating at the same time. I want to keep the shooter guessing on where I'll be next. Can we go back to the park and take another look around in broad daylight? You've still got officers working the area, right?"

"DuPree is there now, and I think he'd like an expert witness's take on what went down last night. Getting away from here for a while might be a good idea anyway, Charlie. The press will come looking for you now that word is out, and the less they show your face the harder it'll be for a potential sniper to identify and target you," Nancy said. "Worse-case scenario, of course. How about you, Gordon? Can you get away for an hour or so this morning, maybe do the driving for Charlie?"

"I guess, at least for a while. I'm working on something new here in the shop, but as long as I'm back in a few hours it should work out. Can you guys handle things if we take off until, say, ten thirty?" Gordon asked, looking from Jake to Ruth.

"Ruth?" Jake asked.

"Of course. And you'd better get going," she added, pointing to the monitor. "Check the sidewalk camera out front."

A local TV station's van had just driven up to the curb.

"Follow me, guys," Nancy said, nodding toward the back door.

Nancy drove north in her unmarked vehicle, Gordon following closely in his big pickup with Charlie riding shotgun. Both had their concealed carry beneath light jackets.

They crossed the Rio Grande on the Paseo del Norte Avenue bridge and within fifteen minutes Gordon pulled up to the curb that defined the grassy, egg-shaped park. The lawn was about the size and shape of a high school athletic field.

Unable to find a space near Nancy in the line of official-looking vehicles, mostly marked and unmarked law enforcement units, Gordon had to circle the park to find a spot on the opposite side. Cars and trucks of all shapes and sizes surrounded the park and the adjacent streets, and more than a hundred civilians were congregating at the west end of the park, outside the restricted area. That section, halfway across the big lawn, had been delineated by yellow crime scene tape. Flowers lay scattered along the boundary, accompanied by lit candles of various sizes, most of them in glass jars.

As Charlie climbed out of the pickup, he noted that several folding chairs had been set up in what appeared to be their positions last night before the attack. Gordon came up beside him, and they crossed the grass and met Nancy at the halfway point, ducking under the tape.

"That where you and the victims were seated?" Gordon asked.

Charlie took a careful look at reference points, including the monument, then nodded. "I'm guessing that they're hoping to re-create the scene and get a better idea of how things went down." He'd already identified a cop who was standing in the front row, looking off to the southeast. It was Detective DuPree, this time in a light blue APD windbreaker instead of his weary, checkered sports jacket.

"Looks like a crowd is gathering." Gordon glanced over his shoulder toward the west end. "Now that there might be a terrorist angle, this is going to be an unfortunate attraction for a while." He stopped and looked up at the ten-foot-tall, foot-thick, polished granite monument shaped in the roughly square outline of New Mexico, pegged on the bottom left. Carved into the sides were terms and expressions used to describe those who put their lives on the line—patriot, first responder, Marine, soldier, sailor, medic, police officer.

"Today that slab of granite reminds me more of a tombstone," Nancy commented sadly. "I wish I'd caught up to that bastard last night. Every hour this event is in the news there's someone overseas cheering about the death of another American."

"This guy is living on borrowed time, and if someone was working with him, they're both going down," Gordon replied, catching up to Charlie and Nancy.

DuPree nodded to them as they approached. "Thanks for coming back, Charlie. I wanted to get your confirmation regarding the location of the chairs last night, and the victims. I've been tracing the shooter's field of view based upon where we found the .223 brass. Check it out and give me your feedback."

Charlie took a quick look around. There were colored and numbered flags on wires stuck into the grass identifying the location of victims, blood, and the position of chairs and other items after the shooting had occurred. "Okay if I sit down to re-create my field of view?"

"If that helps," DuPree replied.

When he and Ruth had been led to their seats in the front row, he introduced himself and Ruth to those already there, including Captain Whitaker and his sister, Janice, to his right, in the seats beyond Ruth. To Charlie's left had been Olivia Benevidez, an APD police officer who'd been shot a year ago while attempting to arrest a drug dealer. Her husband, a private school teacher, had been seated in the next chair over.

Choosing the seat he believed was in the same position during the ceremony, he sat and looked to his two o'clock, southeast from where he was facing. Across the park, beyond the street, were houses in a row, and in the space between properties, he saw a red flag on a wooden post, and a utility pole within a few feet. An officer was standing beside the pole, looking in his direction.

"The red flag is in the right position, or very close to it, as I recall. That's where I saw the muzzle flash. I'm ninety percent sure that's where the shooter was positioned. It looks to be about a hundred and twenty yards, give or take."

"A hundred and twenty-five, to be precise. Good estimate."

"Not a difficult shot, assuming the weapon was equipped with a scope, and there was still ambient light here in the park."

"Agreed. You didn't get a look at the shooter, is that correct?"

DuPree asked. "Not enough for any description, even a general height, weight, or like that?"

"No, the sniper was in deep shadow, and the sun had already gone down. It was essentially dark at that location. I do recall seeing the pole from the flash when the second round was fired. It was to the left of the shooter, probably."

"That makes sense. We also found a nail driven about an inch into the wooden pole forty inches off the ground," DuPree added.

"A rest for the rifle to steady the aim of a right-handed shooter?" Gordon suggested.

"Based upon the position, that makes sense," Nancy said. "We believe the shooter was kneeling, Gordon, and not a little person. That confuses the actual height of the shooter."

Gordon frowned at Nancy, who was six inches taller than him.

"The attack took some planning," Charlie said. "I can't help but believe that the shooter had a specific target in mind, at least for the first one or two rounds."

"But two more people were shot."

"The man who died was only struck once, then the shooter switched targets," DuPree pointed out. "That supports the theory that the shooter wanted to kill more than one person, which goes to support the terrorist claims that we read in that letter."

"An attack by a very careful terrorist, then, but not a trained sniper. With a limited-capacity, old-school magazine—five rounds—if that's what it was, then hitting a target sixty percent of the time isn't that bad," Gordon confirmed. "By the time the third round was fired, everyone was diving for cover. That's how it went down, right?"

"Yeah," Charlie said, turning around to look in the second row, then back at the flag in the distance. "Those guys back there, they were seated pretty much in line with the captain."

"Looking from where the shooter was, the field of fire was pretty limited. Even with a twenty or more round magazine, he could have only taken out a maximum of four to five people in the front row, the captain, his sister, Ruth, Charlie, and the lady cop, Officer Benevidez. Plus those seated behind you and to your left, Charlie," DuPree said.

"So did the sniper's position determine the targets, or did the target determine the position selected by the sniper?" Gordon asked.

"Either way, if killing one of the heroes was the objective, the attack succeeded," Nancy said. "We have to . . ."

The sound of an amplified voice coming from the west end of the park drowned out the rest of her comment.

"We are under attack, fellow Americans," came the angry words. The cheers and shouts from the crowd echoed across the park.

"That's Ed Humphrey, the state senator," Gordon said, "the mirror image of an Islamic extremist. This is his district, isn't it?"

"Yeah, and he's up for reelection," Charlie commented. "I'm glad he's on our side . . . kinda. Humphrey says exactly what the undereducated want to believe, and they follow him like ants to sugar."

"If this attack was really the work of a lone-wolf terrorist and not some local nutjob, old Ed is certainly going to get more traction, even among the moderates. Targeting the heroes who've gone the extra mile for community and country pisses off all Americans," DuPree said.

"The people who hate America can't beat us this way," Gordon affirmed.

"Or on the battlefield. But attacks like this will continue to fuel the fight between the political parties, where power and partisan control trumps unity," Charlie said. "Hopefully this won't all blow up in our faces. Our politicians feed on these incidents."

"Agreed. Not even freedom of speech is free anymore. But enough of that. Today we need to close our ears to the posturing and just do our jobs," Nancy replied. "Hunt down this killer before he strikes again."

"God's ears," Gordon said.

DuPree suggested that they walk over to where the shooter was positioned to get a quick look from that perspective, and see if any new ideas or insights came to mind. Five minutes later, they'd merely confirmed what was already known. Charlie, having observed with a chill that Ruth had been in the center of the field of fire, decided to look in other directions, trying to determine how the sniper had escaped.

He turned and looked into the graveled alley behind the location. It ran parallel to the street on this side of the park, dividing the block of new, middle-class homes along the rear of each property. Only a few had any kind of fencing, mostly split cedar walls standing six feet high that gave backyards some privacy. The houses on either side of the shooter's position had chain-link fencing, about four feet high. The residence to the left of the pole was unoccupied, with a FOR SALE sign out front in the dried-up lawn. The area around the utility pole and down the alley in each direction for the length of both lots had been blocked off by more yellow tape.

"Did you get any vehicle tracks or find any residents who saw what the shooter was driving?" Gordon asked, also taking in the scene.

"Only tire impressions in the gravel," Nancy answered. "There were a few spots farther down the alley toward the intersecting streets where actual tread marks were photographed, but we don't even know if the shooter was parked along the alley or came in on foot."

"We interviewed the residents for this block, and those in the next block in both directions, and nobody recalls a vehicle in the alley. Of course most of them were in the park watching the dedication ceremony," DuPree said.

Gordon looked at the space between the houses opposite the park. "The shooter could have parked a block farther south, east or west side, then approached, headed north, between these two buildings. Neither house has a window facing toward their neighbors."

"But how do you hide a rifle, walking down the street?" Nancy asked.

"A carbine, placed in a golf bag, maybe?" Charlie suggested. "The new municipal course is just three blocks west of here, right?"

"Or maybe the car was parked along the curb, one street over, and everyone was focused on the events in the park," Gordon ventured.

"And it was getting darker by the minute," Charlie said.

"Guys, we had officers roaming the neighborhood all last night and this morning, trying to find anyone who saw or heard anything useful. Some of the homes have security cameras, and the images for the past week are going to be examined. The park dedication was well publicized, so the terrorist, or whoever, had days to come by and survey the site, making plans on where to position themselves. Depending on how and where the guests were seated, the shooter probably had a backup plan. My people have been checking all around the neighborhood, trying to find out if any strangers had been seen walking the sidewalks or alleys," DuPree commented. "If anyone saw anyone, we'll at least have some potential suspects."

"What if the shooter was a local, maybe even someone over there in that crowd?" Gordon asked, pointing toward where the politician was speaking.

"It'll be harder then, or maybe easier. We're going to find out who, in this area, may have immigrated from one of the trouble spots in the Middle East or Africa. Or who traveled to, say, Turkey, within the past year or so," Nancy said.

"Or what if the shooter was the ex-husband all along, and he's managed to mislead the investigation? What if this is simply jealousy?" Charlie asked.

"Then we'll have to sort all that out ASAP," Nancy responded. "Before the crap hits the proverbial fan."

"Exactly, which means we have to get back to work. Thanks for coming over and sharing what you know, guys," DuPree said, turning to walk back toward the park. The others followed.

"I've arranged for an increase in patrols on the streets near your shop, Charlie. You and Gordon need to behave as if there's a sniper out there with you on his list. Keep a low profile," Nancy added as they stopped at the curb to wait for a KOB-TV van to pass.

As they stepped up the curb onto the pea-graveled walking

path that circled the park, uniformed officers were taking down the crime scene tape. The numbered markers and chairs had already been removed, and a few people were moving the flowers and candles that had been placed beside the barrier over to the base of the stone monument.

Reporters from at least two TV stations were standing by as their camera crews filmed the activity, and the crowd that had been gathered around the state senator was passing across the path Charlie and Gordon were taking. The guys decided to wait until the gathering reached its destination.

"Here comes another speech," Charlie commented as Senator Humphrey positioned himself in front of the monument, in exactly the same position where the mayor had stood last night.

"Hey, you're Sergeant Henry, Charlie Henry, aren't you?" an overweight Anglo man in slacks and a camo jacket yelled out, stepping away from the crowd toward Charlie. "You were here last night, nearly got shot by that diaper head, right?"

"So you saw the shooter?" Gordon asked, a touch of sarcasm in his tone.

It didn't register with the man. "No, but crap, didn't you hear the news? Damned Muslim left a note at some school taking credit. Said they're just getting started. We've got to run those people out of here once and for all, then nuke Syria or wherever the hell they're hiding."

"You think Senator Humphrey has a plan?" Gordon ventured.

"Damn straight. We've got to kick ass, not just take names. Too bad you didn't kill them all over there in Afghanistan, soldier." He looked at Charlie, waiting for a response.

"You serve, pal?" Charlie finally asked.

"Wish I coulda. Bad back kept me outta the Army. But I'm well-armed, and if any of them A-rabs show up on my street I'm going to smoke them quicker than shit. Thanks for your service, Mr. Henry," he added, holding out his hand.

Charlie took it reluctantly, limiting the shake to a light squeeze. "Thanks. Just keeping it real, sir. Seriously."

The man nodded, then turned away toward the crowd and ducked his head as the senator started his presentation with a prayer.

Charlie motioned to Gordon. "Let's get the hell out of here before anyone else spots me. I'm not in the mood."

"Yeah, and if they're all intellectuals like Beer Belly, you're outmatched anyway," Gordon said. "The further they are from reality, the tougher they talk."

"Fortunately most Americans can still think for themselves, Gordon. I'm just hoping we've seen the last of the shooting."

"The only thing that's going to settle things down again is catching the sniper."

"Yeah. Especially if he's really out to kill the heroes. You could be next, pal," Gordon said, glancing down the long line of vehicles waiting beside the park as they approached his pickup. "But don't worry, I've got your back."

"And I've got yours," Charlie responded, then he took a look back at the crowd listening to the politician. "But what about Dawud Koury?"

Chapter Three

"Hadn't thought of him, but you're right," Gordon responded. "He and his family live just a few miles north of here. But they're Christians."

Dawud Koury had been their local interpreter in Afghanistan, and had accompanied them on most of their operations. The man had risked the safety of his own family to save their lives in more than one violent encounter, and they, in return, had helped him and his family immigrate to the US. Dawud, his wife, and their two children were now US citizens, attempting to assimilate.

"They'd be dead by now if they hadn't been allowed to enter the US," Charlie said. "Last time I was in their shop, he and his wife were keeping a low profile after vandals had done some damage to the place."

"The same thing happened to the Japanese Americans during World War Two," Gordon reminded.

Charlie nodded. "Let's go back and listen to what Humphrey has to say. Maybe he's going to think before he speaks this time."

"Yeah. But keep an eye out for unicorns," Gordon said.

When they arrived, the state senator was talking about the guests at the ceremony, focusing on those who'd been shot. Charlie listened as Humphrey described how Captain Whitaker had landed his Army helicopter under heavy ground fire more than once to recover wounded soldiers and Marines. Whitaker and his crew had received commendations on three different occasions. Just over a year ago, Captain Whitaker, now a civilian, had created a local company called Back Up. The specialized employment agency found jobs for vets, locating sources for full-time and temporary work in a variety of positions around the metro area. Back Up temps worked mostly day labor, construction, clerical, and delivery work, Humphrey explained.

Microphones had been set up on a metal stand, and Charlie knew that Humphrey's words were going to be broadcast nationwide before the day was over.

Before long, Humphrey began to speculate on the attack, adding that if a local Muslim or other radical was indeed the shooter, everyone should be vigilant. It could happen again, and the shooter might be one of their neighbors, someone secretly full of hate for America.

"Here's where it's going to hit the fan," Gordon whispered to Charlie, standing next to him.

"You can't trust those ragheads," came a shout that sounded like the same guy who'd encountered them earlier. "Send them back home along with the wetbacks!"

Cheers and shouts erupted from the crowd, along with several boos as well.

"Let's not resort to insults, sir!" said Humphrey. "We're better than that. But I understand your anger."

"Hypocrite! Does every fool in the state support your racist policies, Senator?" came another loud voice.

Immediately there were cheers, boos, then even more shouts. Ahead, Charlie could see pushing and scuffling, and then two burly men in suits broke free from the crowd. They were hauling away a tall, slender teenager by his arms, half carrying, half dragging the youth, who appeared to be dark-skinned. People cheered as he was led across the street, then he and the security people disappeared from view behind the cars.

Charlie turned to Gordon. "Heard enough?"

"Yeah, let's get back to the shop. It looks like Dawud's produce market is in for a rough week. I'm going to give him a call."

By the time they reached FOB Pawn, Charlie had warned their friend about potential harassment and vandalism headed his way. His wife, Jenna, always wore a headscarf that usually identified her as belonging to another culture, even though she was a Catholic. Dawud thanked Charlie for his concern, and promised to be very watchful for troublemakers. He also advised Charlie and Gordon to be alert and protect themselves if there was a terrorist in the community.

When they arrived at the shop Charlie took a long look down the alley and along the roof line of the adjacent buildings, grabbed his keys, then, along with Gordon, moved quickly to the door and let themselves in.

Ruth and Jake were in the front of the shop, taking care of

customers. Both glanced their way. Jake nodded, and Ruth smiled, waving slightly with her fingertips as Charlie and Gordon walked into the main display area.

"Time to give these two a break, Gordon," Charlie said softly to his pal, making sure the pistol at his belt was still hidden beneath his jacket.

"Copy. Once they're finished with their customers we can send them to an early lunch," he said, checking the clock on the wall opposite the front register. "Maybe they can bring us back a sandwich and we can get some serious work done this afternoon."

It was fifteen minutes before closing time. Jake and Charlie were looking at the various locks they had available for sale, almost all of them sturdy padlocks. Ruth and Gordon were in the office, making sure the inventory was current on the new online site, which they'd named FOB OK. This service, a marketing idea conceived by Gordon, listed one-of-a-kind items that were available for sale to the first customer who came in to make the purchase. The customer could put a hold on the item also for a short period of time, if they'd already agreed on a price.

"Dawud wanted the strongest padlocks he could find, keyed alike if possible," Jake explained as they looked through the inventory of fifteen or so locks in the plastic bin.

"For the business, not his home, right?" Charlie asked. "If I recall, the only keyed-alike locks we have are light duty, or those two deadbolts over there."

"He needs them for hasps on cabinet doors, to secure the outside fruit and vegetable bins along the storefront," Jake explained. "It looks like he's going to have to settle for two keys, unfortunately."

He brought out two massive Master locks with hardened shackles and pry-resistant mechanisms. The keys were taped to the locks.

"These should do the trick. Any stronger locks and a determined thief would force the doors with a pry bar," Charlie said. "He's more worried about vandals than thieves, I'm guessing," he added, looking up at the clock.

"What did he sound like on the phone?" Charlie asked.

"Anxious, though it's hard to say just how much. The guy has become a little paranoid," Jake said, looking toward the front door. "But being a Christian in Afghanistan must have resulted in a lot of looking over your shoulder anyway. Now that the Taliban is on the uptake again, he's lucky to have escaped with his family. The problem is, too many people here in Albuquerque think that any woman with her head covered who isn't a nun is the wife, sister, or mother of the enemy."

"Got that right. Here he is," Charlie added with a whisper as the door opened and a tall man in a red Lobos cap, tropical-style shirt, and khaki slacks stepped inside the shop.

Dawud, clean shaven and wearing sunglasses, looked around carefully before spotting Jake and Charlie behind the counter. "Gentlemen," he greeted with only a slight accent, holding out his hand to Jake, shaking it vigorously.

Charlie stepped out into the aisle, and they man-hugged as usual. "Good to see you again, friend," Charlie said. "You look like a tourist visiting from California, or maybe Florida. Congratulations."

"What's the saying? When in Rome . . ."

Dawud smiled again, then grew serious and looked around the shop again, spotting Gordon in the office window. Gordon waved.

"Just the staff here at the moment," Charlie said, recognizing that his old friend was alert for trouble. It was sad that the Afghan man, now an American citizen, still had to live in fear after all he'd done to fight the Taliban. Maybe the extra padlocks would help just a little.

"You wanted to buy some locks for your shop?" Jake asked, bringing out two pairs of locks onto the counter, one the small, keyed-alike set, and the other the larger, much sturdier pair that required separate keys. "Here's all we have, but the price is very reasonable."

Dawud stepped over, then pointed to the small locks, checking the price tag at the same time. "These two will do the job. They're just to deter shoplifting, not the serious thief. Most of my regular customers are well-educated professionals looking for nutritious fruits and vegetables, and I rarely have a problem except for those who come in looking for trouble."

"Still experiencing some harassment?" Charlie asked.

"There are a few younger men who seem to come by every time there's an attack, whether it's Paris or California, plus a white-haired retiree or two with anger in his voice. They call us names, make accusations, and sometimes damage or throw fruit and vegetables. I have installed cameras inside, and after a few arrests the incidents have died down. I only have three part-time employees, but they are very loyal and they sometimes know the troublemakers on sight. But now . . ."

Charlie nodded. "Now that a vet was killed by someone claiming to be a terrorist, you're thinking that it'll get worse."

Gordon came up just then, greeted Dawud with a hug, and then stepped back. "What'll get worse? Someone giving you a hard time again?" he asked.

Dawud shrugged. "Not as yet, but I can see it coming, friend. The police are on alert, the community is angry, and those of us from that part of the world are automatically suspect. You know that is true."

"Do you and your family need our help?" Gordon asked.

"Thank you, but no. What I need is a weapon—a firearm," Dawud said softly.

Gordon nodded solemnly. Jake, meanwhile, looked at Charlie with raised eyebrows.

"You don't already have one to protect your shop?" Jake asked.

Charlie knew that Jake was referring to the loaded shotgun on a shelf below the counter not three feet from where his employee was standing. Jake had been forced to grab for it once already, a year ago, but it had never actually been fired.

Dawud shook his head. "As I said, most of my customers are not stealing fruit or a hundred dollars in cash from my register. I see more credit or debit cards than twenty dollar bills, Jake, and I have one of those scanners for the smartphones."

"You want to protect your family—at home," Charlie concluded.

"Yes. Only in self-defense, a last resort, as you say. If the killings continue, there are those in the community who will want revenge. We're different, Afghan, and many people incorrectly assume we're Muslim. We had to leave our own country because we chose to follow Jesus, not Islam, but to some we are still the enemy."

"What kind of support do you get from your church?" Gordon asked.

Dawud lowered his head, avoiding eye contact. "Just prayers and sympathy from those who know my family. We stopped attending services after our car was vandalized in the church parking lot—two times. Our vehicle was the only one damaged, no others. Someone didn't want us there. Now we read the Bible and pray at home."

"We keep our guns locked up in our secure area, but I can show you what we have to sell right now, then give you some basic handling and safety instruction," Gordon offered, taking a quick glance at Charlie, who nodded with his eyes.

"Thank you. Please let me know what you would recommend. I will need something that my wife or children can use to defend themselves if I'm not there," Dawud explained.

As Gordon and their friend walked down the aisle toward the rear of the shop, Jake stared at the floor.

"What's on your mind, Jake? You think we should send him away empty-handed?" Charlie asked.

"If, and this is only hypothetical, if Dawud or his family ever end up firing a weapon at someone, whoever sold it to them is going to be in the hot seat. You know that," Jake spoke up immediately. "Even if it's clearly self-defense. There are some nutjobs out there who can't be reasoned with or are incapable of rational thought."

"Yeah, we have our own bad guys. I ran across a few in the Army, soldiers with that old Vietnam-era mind-set, kill them all and let God sort them out. Well, maybe not that bad, but bad enough. You know we can legally sell to people who are even on the no-fly list, or crazies who've been identified as mentally ill. I know Dawud personally, and he's the kind of American who would have *my* back under any conditions. We have to give him the means to defend himself and his children."

"Yeah, well. I still have my doubts, for the record. Your judgment has always been pretty solid, and you're the boss. I just don't want any blowback to come our way."

"Gordon has good instincts. He's not going to offer up any weapon that would be attractive to a potential terrorist, like an assault-style rifle with a high-capacity magazine. We're also going to send the usual notice of the purchase with a copy of his driver's license. Koury is a US citizen and he already has a lot of documentation with the Feds."

"Mr. Koury has a son in high school, doesn't he?" Jake asked.

"Yeah, good point. Maybe a trigger lock would be appropriate. Any kid that age can fly off the handle in a second if he starts getting any flak from hotheads at school," Charlie said.

Ruth came out of the office just as two potential customers entered from the front, followed by another, and soon they were involved in asking questions, and, with Jake, arranging for the pawn of a watch and wedding ring.

Ten minutes later, it was time to lock up for the day. Ruth left immediately to pick up Rene from the sitter, and Charlie helped Jake close out the two cash registers and complete the paperwork. Shooing Jake out the back door, Charlie picked up a broom and started to sweep.

"You missed a spot," Gordon joked as he and Dawud came out of the secure area. Gordon was carrying a 12-gauge Winchester slide-action shotgun pump with a short, twenty-inch barrel.

"Good choice for a home defense weapon. Scary big barrel, short enough to aim, and not likely to penetrate through walls and hurt unintended targets," Charlie observed.

"Especially with number four buckshot," Gordon said, glancing over to Dawud, who was carrying a box of shells.

"I don't ever want to fire a weapon again," Dawud replied, "but my wife and children have to be defended by something with more force than a fist or kitchen knife. I have a baseball bat at the shop, and that's going to be it. However, at my home, I draw the line."

"I gave him the basics in weapon handling in the secure area, but will you test Dawud on safety one more time while I write this up?" Gordon asked Charlie.

Ten minutes later Dawud left out the front door, carrying the unloaded shotgun in a hard-side case along with a bag containing the shells, a trigger lock and keys, and the two padlocks selected earlier. Gordon had thrown in a cleaning kit along with the purchase.

"He handled that shotgun like it was made of glass, bro," Gordon said. "I wonder if he'll even take it out of the case. You remember the firefight behind that burned-out mosque? First and last time Dawud ever used his weapon."

"If he hadn't fired off that clip into the doorway, we both might be dead. Neither of us had any idea there was a sniper in the back of the room," Charlie replied.

"Two snipers. I'm including the guy with the RPG."

"Dawud saved our butts, but it blew his cover. He and his family were dead meat from that moment on. Talk about a life-altering moment," Charlie said.

"Yeah. We've had more than our share of those lately. Which brings up the current situation. I haven't heard any news on yesterday's events or the status of the investigation. You?"

"Naw, just been keeping busy. I suppose Nancy or DuPree would have called if there were any developments. Unless it was still going on. If they have someone cornered and SWAT is there, it may take hours for a resolution," Charlie observed.

"I'll put on the news while we clean up. If there's a situation it'll be on every channel right now." Gordon walked back into the office and turned on the TV.

As Charlie swept the aisles, Gordon emptied the waste baskets into a larger container in the small hallway that led to the restroom, secure room, their office, and outside the back door.

Five minutes later, they set the timer on the alarm, turned off the main lights, and stepped out onto the small concrete porch and loading dock, which was illuminated by a light up on the outside wall. "I'll lock up, Charlie. Go on home. Keep alert and stay away from trouble."

"Okay, Gordo. You too," Charlie replied, walking down the three steps. His purple Dodge Charger was parked in the first slot south of the loading dock. He thumbed the fob on his key and the Charger beeped twice. Then he saw a vehicle straddling the alley at the end of the block, lights out.

"That look like a cop?" Charlie asked, pausing beside the passenger-side front tire.

A muzzle flash and a simultaneous blast answered his question.

"Cover!" Charlie yelled, dropping into a crouch beside the side of the Charger as a second bullet ricocheted off the brick wall three feet away. Long-developed survival instincts were already taking control. In his right hand, Charlie already had his 9mm Beretta out, barrel up.

"He's not sticking around!" Gordon yelled as Charlie heard the squeal of tires at the far end of the alley.

"My car! Let's catch his ass," Charlie ordered, scrambling around to the driver's side as he jammed his pistol back into the holster. As he put the key in the ignition, Gordon slid into the passenger's seat. "Go!"

Charlie spun the Charger back and around, then turned on the headlights as he hit the gas, accelerating down the narrow alley. He swerved around the Dumpster behind Frank and Linda's grocery, touched the brakes and slowed past the parking area of Melissa's laundry, then screeched to a stop at the end of the alley.

"He went to the right," Gordon called out.

Charlie pulled out into the street. "Crap," he exclaimed, hitting the brakes hard as a laundry patron, basket in hand, stepped off the curb. The woman jumped back, nearly dropping her load.

"Sorry!" Charlie yelled, edging forward and around the startled lady.

"Call 911!"

"On it," Gordon responded, holding up the cell phone in his hand for Charlie to see. "And by the way, there was a big manila envelope on the pavement next to Melissa's back entrance."

"Could be another terrorist tabloid," Charlie suggested. "Hopefully it won't get thrown away before we get back."

At the next street corner, they looked in both directions. "Clear on my side," Gordon yelled.

As he made a quick left out into the wide, four-lane street, Charlie could see three or four vehicles headed south, and a truck approaching. "Taking a guess here, Gordon."

"Left?" Gordon suggested, then he told Dispatch about the

ambush, the possible direction and street the shooter had taken, and the envelope at the end of the alley.

Charlie picked up speed, hoping to get close enough to the vehicles ahead to at least establish makes, models, and get a look at the tags. A car in the outside lane turned right into a residential neighborhood. He decided to follow and made the turn as subtly as possible, without a signal.

"Did you recognize the shooter's vehicle?" Gordon asked, his phone still in hand as he looked ahead at the car, a block away now.

"No, just trying to psych out the shooter. I turned on a hunch," Charlie responded. "Cops on the way?"

"Copy. Officers are going to the shop. They're sending additional units to patrol the area, and warning calls are being sent to the guests who attended the ceremony. I wish we had more to go on," Gordon said.

Charlie shrugged. "All we know is that someone, probably using a rifle, in a car of an unknown non-dark color, took a shot and drove off, maybe leaving another message on the asphalt. Unless the shooter creates enough attention to motivate a cop to pull him over, and the officer discovers a rifle inside that's just been fired . . ."

"Basically we're screwed."

"At least we're not shot."

"We? I wasn't the target. It's a good thing you were on the move and had just stepped away from the light, Charlie."

"Yeah. If I'd have been locking the door instead of you, we might not be having this conversation. Or following this car right now, hoping it contains an armed attacker trying to kill me."

"Which sounds a little stupid, when you think about it."

Charlie nodded. As they approached the possible suspect car, the sedan turned into a driveway, then came to a stop in front of a two-car garage door. Charlie slowed, wondering if the shooter knew he was following, and was prepping for a gunfight. Charlie's Beretta was on the bucket seat beside him, and Gordon held his matching weapon across his right thigh, his window down so he could return fire.

As they drove past the driveway, an elementary school-aged girl wearing soccer team shorts and a numbered jersey jumped out of the passenger door and ran toward the front porch of the house.

"Well, so much for instincts," Charlie said. "I made the wrong call, so there's no sense in driving around anymore. Let's get back to the shop and meet the cops. That envelope should still be there, but I doubt anyone will be able to recover a slug. The only hope is that it struck the empty rental place on the next block. Their end wall is stucco and timber, not brick."

"There should at least be a chunk or furrow where the bullets struck the brick wall and left metal streaks. I heard the impacts. They looked like clean misses by, what? Three feet?"

"That's about right," Charlie said, circling the block and heading in the direction of FOB Pawn. "I should be grateful the shooter couldn't hit a moving target. Come to think about it, I'd just stopped to look at the car, like an idiot. If that was the same sniper, I should have taken a hit. It was an easy shot."

"You should be grateful that you were lucky, pal."

Chapter Four

Less than five minutes later, Charlie turned down the street adjacent to the north end of FOB Pawn and parked at the curb. An APD unit was blocking the alley exit, and he'd already noted another unit at the south end of the block, behind Melissa's laundry.

"Guess the entire alley on this block is now a crime scene," Gordon commented as a dark-blue-uniformed officer appeared at the back corner of the shop, looking them over. His hand was resting on the butt of his holstered service weapon. "Ah, an old friend. Officer Roseberg," Gordon said, recognizing the patrolman as they climbed out of the low-slung Dodge.

"Mr. Henry, Mr. Sweeney," Roseberg greeted. "Detective Medina is waiting."

They followed the slender but fit officer down the alley, past another police car with flashing lights that was parked beside the loading dock of the brick office building across the alley from FOB Pawn. The vehicle's spotlight was directed against the rear wall of their shop. Below was Gordon's big pickup, which was still in the parking slot.

About halfway down the alley Charlie spotted Nancy walking in their direction, accompanied by a male, uniformed APD officer. "Looks like they found the envelope." Charlie observed what Nancy was carrying in her gloved, left hand. "I hope it's not just somebody's displaced mail."

"Charlie," Nancy called out. "Any luck tracking the shooter or getting an ID on his vehicle?"

"No, and I wasn't even sure the vehicles I was trying to catch up to also included the one with the sniper. The car, and I'm certain it was a lighter-toned sedan of some kind and not an SUV, was parked about where the patrol car is now." He pointed down toward the laundry.

"There were no headlights on," Gordon added, "and I saw less than Charlie from where I was, standing in the glare of the loading dock light."

"We took cover after the shot, and when we looked up the car was already gone. From the direction the vehicle was facing, I think it went west to Fourth Street, then south. When we got to the corner, the only vehicles within range were also heading south," he added, stopping to face the woman detective. "I ended up following a soccer mom and daughter, not the shooter."

"Marty, go help Roseberg set up the perimeter," Nancy instructed another officer.

"Was this what you asked our officers to collect?" She held up a manila nine-by-twelve-inch envelope, the type with fold-over metal flaps. She turned it over, revealing a paper cutout of an ISIS flag glued to the outside.

"I didn't seen that side, it must have been facing down. But it's the right size, Nancy," Gordon said. "Charlie was too busy not running over a woman carrying her laundry to notice what was on the asphalt."

"I'm going to open this in a while and take a look at what's inside," Nancy said. "It feels like a sheet of letter-sized paper, probably with another message. In the meantime, I need you two to reconstruct what exactly went down and where you were positioned at the time."

"I'm afraid we won't be able to tell you much more than we've already said," Charlie answered. "The shooter's vehicle was parked down there, blocking the alley." He turned and pointed. "The muzzle flash came from the front seat, so the bad guy was probably leaning across, using the passenger-side door as a rest. I can't swear to those details, of course."

"So the APD unit is parked in pretty much the same spot?"

"Yeah, but if there are any tire impressions or tread patterns, hopefully they can still be found unless the officer pulls out in that direction and distorts the images," Charlie said.

"He's not moving until I give the word," Nancy answered.

"Is this envelope similar to the one left at the school?" Gordon asked.

"Looks identical to me," Nancy replied. "But keep that to yourselves, guys, we're keeping the details from the public to help screen out possible copy-cat attackers or cranks."

"Any leads on the killer yet?" Charlie asked. "We didn't hear anything new, not from the local or national news, the internet, or law enforcement."

She shrugged. "The techs at the crime lab have matched the

ejection marks on the .223 shell with a Ruger Range rifle, an older model carbine-sized weapon which originally came with a five-round magazine, though higher-capacity after-market mags are available. That's all we have on physical evidence. As for the politics, there's the usual rabble-rousing among the politicians and the wingers. We're lucky so far that nobody has retaliated against the local Muslim community. There are a couple of mosques in the area and they've hired extra security, just in case."

"What about that teenager this morning in the park?" Gordon asked. "The one who caused the outburst during Mr. Humphrey's speech. What happened to him?"

"He was a sixteen-year-old kid who'd ditched Cibola High School. He's an immigrant from Afghanistan and has lived here just a few years. Humphrey's people roughed him up a little, checked his ID, and then let him go."

Charlie and Gordon exchanged glances.

"You know who this kid was?" Nancy asked.

"Maybe," Charlie responded. "Is his last name Koury?"

Nancy nodded. "Caleb Koury. Sounds like you need to tell me something, guys. What's going on?"

As they walked up the alley toward FOB Pawn, Charlie and Gordon told Nancy about Dawud's visit to the shop, his fear for his family's safety, and the items he'd purchased.

Nancy's eyebrows went up immediately when Gordon mentioned the shotgun. "You know you're going to take some heat if that weapon is ever used, self-defense or not. People like Ed Humphrey are going to scream that you're arming terrorists. At least it wasn't an assault rifle."

"Jake's already pointed that out to us," Charlie admitted. "But we have a history with Dawud, and we trust him to do the right thing."

"Is this the man who worked with you in Afghanistan? The interpreter?"

"Yeah, and he's a Christian, which put him in a very dangerous situation in his birth country. He and his family would probably be dead by now if they hadn't been able to get out when they did," Gordon reminded.

"But what about the kid, Caleb? Did your friend mention the incident with his son?" Nancy asked.

"No, but we were already considering what might happen if Caleb or Justine, Dawud and Jenna's daughter, were harassed to the point where they felt the need to take action. Dawud also bought a trigger lock for the weapon and only he and Jenna, supposedly, have a key," Charlie said.

"I hope he uses the lock," Nancy replied. "I'm betting that someone's going to go after Caleb, his family, or their business sooner or later."

"And once tonight's ambush hits the news . . ." Gordon added.

It didn't take long for the reporters to arrive, but they were kept outside the yellow tape as officers walked the length of the alley, looking for any potential evidence. Nothing was found that could be established as relevant, and no images were captured on the pawnshop alley camera, which only covered the parking area at the rear of the shop. No crime scene van was dispatched—there was no need—and there was only a metal-streaked smear on a small piece of brick that was found to have been dislodged by a bullet impact.

Finally, in the shop office, Nancy slit open the recovered

envelope from the bottom using a pocketknife. She gingerly removed a sheet of paper with a printed head shot of Charlie in his Army uniform, the one that had recently appeared in the local newspaper. It had a big red X across his face, and below the image was a typed message in large fonts. "One more godless 'hero' dead. Many more face our wrath," Nancy read aloud. "Praise Allah."

"This reads like television or a B action flick. Don't terrorists ever say anything that's not a cliché?" Gordon said.

"At least this confirms I was the target," Charlie observed.

"And that it was either the same shooter, or someone working with him," Nancy replied, sliding the paper back into the envelope, then placing the envelope into a larger, paper evidence bag that had already been labeled with her name and other essential information. She sealed the bag and stood.

"Think the lab techs will get anything from this?" Charlie asked, walking with her to the back door. "Besides alley pavement grit."

"Probably not, but we have to try, Charlie. Want me to see if I can get a detail assigned to watch your house?" Nancy asked.

Charlie shook his head. "No, I'm good. This shooter appears to be too worried about getting caught to confront me up close. All I have to do is be more careful when I go outside and not present an easy shot. I don't think the shooter knows where I live either."

"Even so, stay away from windows," Gordon added. "You can sleep over at my place if you want to keep the sniper guessing, pal."

"If it comes to that. Do you think the shooter will make another move at me now that he missed his first try?" Charlie asked.

"I have no idea. This sleezeball isn't behaving like the typical wild-eyed fanatic. Like you say, the shooter is careful not to get caught or ID'd. He may move onto someone else on his list, then try again with you later. That'll make any new attack he carries out risky," Nancy speculated. "I'll talk this over with DuPree and get his take. We'll also talk to the Feds."

"You know I'm not going to hunker down, Nancy. Not for a terrorist, not for anyone."

"As always. All this does is motivate you to find the bastard and kick ass."

"Exactly. Looks like it's time for me to take up the hunt. Any suggestions where to start?"

"We've got law enforcement teams looking for self-radicalized nutjobs and potential lone-wolf terrorists all over the state right now and, of course, watching locals who've traveled to the Middle East recently. Especially anyone with an arrest record and the typical age group. The usual profiling, legal or not." Nancy yawned. "Well, I've got to finish up outside. Miles to go before I sleep. You guys be careful," she added, giving Charlie, then Gordon, a hug.

Nancy walked down the short hallway and stepped out into the alley.

"You hungry?" Gordon asked as he stood.

"Yeah. Let's check out the new Firehouse Subs, the one over by Corrales," Charlie suggested.

"Okay, but let's take my pickup and I can drop you off here to pick up your car after dinner. The cops will have cleared out by then," Gordon said.

Less than an hour later Gordon dropped off Charlie at the FOB's end of the alley. Except for his Charger and the trash containers behind each of the businesses down the alley, there was no sign of activity, not even a stray cat. A crescent moon was high in the sky, and there were just enough street and building lights to block out the stars. He stood there for a moment, looking at the loading dock, really nothing more than a roofless, raised block of concrete with steps leading to the heavy steel door. Several feet above the door was the hooded light, and, closer to the roof parapet, a surveillance camera that covered the loading dock and four parking slots, defined by white lines painted on the asphalt.

His keys already out, Charlie walked around the rear of the Dodge to the driver's side, then pressed the key fob and opened the door. Out of the corner of his eye, he saw sudden movement inside the car. Jumping back, Charlie pulled out his Beretta as someone sat up in the backseat.

"Stand down, Henry. It's me, Davis," came a vaguely familiar Southern accent, then the guy leaned forward into the light, showing his face and empty hands, up by his shoulders.

Davis, which was not his real name, was so physically ordinary in appearance that his face was probably placed next to "generic" in the dictionary. His face was flat but not too flat, his eyes and hair brown, his nose just about right, and he was neither handsome nor ugly—a five in every way.

The man was CIA, the contact he and Gordon had worked with in Afghanistan. Davis was smart, well-trained, and extremely dangerous. He was lethal with any weapon, and knew his trade craft so well he was capable of getting lost in a crowd of three.

The night that he and Gordon had shipped out of 'Stan for the last time, Davis had been there at the airstrip. There had been no handshake or good-bye, just a nod. That was the last time they'd seen or heard of the guy, and it had been over three years ago. So what was he doing here tonight?

"Get in and drive, Charlie. We need to talk about your safety, and I want to do that while on the move," Davis said softly. "Circle the neighborhood. I'll need about fifteen minutes to read you in."

"What's the company doing getting involved in domestic issues, Davis?" Charlie asked, climbing in and starting up the Dodge. "You been tracking the shooter?"

"Wish I could say that, Charlie, but no. The current assignment is insuring your safety, and the safety of those other vets under attack. I'm here to keep you alive, and hopefully at the same time, take out the person or people behind this assault on Americans," Davis replied, his head swiveling from side to side, watching for a tail as Charlie drove north down Second Street.

"How long have you known about the shootings? It's only been a little more than twenty-four hours."

"I caught the next plane after hearing about it last night. You were seated two chairs away from Captain Whitaker. We can't afford to lose any more people like Whitaker, you, or the civilians who were also hit."

"I'm a civilian now, and so was the chopper pilot," Charlie reminded, not wanting to voice the name of the dead aloud— another Navajo taboo. He focused back on his driving, passing an old pickup on the otherwise empty street.

"Okay. But you've served your country under special circumstances, and like Whitaker with his work with vets, you're going above and beyond to help total strangers. You've made the national news more than once, and not just in a Fourth of July parade. I've been following your activities since you left the Army. I've read about your work with local law enforcement, the Bureau, and how you've stepped up and saved lives. It's not just patriotic, it's who you are, and what you're doing."

"The CIA is now saving the heroes? That's a new spin on the flag, grandma, apple pie, and baseball. You're not our guardian angels, Davis."

"Yeah, but there is always a connection, isn't there? So much of our work has been tainted with political goals, doing things across the board to protect our country from the rest of the world, even when it means coloring outside the lines. You and Sweeney are much more than shop owners. You've kept up the fight and become advocates of victims. Proactive advocates, actually. Of course, what I'm here to do is off the books. No one but Sweeney can know who I am or why I'm here. Not the detectives, not the Bureau, not HS, not Jake or Ruth, even. Or her son."

"I see you've been doing your homework."

"That's who I am, Charlie. And call me Turner. Russell Turner."

"That your real name?"

"It'll do for now."

"Okay, what's the plan, Russ?"

"I'm going to hang around the perimeter of your life, trying to locate whoever might be watching you. The sniper may not strike at you again, at least not right away. This likely lone wolf is paranoid about being caught. None of that rush for martyrdom shit, and no suicide belt, but I'm not making any hard and fast assumptions. There are other agencies, including APD, that have stepped up security and are trying to screen you people, but they all have gaps in their coverage and a lack of reliable intelligence. My theory is that the sniper is going to search out a safer target. Meanwhile, I want to make sure that you're covered," he added.

"We've got some smart cops around here. If you're not coordinating with them, they might just detect your presence," Charlie asked.

"I'm not cleared to work with anyone outside the agency, and if you hadn't noticed, I'm pretty good at keeping a low profile."

"Okay. But the shooter is careful in setting up the attacks. We have no idea at all what he looks like, the vehicle he uses, except for a medium-toned sedan tonight, and so forth. He could be a pro," Charlie reminded.

"Not likely. He's careful, and hasn't made any mistakes yet, but he's definitely not a pro. You're still untouched."

"Good point."

"Here's my phone number if you need to reach me. I already have yours, including your cell," Russ said, reaching through the gap between the bucket seats and laying a card on the empty passenger seat. "And it's okay to tell Sweeney, but only Sweeney, that I'm here. But you were going to do that anyway."

"Of course," Charlie said, circling back toward the street with FOB Pawn. "Now what?"

"Drop me off at Sweeney's apartment building where I parked my vehicle. I walked the four blocks to your shop."

"You didn't damage anything getting into my car, did you, Russ?" Charlie asked, glancing around at the windows.

"Not at all. You clearly like this car. A bit flashy, though."

"Purple suits me. Back here in the States, I no longer have to blend in," Charlie said.

"Yeah, well, you might want to rethink that and get a generic rental—at least until we nail the terrorist."

Charlie had no comeback for that. He pulled over and parked next to the curb on the street beside the small apartment complex where Gordon lived.

Turner stepped out, yelled, "Thanks for the ride," and walked toward three cars parked side by side. Charlie drove off, looking in the rearview mirror, wondering which car was his—and what Davis, now Turner, was really doing here.

Once Turner was out of sight, Charlie brought out his cell and called Gordon. His gut told him it might be a good idea to stay at his pal's apartment after all, at least for tonight.

Chapter Five

"Ruth's here," Gordon announced, looking up at the camera monitor on the office wall from his side of the big desk. Charlie, looking over the inventory on the FOB OK website, turned his head toward the door, hearing a key in the lock.

Ruth stepped inside, then looked toward the office, eyes open wide and her lips tightly pressed together. "Charlie, are you okay? I heard about the shooting last night on the radio coming over here."

Charlie stood. "I'm fine and the police are already on the job. Nancy—Detective Medina—was here and is handling the case. So far, like the shooting in the park, they don't have any idea who's behind the incident."

"Almost getting shot and killed is 'an incident'?" Ruth exclaimed, coming over and giving him a warm hug. She glanced over at Gordon, who was also on his feet. "Were you there too, Gordon?" she added, stepping back from Charlie and wiping away a tear. "The reporter said there was a witness, but didn't mention a name. The authorities suggested that it was the same terrorist that attacked us all in the park."

"Good morning, Ruth," Jake greeted, now entering the office. He'd been out front, placing the cash drawers in the registers. He put his arm around her shoulder and gave her a comforting squeeze.

"It's time to be more careful with our safety here at the shop. A while ago we were talking about this," Gordon said, "and we're now going to follow a new protocol." He nodded to Charlie.

Charlie's words were clear and clinical. "Nobody stays here after dark, and we always check the cameras, front and back, before stepping outside. If another vehicle or person who we don't recognize is visible anywhere down the alley, we need to be extremely careful. If we're at all uncertain, we need to take someone with us, or call the police."

"Also, be alert to anyone passing by to the north along the side street," Jake added, looking to Charlie, who nodded.

"A drive-by from that direction would be at nearly point-blank range," Ruth said. "At least, the way we park, nose in, the driver's door is on the south side. We'll have the vehicle for protection." She sat down in a chair Charlie had moved over for her.

"True, and Gordon got permission to redirect Frank and Linda's north-facing alley camera to get a wider angle," Charlie said. "It's not going to give us a warning view, but maybe we can get a look if the guy with the rifle decides to do a recon first. We might end up with an image and a possible face to connect to the shooter."

"If you think it'll help, I can call Rick and have him put one of the door locks on the front, the kind with a buzzer, where one of us has to let in the customer. Like with those big-city apartment buildings," Jake said. "It'll give us a moment to take a look at who wants inside."

Charlie looked at Gordon, who shook his head.

"That's going to annoy our customers, guys," Gordon said. "And, unless the terrorist, or whoever the shooter is, suddenly decides to go postal, we're not likely to have someone burst in here with a gun."

"Yeah, it's not like that's ever happened," Jake said with a straight face.

Ruth groaned. "At least not recently."

She turned in her chair and reached onto a low shelf for her coffee mug, the one with the Philadelphia Eagles logo. The phone in her purse began to chime and she grabbed it instead. "Who could that be?"

Charlie saw the smile on her face turn sober, then grim, as she listened to whoever was calling. Hopefully, nothing had happened to Rene, who was supposed to be at school. Charlie looked away and tried to focus on something else, thinking it rude to listen in, but when she spoke the caller's name he immediately knew who it was.

"I'm at work," Ruth said, then paused for a response. "I'll call Rene's school and let them know what's going on, and I'll meet you here at FOB Pawn in an hour. Yes, I'll stay inside. Good-bye." She ended the call, then noted all three men were waiting for details.

"I'll tell you what's going on, but first I need to call Principal Bennett and ask her to check on my son. They need to keep him inside at school." She looked down at her phone, entered a number, then stood and walked out of the office into the hall.

A few minutes later, she returned. "Rene is safe."

"It sounds like there's a problem that you needed to know about," Charlie prodded.

Ruth nodded. "That was Deputy Marshal Stannic, my contact with the witness protection program. He's got some bad news he needs to share with me—us, actually. He's on his way here now."

"Is this about Lawrence?" Charlie asked. Lawrence Westerfield was Ruth's ex-husband.

"Unfortunately, yes. According to the authorities at the federal prison where he's been locked up, Lawrence has disappeared."

"Disappeared, as in escaped?" Gordon asked.

"Apparently," Ruth replied. "That's why I'm being warned."

"When did Lawrence disappear?" Jake asked softly. "Last night?"

"No. Six days ago," Ruth whispered, her voice fading away.

"Crap!" Charlie muttered. Ruth's ex-husband was the lowest excuse for a human being. Lawrence had kidnaped Rene, then tried to kill Ruth, Charlie, and Gordon before he'd finally been taken into custody. The man had been convicted of kidnapping, murder, and a host of major financial crimes, thanks largely to Ruth's testimony and the physical evidence she'd managed to provide. Ruth had only recently felt safe enough to leave the witness protection program and begin using her maiden name.

"If he's had that much time on the run, he could have been in this area for maybe two or three days," Jake observed softly. "More than that if he flew here."

"Maybe you were the target all along, Charlie. Westerfield promised to kill you, remember?" Gordon replied. "What if he missed during the ceremony and hit the wrong guy, then tried to make up for it in the alley last night?"

"And tried to misdirect the cops with a fake terrorist threat," Charlie concluded. "It's thin, but feasible, I suppose. The guy is a skilled manipulator, and he's been in this area before. He also knows where I work."

Ruth sat down and reached for her coffee mug, her hand shaking. "Lawrence was an avid hunter and he had several rifles and shotguns. Just when I thought we were safe again."

"Even if the shooter isn't connected to that weasel, we still have to be very careful, guys, and look after Ruth and Rene," Jake said, gently putting his hand on Ruth's shoulder.

"Let's get proactive," Charlie suggested.

Charlie was out with Jake by the front register, standing by while a couple in their late twenties searched through the vinyl collection of perhaps five hundred albums of all genres. The front door opened, ringing the bell atop the doorjamb, and in walked Deputy Marshal Peter Stannic. Wearing jeans, a polo shirt, and poplin jacket, the man was dressed in New Mexican casual rather than the business suit that would have made him stand out in this neighborhood.

He nodded to Charlie and Jake, both of whom he'd met on earlier occasions when the Feds had been protecting their key witness, Ruth. Spotting Ruth and Gordon in the office, he nodded in that direction. "I'll be in there, boys. We all need to talk once you can get away."

Jake turned to Charlie. "Go ahead, boss, I've got things handled. I'll join you later."

"Okay, but if you need any help, just call out," Charlie said, then walked down the aisle to join the three already in the back.

Ruth was still seated, but Gordon and the fed were standing when Charlie joined them.

After a quick handshake, Stannic began. "I'll brief you on the events as I know them, then I'll answer as many questions as I can. But first I have a very important question," he added, looking from Charlie to Gordon.

"Do we think the shooter could have been Westerfield or someone he hired?" Charlie asked. "It's possible he might have been gunning for me, and the shooter ended up thinking I was the guy to the right of Ruth, not the left. At that distance and in twilight and shadows, it could have been a simple misidentification. The pilot and I were the same height, build, and hair color, and neither of us were in our Army uniforms."

Stannic nodded. "I've had some conversations with law enforcement, including APD detectives Medina and DuPree, and although they agree that the attacker in both incidents was probably the same person, they've concluded that it's a lone-wolf terrorist, not Westerfield, and his escape from prison is coincidental. They're basing their theories on the claims made in those notes delivered to the school and the one last night. Found near here, right?"

"At the south end of the alley," Charlie confirmed.

"But it *could* have been Lawrence, or one of his people?" Ruth asked. "Is that what you're suggesting?"

"I'm here because we can't rule that out, Ruth. Your ex kidnapped your son and caused several deaths—not to mention his history of abuse," Stannic explained.

"The bastard is capable of anything," Gordon proclaimed. "But he was supposed to be locked up in a federal prison. What happened?"

"Okay, here's what I know. Westerfield was attacked by another inmate during an exercise period when several prisoners were in the same area. He took a considerable beating, apparently, and was transported to a hospital ER for treatment. Now local law enforcement have concluded that Westerfield set the whole thing up. On the way to the hospital the EMT vehicle was disabled and attacked by four men wearing masks. One of the guards was shot. The other guard and two medics were Tasered. Westerfield fled with the assailants, and it took a while before officers arrived on scene. The attackers took all their victims' cell phones and radios, and put the vehicle communication gear out of action. The victims had to flag down a passing motorist. Fortunately, the man who was shot will make it."

"Why wasn't Ruth notified immediately? Who in the marshal's office dropped the ball?" Charlie demanded.

"It was a major bureaucratic screwup, and all I can do is apologize. With Ruth no longer in the program, WITSEC wasn't informed that Westerfield had escaped until last night. Prison officials and local law enforcement were scrambling to protect their local community, focusing on finding the fugitive and his accomplices before they did any more harm. I didn't know about any of this until I got a call from my superior. The marshals service already has a fugitive task force at work trying to locate him, but hadn't notified witness protection until they'd run out of leads and began probing into Westerfield's background. We're forced to be very compartmentalized, and the identity and location of our witnesses are based on a need to know. I was told that those involved thought Ruth was still under our protection."

"Are you saying that there are no leads at all concerning

Lawrence's location right now, and that Charlie and I are in danger?" Ruth asked.

"We just don't know," Stannic replied. "I'm here to offer you protection until your ex-husband is back in custody. Mr. Henry, I'm sorry that we can't do the same for you—your testimony was never used in court. All this despite you and Mr. Sweeney's help in recovering Rene and apprehending Lawrence Westerfield."

"I'm capable of looking after myself," Charlie replied, "and so is Gordon. But how are you going to keep Ruth safe?"

After last night's inaccurate gunfire, he was now wondering if Ruth *had* been the primary target at the ceremony as well, and the sniper had missed, striking Whitaker instead. Ruth's ex-husband had abused her during their marriage, and hunted her for over a year after she fled her home with their son. She'd later provided testimony that had sent him to prison for life. Lawrence wanted revenge, he'd made that clear months ago. Maybe he was just a lousy shot.

"We'll put her in a safe house in another community, in Arizona or Utah. And she'll need a new identity, of course. It may just be temporary, but that all depends on how quickly we locate Westerfield," Stannic answered.

"So the only good news for Ruth is if there's really a terrorist sniper out there, shooting at our most decorated people," Jake called out, having arrived in the office just a minute ago. "And we won't know that with any certainty until the next attack."

"I agree with the terrorist theory. Either way, I'm not running and hiding anymore. We defeated Lawrence once before and we'll do it again. I'm staying right where I am," Ruth said, reaching over and placing her hand on Charlie's. "I feel safer around the people I love. Forget about the relocation, Deputy Stannic."

"We'll change our routines and look out for each other," Charlie said, looking over at Gordon, who nodded. Russell Turner was out there now as well, keeping watch, and Charlie had already decided to let the CIA operative know how important Ruth and Rene were to him.

"The sniper, regardless of who he is, may not know where any of us live. If he's going to make another move against any of us, he'll have to follow us home," Gordon pointed out. "If we can predict his movements . . ."

Stannic nodded. "Then we locate him, set up a trap, and hopefully take him down. Fugitive retrieval is one of our primary missions, but we'll have to do this without any additional support from the marshal's service unless we get some evidence that Westerfield is connected to the attacks. But I'll be keeping an eye on Ruth, especially at night and when she's out on the road with Rene."

"And if you only catch a terrorist who'd just shot and killed a decorated soldier, that won't hurt your résumé," Jake interjected. "I like a good offense, people. If there's anything I can do to help, count me in."

Charlie looked from face to face, a plan forming in his head. "Let's contact the detectives and our other sources and see what we can set up for this afternoon and evening. But don't anyone go outside without backup—just in case."

It was six o'clock in the evening, and Charlie was sitting between Ruth and Rene on the sofa in her apartment, having dinner on old TV trays borrowed from FOB Pawn as they watched the local news. The seven-year-old seemed to be enjoying his meal, a take-out sandwich from Firehouse Subs, but Ruth ate slowly, her attention focused on the television.

The lead story had focused on the new terrorist threat to the community, and Charlie had been mentioned as the most recent target. The death of Captain Whitaker and the hunt for his killer was the main focus, of course, and sidebar interviews followed with law enforcement officials, politicians like Ed Humphrey, and a brief, anguished comment by Whitaker's sister, Janice. The captain's ex-wife, Patricia Azok, was mentioned by name but not interviewed.

Charlie looked over and saw tears in Ruth's eyes. She caught him looking, then shook her head, trying to smile.

"I'm so sorry for all the innocent people who've been part of this nightmare, Charlie, and especially the victim and his family. But I feel guilty right now. I was annoyed because we have to sit here eating our dinner off of TV trays instead of at the dining room table. We'd gotten used to staying away from windows when Rene and I were on our own. But this last year I thought we didn't have to worry anymore about being seen."

"I'm sorry, but we have to be very careful for a while, Ruth."

"Hey, I like eating and watching TV at the same time," Rene exclaimed. "Besides, Mr. Henry, Mom says you'll keep us safe from any *dangerous* people."

"You can count on me, Rene," Charlie said, trying to manage a serious smile, if one really existed.

"Don't get too used to this, Rene. Civilized people eat together at the table, with family, and we don't watch TV or text during dinner," Ruth said softly, looking over at Charlie, who had his smartphone beside his plate.

"We don't have to be civilized *all* the time, Mom. That would be uncivilized," Rene responded with a grin. "Besides, what about the Super Bowl? We watch it from the couch and always eat hot dogs and stuff."

"I think he's been spending too much time around Gordon," Charlie whispered. "Sorry about the phone—I need to stay in touch with our watchers."

"I understand," Ruth replied. "I don't know if I'm hoping they find someone out there, or that they don't."

"I prefer bad news or good news more than no news. If we want this to end . . ."

"I so wanted to get on with my life, Charlie. Our lives," she said softly, placing her hand on his. Then she crinkled her nose with a teasing grin.

"Are you flirting, or was that an itch?"

"You decide."

Charlie gazed into her sparkling blue-green eyes, his heart beating faster. "No offense to the offspring, but this wasn't the way I wanted us to have our first dinner, Ruth."

Rene looked at him for a moment, his eyebrows furrowed in question. "You mean, back at the table?" he asked. "Or are you and Mom talking in code?"

Ruth laughed, then so did Charlie.

It was ten in the evening now, and Rene had long since been put to bed. Charlie, pistol by his side on the sofa, was checking his cell phone once more. Nobody had reported seeing anyone sitting in their vehicle in the area, or had observed anything other than a police unit pass by more than once. Gordon had been approached by an officer who was checking *his* presence, but that had been cleared up with a call to Detective DuPree.

The lights were off now except for a light in the hall outside Rene's room, and Charlie was adjusting his pillow, ready for sleep, when Ruth walked silently into the living room, clad in a terry-cloth robe. Somehow, she still looked incredible.

"It looks like tonight is going to be peaceful after all, Charlie, and I appreciate you looking after us like this," she said softly.

"There's no place I'd rather be right now, Ruth," he admitted.

She sat down beside him on the sofa. "This wasn't the way I wanted to spend the night together," she whispered.

"Me neither," Charlie replied, realizing just how much he wanted to spend time with this woman.

Ruth leaned forward, kissed him gently, but before he could put his arms around her, she slipped away and stood.

"For now, that'll have to do," she said, then walked across the room. "Get some sleep, Charlie," she added before disappearing down the hall.

His heart was beating so loud for a moment he was feeling light-headed. "Like that's going to happen now," he mumbled, leaning back against the cushion, wondering if this was what it felt like to be in love.

Chapter Six

Charlie heard a sound and woke up abruptly. As he reached underneath the comforter for his pistol, he realized Rene was standing there in his pajamas.

"Sorry Charlie, um, Mr. Henry. Did I wake you up?" Rene said, a sleepy smile on his face.

"Rene, get into the shower and get dressed. We're running late," Ruth called from across the living room.

"Yes, Mom," Rene replied, turning to look at her. "I was just checking up on our guest."

"Check's over. Get moving," she replied.

As Rene passed by his mother, she grabbed him and gave him a hug. "Hurry up, sweetie; there are three of us that need a shower this morning. You're next, Charlie."

As soon as Rene entered the bathroom and closed the door, Ruth spoke. "I wanted to ask while Rene wasn't around. Did you get any news last night?" she asked, walking over to him.

"My brother Al called from Shiprock, asking if I needed any

extra manpower. I told him to hold off for now," Charlie said, checking his cell phone for messages.

"He's still with the tribal police, right?" Ruth asked.

"Yes, and he's been promoted back to his old rank now, sergeant. Al's had his problems, but he's a good cop. And a good brother too," Charlie responded.

"Nice to have family ties, Charlie," Ruth replied. "And speaking of family, I'd better get started with fixing us some breakfast. Oatmeal, berries, and toast okay with you?"

"And coffee. Let me help, I'm almost dressed," he added, having slept in his pants. As he sat up and pushed away the blanket, Ruth saw he was shirtless. She stood there for a moment, staring at his chest.

Finally she spoke. "Okay, I'm impressed. Now put your shirt on before I get distracted." She spun around and moved toward the kitchen side of the room.

Charlie laughed, then reached for yesterday's shirt, which was laid out across the back of the sofa.

They were seated on the sofa having breakfast when Charlie's phone buzzed. He looked at the display, saw who was calling, and set down his coffee cup. "It's Nancy. I've got to take this."

"Want us to leave the room?" Ruth offered, looking at Rene, who was drinking his juice.

Charlie shook his head. "I'll be cryptic if necessary."

"What's crippic?" Rene asked.

"I'm here," Charlie spoke into the phone.

"Detective DuPree and I are going to interview your friend from Afghanistan this morning," she said, referring to Dawud

Koury, "and we'd like you and Gordon to be there to put him and his family at ease," she added.

"Okay. When and where?" Charlie asked.

"How about nine at the Koury produce market?" she suggested. "Their children will be in school, hopefully, unless the boy has gotten himself suspended again."

"Rene will be in school, but I'm not leaving Ruth at the shop, even with Jake there," Charlie said, looking over at them. They both had been listening intently, though he doubted they'd heard Nancy clearly.

"Hold on a second," Nancy responded.

Charlie waited, watching for Rene, who'd walked over to put his empty bowl and juice glass in the sink. Ruth had stood, but remained beside the table.

"Okay, Charlie," Nancy said, now back on the line. "How about you drop Rene off at school, then bring Ruth with you. Will that work?"

"I'll call you back in a few minutes."

"No, deal with it now. I'll hang on," Nancy replied, her tone edgy now.

"Charlie, tell her yes," Ruth whispered. "I can hear."

"Ruth says that's fine," Charlie said. As he'd learned from his parents while growing up, women were more than equal partners in any good relationship, and the woman beside him could make her own choices. Like his father, he was also very protective, and Ruth would be safer with him around.

Charlie and Ruth were with Gordon in his pickup as they approached Albuquerque's small west side minimall where the Koury business was located. Maybe two dozen people were gathered in the parking lot in front of Koury's American Produce. The market was positioned in the center of the multibusiness structure that included a clothing store, smoke shop, UPS store, and a Kentucky Fried Chicken at the far end.

Gordon glanced at the oversized Target which stood at the opposite end of the mall. "I hope this doesn't hold some special meaning today," he commented softly.

"You would think of that," Ruth replied, shaking her head. "I count at least four police cars in the lot, however, and see several uniformed officers, including the sheriff's department."

"The threat is more likely somewhere in that crowd of protestors," Charlie pointed out, noting several signs held by various people along the sidewalk beside Koury's market. "I estimate thirty, and there are more people walking in that direction."

"There's an American flag on a pole above the door to their business," Ruth said. "Shouldn't that gather some respect—not to mention the name the Kourys have given their shop?"

"You'd think so. Dawud put the flag up there the morning he opened for business," Charlie said. "That was a year before we bought the pawn shop."

"There's Nancy and DuPree," Gordon said, driving down a line of parked cars toward two generic-looking sedans. The detectives were standing together in an unoccupied slot, eyes on the activity.

"Right on time," Charlie noted, looking at this watch. "I guess they were waiting for us to arrive before they entered the market."

DuPree motioned them toward the parking space, and he and Nancy stepped aside as Gordon parked.

Charlie was watching elsewhere, searching the perimeter of the two-acre asphalt lot, trying to determine if any of the vehicles farthest from the businesses were occupied. The main street that ran parallel to the mall was heavily traveled, and no one had attempted to park at the curb, which would instantly draw attention.

"Searching for a sniper?" Gordon asked as he glanced at Charlie past Ruth, who was sitting between them on the large, bench-style seat. Gordon's oversized pickup could seat six, with the twin cab layout.

"The shooter so far has chosen to attack in low light or darkness, but sometimes the most successful tactic is to be unpredictable," Charlie added. "But we're probably safe here," he said, reaching over and putting his hand upon Ruth's, giving it a gentle squeeze.

"But stay close, Ruth," Gordon said. "Ready, people?" he added, opening his door.

"How long has the crowd been here?" Charlie asked DuPree immediately. Then he turned and gave Ruth a steadying hand as she climbed down onto the running board, then to the ground.

"According to Dispatch, Mr. Koury called to report some vandalism when he came in to open up the business around 7 AM. There was some graffiti and a broken window, and a few people standing around, shouting insults," DuPree replied.

"Nothing physical, at least not yet," Nancy joined in. "You guys ready?" she said. "Ruth, stick with Charlie and Gordon, okay? And, oh, good morning, you three."

"I guess we'll see about that," Gordon said with a grin.

As they approached the gathering, Charlie noted two APD

uniformed officers standing by the glass entrance to the market, which had a piece of cardboard duct-taped over what was probably a hole in the double door. Dawud was using a wire brush to scrape dried paint away from the textured block wall below the window, which was also taped up in three spots.

The small crowd grew quiet and parted in the center to let them through. Perhaps they'd observed the weapons and badges on the belts of the two detectives, plus Charlie and Gordon's sidearms, holstered on their belts beneath their jackets, which were unbuttoned. Ruth remained in their center as they passed through, looking at the people's faces. Some stared, while a few scowled or narrowed their eyes.

"Arrest the rag head for littering the neighborhood!" came a shout from a pot-bellied man in his late forties, as Charlie followed Nancy toward the sidewalk and storefront.

Charlie turned his head to stop and stare at the redneck, who was wearing a stars and stripes cap and a white T-shirt with the black target image of an Arab holding an AK-47 and an X in the middle of his forehead.

"You work out?" Gordon asked quite clearly, looking at the guy's midsection.

Several people laughed and the guy shot them angry glances.

Dawud, who'd been trying to ignore the crowd, turned when Gordon spoke and grinned.

"Good to see you, pal," Gordon said, reaching out his hand to shake.

Charlie stopped to greet the Afghan man as well, then turned to face the crowd, for once hoping someone would recognize him. Nancy, behind and to his left at his eight o'clock, had positioned

Ruth out of the way, blocking her from anyone out in the parking lot, so she was safe.

"That's Charlie Henry, the Navajo soldier from Shiprock," someone said aloud. "He was beside Captain Whitaker in the park."

"What are you doing *here* with the enemy?" a skinny woman in tight jeans and a red, white, and blue sweatshirt asked.

Charlie saw his opening. "What enemy? I've come to visit my friend Mr. Koury. He saved American lives, including mine and that of my buddy Gordon, from the Taliban. He and his family are Americans now and we owe him our thanks and protection, not our paranoia."

"Why don't you people free up the police to track down the shooter instead of forcing them to work crowd control," Gordon suggested. He turned and joined Charlie in escorting Dawud into the market.

Several minutes later, Nancy and DuPree were interviewing Dawud and his wife, hoping to get the names of any possible rad- icalized Middle Easterners they might have come into contact with in the community. Their introductions complete, Charlie, Gordon, and Ruth were ready to return to work.

Charlie and Ruth watched, from just inside the market, as Gordon walked out to bring his truck around to the front of the business. With only a few people still outside and a clear field of fire now, they were once again concerned about a potential sniper.

Gordon had reached his truck when a figure suddenly came into view from around the front of the big Dodge.

"It looks like that troublemaker, the one Gordon ridiculed, Charlie," Ruth exclaimed. "Gordon's in trouble!"

"No, Beer Belly is in trouble," Charlie said.

"The man outweighs Gordon by fifty or more pounds. He's as big as Jake."

"Jake can handle himself, but I bet this guy is all hat and no cowboy."

Ruth laughed. "He's wearing a cap."

"Don't know any cap analogies," Charlie responded, still watching Gordon, who appeared to be in a serious conversation at the moment. He wondered if the guy with the target on his chest knew Gordon was packing—not that Gordon would shoot the guy.

After a minute, the two men shook hands, and the guy in the cap walked away. Gordon turned, looked toward the market, and waved.

"It's okay now," Charlie commented, waving back.

A minute later, Gordon pulled up next to the curb, with the passenger side nearest the market, and Ruth stepped out and climbed into the cab, Charlie right behind her.

As Gordon put the truck into motion, Ruth was first to speak. "What was going on between you and that guy?"

"The guy's name is Donnie, no last name, and he's former Navy. He Googled us on his phone while we were inside talking to Dawud and his wife. Donnie wanted to apologize for disrespecting us—his words—and he thanked me for my military service."

"What did he say about Dawud?" Charlie asked.

"He said he still hates Muslims, but that if we say Dawud is okay, he can go along with that. He won't be bothering the Kourys anymore," Gordon replied.

"The Kourys are Christian, aren't they?" Ruth asked.

"Yes, which is one of the reasons Dawud helped us out. I wonder what Nancy and Wayne are getting from their interview?" Charlie speculated.

"Wayne?" Ruth asked.

"Only God and Charlie can call him that," Gordon responded. "DuPree hates me."

"Naw, he just can't stand you," Charlie said.

Ruth smiled. "Not to change the subject, guys, but Nancy told me she'd be stopping by FOB later. Meanwhile, we need to get back because there's work to do and Jake's handling it alone. Gordon, you want to work on the new website while Charlie and I help out front?"

"Jake can finally take a break," Charlie said.

"Uh-oh, he drinks a *lot* of coffee. Pedal to the metal," Gordon said, pulling out into traffic.

The rest of the morning was better than routine, with more business coming in, much of it from buyers interested in the one-of-a-kind bargains they'd discovered online. It wasn't until noon that Nancy showed up to discuss the Kourys.

Jake and Gordon brought back sandwiches from the little deli bar at Frank and Linda's grocery, just three doors down the block, so they ate in the office while Nancy spoke to Charlie out front. Ruth was taking care of the register and conducting a transaction with a middle-aged couple selling collectible porcelain figurines, a subject Charlie knew nothing at all about.

"I saw some surveillance cameras outside along the roof line of the produce shop. Did they capture some images of the vandals?" Charlie asked Nancy, who'd stepped behind the counter and was sitting on a stool beside him.

"Hopefully. DuPree assigned one of the sergeants to follow up on that. But regarding possible suspects in the murder and the attempt on your life, neither of the Kourys could suggest anyone who might be involved. They only know a few immigrants from their part of the world, most of them other college-educated people who were also driven from their homes by the Taliban. We got a list of names, and that was pretty much it," Nancy explained.

"What about the younger crowd—the children of those who've settled in the area? Those are the ones less connected to Afghanistan and the Middle East, the ones most susceptible to terrorist propaganda on the internet," Charlie asked, looking across the big room as he spoke.

"Yeah, that's the problem. We confirmed something we already knew, that their son has been in a lot of trouble at school."

"But Caleb was at school today?"

"Yes, but if he gets into trouble again, at least at school, he's probably going to get a long-term suspension," Nancy said. "He's been in three fights this year, according to Dawud. Caleb is taking a lot of abuse, name-calling, crap like that. He won't back down or walk away."

"Kids his age can be evil, and sometimes you've got to stand up for yourself," Charlie answered, having dealt with the being-Navajo issue himself when off the Rez. "Fear and hatred are alive and well after 9-11, and there is so much guilt by association handed out by people who need to strike back at someone."

"I think we're better than that, at least in the long run. Unfortunately, we have to deal with the *now*," Nancy reminded.

"Did you or Wayne ask if they thought Caleb might be involved in the shooting? That would be an extreme way of striking back at the country that has become so hostile to his family, especially if he's become radicalized."

Nancy shook her head. "What they are worried about is that he might turn violent against those harassing him at school."

"Are they sure he's even there?"

"He was dropped off by his father this morning, early, and there's an automated call to the parents if he's counted absent."

"And the daughter?"

"She's thirteen and in the eighth grade—middle school. So far, there haven't been any problems, at least none reported. Justine is coping better, I suppose," Nancy said. "She's made a lot of friends, they say."

"Nice to have allies your own age. Did you have problems when you came out?"

"Yeah, some, but that wasn't until I was a senior, and by then, everyone was too concerned about sports, dating, college, or just graduating high school, to cause any major problems. Besides, I had gay friends and we looked out for each other."

"And it wasn't like you were trying to destroy America."

"Depends on who you ask."

"I get it. So what now?"

Nancy's phone rang, and she looked down. "Hang on, I gotta take this."

Charlie looked away, but listened in once he knew it was DuPree calling.

Nancy ended the call and stood. "Gotta go. You hear that?"

"Only that the terrorist had made a new threat."

"Yeah, this time it's taking a new direction. The guy claims that the next hero is going to die by fire. Burned alive, the message says," Nancy added.

Chapter Seven

"Was the message left at a school again?" Charlie asked.

"You nailed it. The announcement was in one of those envelopes, this time thrown over a wall into a private elementary school yard in Corrales about a half hour ago. One of the kids found it, apparently, and gave it to a teacher."

"No video of the delivery?" Charlie asked.

"Not that we know of, not yet. Apparently there's no camera coverage outside the wall. Local officers are canvassing people in the area, business owner and such, and asking for help on social media. This was on Corrales Road, which has regular traffic, so maybe someone in a passing car saw the guy toss the envelope. Whoever is doing this is keeping a low profile."

"You involved?" Charlie asked as his cell phone began to chime.

"Corrales officers and Sandoval County deputies are handling it," Nancy said. "Go ahead and answer that."

A minute later, Charlie ended the call and looked toward the office. He waved at Gordon to come over, then turned to Nancy.

"Mr. Koury's son has disappeared," he announced.

"You sure about that?" she asked.

"Yeah. Maybe. According to Dawud, Caleb left school early to avoid an after-school fight threat, deciding to walk home. The boy had called Dawud to let him know, but now Caleb's phone keeps going to voice mail. Dawud doesn't want to leave his wife alone at the market, and his part-time employee has the afternoon off . . ."

"So Mr. Koury needs your help," Nancy said.

"Exactly. I'm going to track down Caleb and give him a ride. We've met, and I think he'll trust me," Charlie said. "Cibola High is just across the river. I can get there in ten minutes this time of day."

"What's up?" Gordon asked, coming up to join them.

"Dawud's son may be in trouble and I told our friend we'd check it out. Caleb was going to walk home, but now his dad can't reach him on the boy's phone. You think Ruth and Jake will be safe here?" Charlie asked.

"I've got to talk to Ruth, so I'll be here for a while anyway. Go!" Nancy ordered.

Two minutes later they were on the road, this time in Charlie's Dodge Charger.

"We have any idea what route Caleb will be walking?" Gordon asked, his phone out with a map app on the screen. "I'd recommend we follow the most direct route from school to home. We've both been at the Kourys' so I'll have the app show me the way."

"Yeah, but we'll start from the high school. If he got jumped, that probably happened right away," Charlie said.

"Did Dawud call the school?" Gordon asked.

"He didn't say," Charlie answered, turning onto Alameda

Road, which led across the bridge to the west. The high school was only a few minutes beyond the river, off Ellison Road.

They drove slowly past Cibola High School, on their left, noting the student parking lot full of cars. A few yellow school buses were pulling into a loading zone, but classes didn't let out for another half hour, according to what Charlie had learned.

"Riding a bus must be tough for high school kids, you think? All that pressure to be cool and have a car, or friends with a car," Gordon speculated as they drove west.

"Back in Shiprock when I was in school, most of the kids, especially the Navajos, rode the bus. Low income and all that, plus so many kids lived twenty or more miles away out in the sticks. It was okay if an older brother or sister dropped you off, but riding with a parent—that wasn't manly at all," Charlie admitted. "Peer pressure is probably a lot worse now."

"I walked to school back in Denver, but my friends stuck together. Lots of perverts and drunks on the streets in my 'hood."

"And gangs?"

"Yeah, but they didn't hassle you in the mornings, I guess it was too early after hanging out all night. But if you had to go back to school in the evening, or stayed for athletics, it could be rough."

"That's when you learned to defend yourself?"

"Boys' Club saved my ass, and one of my teachers lived across from our apartment building. Until I learned some skills, he kept me alive. One night he got shot walking home. I wish I'd have been there to have his back."

Charlie shook his head. "You'd have been shot too, Gordo."

"We'll never know." Gordon looked at the phone. "Turn here," he nodded to the right.

Charlie drove into a nice middle-class neighborhood with similar-looking, two-story, single-family homes placed less than twenty feet from each other. There were no power lines or telephone poles on these streets, all the wires and cables were underground.

"Barely any vehicles in the driveways or along the curb. No junkers, and nice and clean. I wonder if everyone is at work," Charlie observed. "Nobody on foot, so either he's between houses or standing in one of the recessed entryways."

"He could have gone another way, of course, or ran like hell and is farther ahead."

"You watch your side. If you spot any residents outside, let's stop and ask if anyone's seen a kid passing through."

"Suppose Caleb knows anyone in this neighborhood?" Gordon asked.

"This is in the school's district and Cibola has a lot of students, so it's likely. But I got the idea that Caleb hadn't made a lot of friends, and Dawud reported that Caleb said he was alone," Charlie answered.

"So we'll cruise the 'hood. The backyards are all walled in, but there's a utility easement that we can't see from here. If I was hauling ass away from school on foot, I'd take that route. You'd be invisible to anyone cruising the streets looking for you," Gordon reminded.

"You're right, city boy," Charlie affirmed. "I'll turn at the next intersection so we can get in position to see down the alley."

The street ran for a dozen or more blocks created by several intersecting streets just along the west side, before finally reaching another road that went in the right direction. They stopped and looked south. To the east was a long, empty flood-control canal, and along the west side of the canal was that easement. The dirt utility road curved back and forth—the houses following the undulating terrain rather than a straight line—so they couldn't see the entire length of the route.

"Drive down the easement, Charles," Gordon suggested.

"Yeah, unless he's already gone past this point."

"If he's already made it this far, chances are he's alone and probably safe," Gordon said. "If he's gotten into a fight, he could be hurt somewhere along the way, maybe even got tossed into the ditch."

"Here goes, then."

The unpaved easement was in good shape, with recent tire tracks from utility vehicles or joyriders, and at the halfway point, they discovered a small enclosure in the cinder-block walls located between adjoining properties that contained some kind of electrical transformer protected on three sides by the high walls.

"There he is!" Charlie said, slamming on the brakes and raising a cloud of dust.

Caleb Koury was in a corner, fists up, facing three young men. Book bags and papers were strewn across the dirt.

Gordon was out first, closest to the enclosure. "Walk away, guys. Get back to school before the cops arrive."

"Screw you, shorty," yelled one of the teens, a sturdy-looking linebacker-size seventeen-year-old who stood a head taller than Gordon. "You get the hell out of here before you get hurt. We're teaching this Arab a little respect for America."

"Quit talking trash and walk away, brain dead," Gordon warned. "You too," he added to the other two teens still blocking Caleb in the corner.

Charlie came around the front of the Charger and got their attention instantly. He was taller than them all, and had on his mean face. "Want me to hold your weapon while you crack a few skulls, Gordon?" he suggested, sliding back his jacket enough to show his holstered Beretta.

"Louie, they're carrying!" one of the teens exclaimed.

"Hey, Mr. Henry," Caleb greeted, managing a weak smile. "Just let them go."

"Or we could beat the crap out of them," Gordon said, grinning now.

"I'm outta here," one of the two in the back called out. He turned, grabbed the shoulder strap of a book bag, then stepped out and began walking down the easement in the direction of the school.

"Wait up!" the other one yelled, grabbing another bag and hustling away.

"Well, son, it's just you and us now," Charlie said, stepping up beside Gordon. "What's it gonna be?"

"Who the hell are you, anyway?" the young man exclaimed, his voice now a little shaky despite his size.

"Your friend or your worst enemy. It's your call . . ."

"Louie. Louie Edmonds."

"Good to know you, Louie Edmonds. We done here?"

Louie nodded, then started looking around for something.

Caleb stepped up and handed him a book bag.

"Thanks," the big guy mumbled, then turned and hurried to join his two companions, who were waiting about fifty feet away.

"Thanks for finding me, Mr. Henry, and Gordon, uh, Mr. Sweeney. Did my father send you?"

"No. We volunteered. He couldn't get you on your cell, and with all that was going on, he didn't want to leave your mother alone at the market," Charlie said. "Or bring her with him if they'd be heading into trouble. I talked him out of closing the shop, then said we'd give you a ride."

"My father is very protective of our family. He didn't want me to go to school today," Caleb said, bending down to examine an open backpack on the ground. The contents were scattered, including notebooks, pencils, and two books.

Gordon and Charlie joined him, picking up the supplies. They were quickly stowed in the pack, which had been torn open at a zipper. "What happened to your cell phone?" Gordon asked.

"When my classmates jumped me, they tried to take the phone. I threw it over the wall into the backyard of that house," Caleb said, pointing to his left.

Charlie stepped back out of the enclosure and looked at the eight-foot-high wall. "I hope the residents don't have a dog," he mumbled, jumping up and pulling himself to the top of the wall.

He glanced at the rear of the house, where there was a covered patio with a small mosaic tile table and chairs. Fortunately no one was visible, neither man nor beast, so he dropped down into the backyard. Quickly he found the phone atop some landscape bark, put the device in his jacket pocket, then leaped up and pulled himself back over the wall, landing in a crouch back in the alley. "This it?" he asked, handing Caleb the phone.

"Yessir. How'd you make it over the wall so easy at your . . . well, thanks again," Caleb said, checking the phone's display.

"At his advanced age? Charlie can barely walk." Gordon chuckled, handing Caleb a Sharpie he'd found on the ground.

"You'd have needed a boost, or a ladder. *Shorty*, is that what Louie called you?" Charlie said, smiling.

"I could have made it in a single bound," Gordon argued. "Did you get all your stuff, Caleb?" he added, turning to the teen.

Caleb took a quick glance around, then stared down the easement in the direction of the high school. The ones who'd cornered him were out of sight now, apparently having cut between two adjacent houses and onto the street to the west. "Good to go. That the expression?"

"Your English is nearly perfect," Charlie mentioned, walking toward the Dodge.

"Before Christianity was banned, both my parents learned the language from their parents. My sister and I were taught at home," Caleb explained. "But I'm still discovering what my father calls street English."

"I grew up on that. You'll learn," Gordon commented as they climbed into the car. "Okay, now tell us what went down this afternoon."

A half hour later, Charlie circled the block, then drove into the alley and parked in his slot beside the loading dock of FOB Pawn. "What do you think that threat of fire meant, coming from the supposed terrorist?" he asked, stepping quickly out of the car and moving toward the loading dock, key in hand.

"The idea of a flamethrower sounds ridiculous, but a car bomb, maybe, or their house or apartment set on fire?" Gordon responded, looking everywhere except at Charlie as he followed him up the steps.

"Hopefully not my place. That house has taken a beating since

I moved in, and I bet Nestor is thinking that renting it to his cousin was a really bad idea," Charlie said.

They were inside, the door closed, less than five seconds later. Charlie glanced toward the office. It was empty, but he could see Ruth and Jake in the main room, working together at the front register with customers. There were two other people standing, waiting their turn to be served.

"Looks like FOB OK is working," Gordon muttered, then headed out to greet the people waiting, motioning them toward the second register at the back counter.

Charlie started forward to help out, then the phone in the office rang. "I've got it," he called out. He was almost disappointed to find out it was a business call.

Charlie left with Ruth to pick up Rene at school while Gordon and Jake took care of business. Once the three were back, that allowed Jake and Gordon to leave for the day. Rene stayed in the office, doing homework and reading, while Charlie and Ruth dealt with the final client of the day and closed up the shop.

Charlie had checked back with Nancy just before closing, and there was no news of any incident that might be related to another attack. Then Ruth called Deputy Marshal Stannic. At least there was progress being made. Three men suspected of helping Lawrence Westerfield escape were apprehended in New York, but those arrested claimed that they'd split into two groups, with Lawrence and another man headed for Canada. Those captured were ex-cons carrying five thousand dollars cash, payment they claimed came from one of Lawrence's stashes. There were no other leads concerning Lawrence, and no description of the man with him, but at the same time there were no reports that he'd been on any form of public transportation since his escape.

The threat against the local heroes took almost all of the law enforcement agencies' attention, but at least the various agencies had been given photos of Lawrence and an ATL bulletin—attempt to locate. The identity of the man with Lawrence remained a mystery.

Charlie and Ruth decided that Westerfield was probably hiding somewhere back east, possibly in a remote or rural area, and that his mention of Canada was just a ruse. Lawrence was obsessed, and if he still had access to money, Charlie had no doubt he'd come for Ruth. She, however, was worried about Charlie, not herself or Rene.

When they finally left FOB Pawn, they decided to go somewhere for dinner, then Charlie could take them home and stay until late. At that point, they'd decide if he should return to his own place or sleep on the sofa again.

Charlie chose one of his favorite north valley restaurants, a popular place with locals that served New Mexican fare, but more importantly, had a congested parking lot filled with old cottonwood trees and narrow rows for vehicles. The shooter would have to get up close, risking being seen, and there were plenty of cameras covering the grounds. So far, even the envelopes he'd dropped containing the threats had been left at locations selected because there was no camera coverage. Basically, Charlie felt they were safe in a well-lit, crowded environment.

As Charlie pulled into the closest parking slot he could find, he noticed a pickup behind him, also apparently looking for a parking place. Glancing into the rearview mirror, he realized something looked very familiar about the driver.

The man cocked his head slightly to the right, a signal that dated back years ago, in Afghanistan, and sent a chill down Charlie's spine. It was Russell Turner—CIA—and the fact that he'd allowed Charlie to spot him was a message. Turner would be watching over them tonight.

"Something wrong?" Ruth asked, glancing in the side mirror.

"No. I guess the guy behind us was thinking we were getting ready to leave, and was waiting for us to pull out," Charlie hedged, looking back as the truck passed by.

"It looks like they have a good customer base here. The lot is almost full. You don't think we're being watched, do you?" she added.

Charlie shook his head, wishing he could talk openly, then recalled how his parents often began conversations, and then stopped abruptly when they knew their children might be listening. He'd have to remember Rene was in the backseat. The boy had spent much of his childhood living in secrecy, and Charlie didn't want to bring the anxieties connected to that back again for Ruth's son.

He climbed out quickly, took a quick look at the other patrons in the lot heading toward the entrance or their vehicles, and circled around to join Ruth, who'd climbed out on her own. He'd been raised old-school, his parents were from a time when gentlemen opened doors for ladies, and didn't know how Ruth felt about that.

Rene was out by now as well, and Ruth took his hand, turning to greet Charlie. "Thanks for coming around, Charlie, but I think we need to get inside."

He had his backup pistol, a small .380, in his pocket, having left the more capable Beretta in the Charger. With his concealed carry permit, he wasn't worried about breaking any important laws. The place had a liquor license, but he never imbibed while on a security detail, no matter how pleasant the company.

Charlie took Ruth by the hand, and together they entered the restaurant's lobby. After leaving his name with the hostess, they found seats on a long wooden bench, waiting for a table. Soon Charlie's cell phone rang, showing only the number.

"This is Charlie," he answered, already aware of who was calling.

Turner spoke softly. "There is no indication that this is anything but a lone-wolf attack, though the shootings have been praised in the Middle East by the usual idiots. I'll be keeping an eye on you tonight, but stay focused. Don't get too distracted."

"Okay, Al. Say hi to your wife and kids for me, okay?" He hung up on Turner, annoyed that the CIA man needed to remain anonymous, and he had to mislead Ruth again.

She smiled. "Your brother checking up on you?"

Charlie put the phone away. "Something like that." He noticed Rene had leaned over and was looking into the room to the left—the bar and lounge.

"Can we go sit on those stools, Mom? There are three with nobody on them."

Ruth laughed. "I don't think you're old enough, not yet anyway."

"They serve alcohol in there, Rene," Charlie explained, "like wine and beer. You'd have to show them your ID."

"I brought mine," he responded, bringing out the lanyard holding his elementary school photo ID. "Just kidding."

They all laughed, and Charlie finally relaxed.

Around 3:00 AM the next morning, on Ruth's sofa again, Charlie woke up with an idea, entered it as a text message, then set it to send to Gordon at 7:00 AM. It took a while to get back to sleep after that, as his mind was racing.

Chapter Eight

"So you're not convinced there's a terrorist out there, Charlie?" Ruth asked, sitting beside him in Gordon's pickup as they waited at the stoplight. It was 9:00 AM, and they'd left Jake and Gordon behind to run the shop. Charlie still didn't want to leave Ruth or Jake unprotected, not that Jake couldn't take care of himself. He was an ex-pro wrestler, smart, fit, and healthy even in his mid-sixties.

Charlie shrugged. "I'm not completely sold on the theory, though the evidence so far is hard to dispute. But there are also so many contradictions to the typical terrorist attacks that I want to rule out the other possibilities. There are hundreds of cops and agents working that angle, and not so many looking elsewhere. Maybe I was the intended target, or you, or the both of us, and your ex is responsible. Or maybe the helicopter pilot, but for a totally different reason."

"Which means those 'kill the heroes' messages are the killer's way of misleading the investigation. I get that. So we're going to find out whoever else might have wanted to kill Captain . . . the guy who died," she said, remembering the taboo.

"There are also plenty of Feds and state agencies back east looking for Lawrence, especially now that they've caught three of his crew. Here, we've got Gordon and other friends to protect us from another attack. I've got to help out where I can do the most good," Charlie answered. "I don't think we're going to be in any danger today, at least not until it gets dark. But stay very close, okay?"

"That's easy; besides, I feel safe when you're around, Charlie. I trust you with my life, and so does Rene. I'll stay alert. I was also wondering why the person doing all this hasn't attacked during daytime. I don't think it's just because they don't want to be identified."

"Okay, Ruth, what's your theory?"

"Well, if the attacker is a local, then maybe they can't get away during the daytime simply because they're at work. Taking time off to shoot at someone, assuming they don't want to get caught, takes away their alibi. Just a thought," Ruth added.

"That also suggests they're not die-hard fanatics on a suicide path," Charlie nodded, continuing down the street, and glancing over at the GPS. "You're making some good points."

"Which leads back to a personal motive, Charlie. Otherwise, why attack a soldier unless they blame someone in the military for the death of a loved one? Or maybe they blame the military for the suicide of a former soldier, or they have a grievance against the Army. I find it hard to believe that you and the man who was killed at Recognition Park have anything in common except having served overseas in Iraq and Afghanistan."

"I also have to consider the possibility that it's *my* enemy, someone who wants *me* dead, but is just a lousy shot. I hate to think of the captain as collateral damage, but there it is," Charlie said.

"In the meantime we're going to the Back Up office to see if the owner had any enemies closer to home."

Charlie nodded. "The person running day-to-day operations right now is Max Mitchell. He's an Army vet, and from his voice I think he's probably in his sixties. Mitchell said we can talk to him and the bookkeeper, if she's willing," Charlie said.

"There's the place," Ruth said, pointing to a small, olive drab one-story block building behind a warehouse along Second Street. "Not much bigger than a two-car garage."

"From what I gather, this is where the boss, his assistant, and the full-time bookkeeper work. Their clients, all vets—check the website, call in, or stop by to find out whatever temporary jobs are available or have been assigned to them. Everything from construction, clerical, delivery, warehouse work, and apprentice or job-training opportunities, I guess," Charlie answered, making the turn off Second Street into a small parking lot. Three vehicles were parked next to the building, and a red pickup was across the street, the driver with a phone to his ear.

Charlie glanced at the driver, who looked familiar for some reason, then took the keys out of the ignition and grabbed his own phone from the center console.

This time when he came around, Ruth waited for Charlie to give her a hand stepping down out of the oversized truck. "Is that a plainclothes officer parked over there?" she asked, looking across the street.

"Maybe. I've seen the guy before, but can't recall where or when."

There was a wide, low concrete pad that served as a porch to the building, and Charlie could hear voices as he reached for the doorknob. As they stepped into what was the front office, Charlie recognized Patricia Azok, the woman sitting at one of two desks positioned side by side. At the second desk stood a bright-eyed, silver-haired, husky man. This was Max Mitchell, undoubtedly, who was wearing a worn leather vest over a long-sleeved, black T-shirt with stars and stripes running diagonally across a sagging chest. The air had the strong scent of cigars.

Patricia Azok looked a little bit better than the last time he'd seen her—at the hospital—just after her ex-husband had died. Charlie thought it appropriate to greet her first, though he was a bit uncertain regarding what to say.

"Good morning, ma'am. We met at the hospital. I want to offer my condolences once more for the loss of . . . Captain Whitaker," he added.

"Sergeant Henry, yes, I remember, and I want to thank you again for all you tried to do to help my . . . Nathan," Patricia replied softly, a hitch in her voice. "Call me Patricia, I still haven't gotten rid of Azok."

"I wish I'd been able to do more, Patricia. I'd like you to meet my very good friend Ruth," Charlie said.

"Ruth! Janice said that you helped her hold it together, and did everything you could to help the other wounded," she said, stepping over and giving Ruth a big hug. "Thank you."

"I'm so sorry. His loss is being deeply felt in this community, and all over the country as well," Ruth responded, joining in the embrace.

Patricia stepped back, managing a smile. "I guess you should meet Mr. Mitchell. Max has been Nathan's right-hand man here at Back Up. He's conducting the daily operations for as long as he's willing to stay on."

Max, who'd stood immediately when they came through the door, held out his hand and gave Charlie a hardy handshake. "Sergeant Henry. Glad to meet you, soldier, despite the situation. Thank you for your service to your country and to your tribe."

"And thank you for yours as well," Charlie responded, noting a ball cap on a coat hook with the distinctive yellow shield, black diagonal stripe, and horse head of the 1st Calvary Division. "Vietnam, before I was born?"

Max nodded. "I was airborne infantry, in-country from '65 to '67. Hate the jungle and the forever rain, which is probably why I moved to New Mexico."

"Smart. I'll take the desert every time," Charlie observed.

"For sure." Max nodded. "Now, let's get down to business and see if we have any idea who might have killed Nathan, then ambushed you at your pawn shop."

Charlie looked up as an attractive blond woman in a striped shirt and jeans appeared in the open doorway leading into the interior of the building. Her eyebrows were raised in curiosity, but her face drooped slightly from obvious fatigue. She must be the bookkeeper, he thought.

"Excuse me, people, I don't mean to interrupt, but it gets lonely back in my office sometimes and I heard voices. You're looking for part-time help at your business, Mr. . . ." She held out her hand to Charlie.

"Charlie Henry, ma'am," he answered, "and no, I'm just here

with my friend Ruth to learn more about Captain Whitaker's associates and contacts, and maybe his enemies."

"Ah, you're one of the vets who was at the ceremony. Sorry I didn't recognize you right away, Sergeant Henry. I'm Anna Brown, the bookkeeper. I understand you've also become a target for this terrorist. Stay careful and stay safe, soldier.

"And hello, Ruth, pleased to meet you as well," Anna added, shaking Ruth's hand.

Patricia spoke. "You said enemies, Charlie. Do you think there is more than one terrorist in our community?"

Charlie explained his ruling-out strategy, and the reason why he and Ruth were here—to get to know more about Nathan, his activities, contacts, and friends, the business, and to determine if the shooter could have been someone with a personal motive for killing him.

"Then why would someone who came to kill Nathan want to shoot at you, Charlie? They'd already done what they came for," Anna asked, leaning against the doorframe. "Did you know Nathan, or have dealings with him?"

"No, but here's my reasoning. If everyone is led to believe the shooter is a terrorist, then the true motive for killing Captain Whitaker might never be discovered. Fake a few more attacks on what the press has labeled heroes, egged on by some fake messages from the shooter claiming his politics, and the shooter misdirects the entire investigation," Charlie explained. "It becomes a terrorist witch hunt, not a criminal investigation."

"And it might take years, maybe never, for law enforcement to realize they'd been led down the garden path," Max concluded. "There is some logic to your theory, Charlie. All of us here knew

Nathan quite well. Can you guys think of any local idiot who might have wanted to kill him?"

Both Max and Anna looked at Patricia, and Charlie suddenly caught on. The guy in the red pickup across the street was Steven Azok! He was clearly a control freak, and must have been extremely jealous of Nathan. Azok blamed Nathan for breaking up his marriage. And right now, the guy was outside, stalking his soon-to-be ex-wife.

"What is it, Charlie?" Ruth asked, reading his expression.

"Tell you later. Um, Patricia, have you had any more problems with Steven since the incident at the hospital?" he decided to ask. It was apparent to him that the other people must also know something about her domestic problems.

"No, I haven't seen or heard from him directly, except at the hospital. My lawyer is handling any required contact with Steven. A few weeks ago, before Nathan died, I was able to get a court order that required Steven to keep his distance and stop trying to communicate with me," she answered. "Anna and Max know about my situation, and how Nathan and I had planned to get together again after . . . after my divorce." Tears came to her eyes.

Charlie doubted that the woman knew her husband was outside watching; either that, or she was afraid of a confrontation.

Everyone waited silently for Patricia to regain her composure, and Charlie quickly texted Gordon as unobtrusively as possible.

After a few awkward moments Patricia was able to speak again. "I'd like to think that the bastard had nothing to do with Nathan's murder, but he's so jealous and possessive I had to tell the detectives. Steven had threatened Nathan once I told him I wanted a divorce. Not that it matters, I suppose, Steven never followed up on that. He just got abusive. Nathan's killer is a terrorist, and even though Steven has a terrible temper, he's very much a patriot. At least he respected Nathan's military service. Steven said so more than once."

He also called Nathan a bastard, Charlie thought as he recalled overhearing Azok at the hospital, and he was apparently quick to arrive after the shooting. Had Azok been watching Patricia, who was at her apartment that night, or did he follow the ambulance to the hospital from the park after taking the shot? A shooter might have done that to make sure his victim was dead.

"We'll still want to speak to Mr. Azok about this, however—just to cross him off the list of possible suspects," Charlie said.

"Do that," Max responded. "The guy—pardon me, Patricia—is a hot-headed whiner who doesn't have the guts to stand up to a man. He's definitely the kind of half-human who'd shoot an unarmed man from ambush."

"I'd have to agree with that," Anna said, nodding her head. "Everyone around here had great respect for Nathan. He returned home with issues—like a lot of us—but managed to get himself together again by starting up this company. Helping vets was his mission, and he stuck with it, operating on a shoestring and putting almost every dollar back into finding jobs and training for those who'd served."

"What she said," Max confirmed. "Nathan was tough and demanding, and not the best businessman, hence the need for Anna, but his heart was in this mission. Thanks to Patricia, we're going to continue his work as long as we can."

"Patricia, you're the owner now?" Ruth asked.

"Good question," Charlie added. "Were you and Nathan still partners, even after the divorce?"

Patricia nodded. "I was a silent partner. This was Nathan's baby, really, something he began while we were still married. Late yesterday I discovered that he'd left his half of the business to me in his trust. That's why I'm here now, hoping to find out exactly where the company stands at the moment."

Charlie took a quick glance at his phone, feeling the vibration of an incoming text. It was Gordon. *He's gone* was the message.

"Excuse me, something from the shop," Charlie hedged, turning his back for a second to tell Gordon to wait outside.

"Back Up serves as a temp service—an employment agency— that gets work for the clients in exchange for a percentage of the pay they receive from outside employers, is that correct?" Ruth asked.

"Yes, the vets who are paid in cash turn over Back Up's percentages directly to Anna, but most of the time the employers send us the paychecks, then we pay our clients their salaries after deducting that percentage. If the job becomes permanent, our percentage is phased out. Often we also arrange for job training, and that cost is shared with the vet trainee, paid back without interest over time. We make just enough money to cover our three-person staff and the office expenses," Max explained.

Anna nodded. "We don't make much, and money is especially tight right now, but that isn't why we're here. I was in the Air Force and served two tours in the Middle East, and if it hadn't been for community college and this place, I might be living on the street right now."

"How about the clients, the vets? Did Back Up—Nathan—ever have any trouble with someone who'd come here looking for work?" Charlie asked, thinking of PTSD and coping with being a civilian again.

"A few, from time to time, but it was usually connected with their employer as well. Some of our clients, well, more than a few, have issues with drinking, drugs, violence, finding housing, family issues," Max said. "That's why they came to us. But I've never seen anything more dramatic than an argument, or Nathan having to tell them he couldn't place them anywhere until they got some help from the VA."

Charlie looked at Anna, who simply nodded. "Same here."

"Okay, then, thanks to you, Patricia, Max, and Anna. If you think of anyone who might have considered Captain Whitaker an enemy, please let me or detectives Medina and DuPree know. Here's my business card." He handed one to each of them.

Charlie and Ruth thanked the three, then said good-bye and stepped outside, closing the door behind them.

As they stepped off the low porch Ruth took hold of Charlie's forearm. 'What was that business with the phone, texting during a conversation? You'd never do that around a client in the shop."

Then she noticed Gordon sitting in Charlie's car, parked just past Gordon's truck. "Oh. So what's going on?"

"Once Steven Azok's name came up, I realized that it was him sitting in that red pickup across the street when we arrived. He's been stalking Patricia, which means he's violating a restraining order."

She looked across the street. "You were hoping Gordon might

catch him sitting there watching, but you didn't want to go after him then and alarm Patricia."

"Right," Charlie answered as they walked over to Gordon.

"Sorry, bro," Gordon said as they approached the purple Charger. "By the time I got here, he was gone."

"It's okay. He'd seen me before as well, and might have been concerned that I'd recognize him and go postal," Charlie said.

"Like I did?" Gordon grinned, looking up at Ruth. "Hi!"

"Don't try and slide past that, Gordon. When did you get rough with Steven Azok?"

Charlie shrugged. "We didn't tell you about meeting the guy at the hospital the night of the shooting. He was manhandling Patricia, so Gordon showed him the door."

"Gordon threw him out?" Ruth replied.

"Wish I had, but no, eventually he ended up leaving under his own power," Gordon said.

"Okay, then we go back to the shop?" Ruth asked Charlie.

Charlie looked up and down the street for several seconds. "How about we circle the block and see if he's just gone out of sight, waiting for us to leave?"

"And if we find him?" Ruth asked.

"He'll get the same level of respect we show all men who abuse women," Gordon said, sliding over into the passenger seat. "You drive, it's your car," he told Charlie.

Charlie opened the backseat door for Ruth. "Buckle up."

She climbed inside, grumbling something that could have been a curse.

He looked back, trying to read her expression in the rearview mirror, and she managed a weak smile. "Be careful," she urged.

"Hey, you know us," Gordon said, fastening his own seat belt.

"That's the problem. No violence, guys, please," she added.

Charlie started the car and pulled out into the narrow side street, heading west down the block. Charlie slowed and looked south down the alley, but saw no pickup.

"Unless you're in danger," Ruth finally added.

The businesses merged into an old residential area just at the end of the block, so Charlie made a left and headed south. All three of them were looking into parking lots and along the street for the red vehicle.

"Gordon, you checked the alley running north, didn't you?" Charlie asked.

"Of course, I'm watching my side all the way," he responded.

As soon as Charlie began the turn back east at the next intersection, Ruth called out, "Is that it?" She pointed across the street, halfway up the block.

"Might be," Charlie commented. "Try to get an ID, Gordon. Ruth and I will keep eyes front so we won't spook the guy."

As they drove past, Gordon looked out of the corner of his eye without turning his head, all part of his urban recon training. "He's got a hat and sunglasses, but I recognize that weak chin. It's Azok. He's got a gun rack in the back—empty though."

"He's a rifle owner, no surprise. Crap, there he goes," Charlie exclaimed as the pickup suddenly accelerated out from the curb and fled in the opposite direction. "Hang on, you two!"

Chapter Nine

With no traffic at the moment and no vehicles along the curb, Charlie was free to go Grand Theft Auto. He whipped the low-slung Dodge around in a moonshiner's turn and raced after the pickup, which was already taking the corner in a wild skid.

"What'll we do if we catch him?" Ruth asked, hanging onto the door handle.

"One step at a time," Gordon interjected. "Hopefully, he won't make a left. Crap, too late."

The pickup swung left, slid sideways, then straightened out and roared down the center of the residential neighborhood. Azok leaned on the horn and three teenagers in the middle of the street fled to the curb just in time.

Charlie took his foot off the gas and slid through the turn with squealing tires. "I'm not going to keep up the pursuit, guys. It's not worth risking some kid or pet getting run over. He's won this one."

"I hope Azok slows down before it's too late," Ruth replied.

"Where do you think he's going now? Maybe we can catch up to him somewhere? His apartment?"

"We can't do much except lean on him and have someone call the cops. There's no way we can prove the stalking. A police officer has to catch him in the act," Charlie reminded.

"Azok is a real nutcase, but he probably won't come back here right away. He knows we'll be returning to Back Up for my truck," Gordon said.

"He's obsessed with Patricia, so where will he go, then? To her apartment, maybe?" Ruth offered.

"Yeah, that's a good bet. We don't know how long Patricia is going to be at the business today, but how about if one of us stakes out Back Up and sees where she goes when she leaves?" Charlie suggested. "And the other can go to her apartment and see if Azok shows up and gets into position."

"We don't know where she lives, do we?" Ruth asked.

"But we know someone who does," Gordon pointed out. "Unofficially, of course."

"Nancy," Ruth replied.

They were back in the Back Up office parking lot in less than a minute, and all the vehicles were still there. After a quick call to Nancy, Charlie had the address for Patricia Azok's apartment.

"What did the detective say?" Gordon asked after writing down the details in a pocket spiral notebook.

Charlie shrugged. "Nancy said don't pick a fight, and don't hurt Azok except in self-defense. If he shows up at his wife's apartment, we're to keep out of sight and call Dispatch. They'll send an officer who can confirm Azok's violation of the restraining order.

And, just in case the guy is actually the killer, we're not supposed to get ourselves shot."

"I can live with that," Gordon responded, getting out of the Charger.

Ruth groaned. "Let's get set up, guys," she said, climbing out of the back. "And this time, I'm riding shotgun."

Gordon drove off, and they waited, parked halfway down the street in the northside alley behind a warehouse that had a FOR RENT sign on the side. They could see anyone coming down the street, and were angled so they could see into the residential area, in the direction Charlie guessed Azok would use for his approach.

Several minutes later, after watching a dozen cars and trucks pass by, Ruth looked over at Charlie with a wicked grin. "Aren't we a little old to go parking?"

"You're as old as you look, and you look young and beautiful. Wanna make out?"

Ruth laughed and Charlie joined in. After a moment, still smiling, she turned to him again. "Thanks, that helps with the tension. I thought for a while we might be heading into another shoot-out."

"Just say the word and I'll take you back to the pawn shop. I never, ever want to put you in danger, Ruth. I know that things get interesting around Gordon and me, and you could earn a lot more money elsewhere. You've got an MBA."

"You know my history, Charlie. I feel safer around you and your friends—my friends too—than anywhere else right now." She reached over and put her hand upon his.

Charlie's phone signaled a call and he reluctantly reached onto the console for it. "It's Gordon." Charlie put it on speaker.

"Charlie. The guy just pulled into his garage, switched to a black Toyota Camry, then took off again. I'm following at a distance," Gordon said.

"How about we try and put the squeeze on him?"

"Yeah, if we can get into position on a quiet street. No sense in getting anyone hurt, or risking a dent in the purple stallion," Gordon said.

"This car?" Ruth asked, rolling her eyes.

'Hi, Ruth," Gordon said. "You know Charlie loves the Charger."

"Enough. Where is Azok headed now?" Charlie asked, eager to confront the guy. If he'd been the one who ambushed him in the alley, Charlie had an idea that another confrontation might goad Azok into doing something really stupid.

"He's heading west on Candelaria," Gordon responded, "and that will make it hard for you to get ahead and cut him off. If he reaches Rio Grande Boulevard, he'll have to go either north or south."

"Or he could make a left or right on several streets before that. What's he up to, and why did he switch vehicles?" Charlie wondered aloud. "Keep following him, but stay loose. I'm going to go north to Griegos, then head for Rio Grande."

"If he goes south, though, there goes the plan."

"Yeah, well. There's also a lot more traffic south. It'll be easier to lose him anyway."

"Okay. Stay on speaker so we'll both have hands free for any sudden turns."

Charlie made the best use of the traffic lights he could, and a few minutes later he was approaching Rio Grande Boulevard. The news from Gordon was good; Azok had reached Rio Grande, turned north, and was coming in his direction. Charlie pulled over to the side and waited for Gordon's signal.

"Something's weird," Gordon said. "It's like he slowed down so I wouldn't lose him. You think he's setting a trap?"

Ruth looked over at him with raised eyebrows.

"He can't know I'm ahead of him on the same street," Charlie pointed out. "Just be careful and don't get any closer until I'm in position. You know the drill."

"Copy."

"What drill?" Ruth asked.

"We did this a few times in-country—Iraq."

"With body armor, plenty of guns, and maybe air cover."

"True. But if Azok shows a weapon, we're backing off. And when this goes down, please do everything I say, okay? I don't want you hurt."

"You've already said that."

"Just checking," Charlie responded.

A few minutes later Gordon spoke again. "Pull up and wait for the next green light, then go. He's approaching the inter-section, but probably can't make the light unless he decides to run it."

"Copy." Charlie pulled out into the street, coming to a stop at the intersection, where the light was red. "The speed limit on Rio Grande ahead drops to twenty-five, so he should close on me a little anyway."

Charlie timed it well, and was soon heading north with Azok's sedan behind him about a half dozen car lengths. After about a mile, in an area with large alfalfa fields on either side, Charlie was primed and ready. Anticipating Gordon's okay, he looked over to Ruth. "Get ready and hang on."

He looked into the side mirror. "Hey, Azok's slowing down." Charlie took his foot off the gas, dropping below 25 mph.

"Yeah," Gordon replied. "I'm closing in. Hit it!"

Charlie slammed on the brakes, but the Camry behind him was already pulling over to the shoulder. They came to a stop, and Charlie put the Charger into reverse, backing up within a few feet of the sedan. Gordon had pulled up right behind Azok, his truck angled to block the man from backing up, and a fence to the right blocked an escape in that direction.

Charlie jumped out, his Beretta at his hip, safety off. "Stay put, Ruth, and get ready to hit the deck if I yell gun."

Gordon was already approaching the car, hugging the driver's side. If Azok had a pistol, or especially a long gun, he'd have to lean out the window or open the door to shoot, and Charlie could see that coming. His hand was down by his holster, ready to draw if required.

"I'm unarmed, Henry. Don't you or your pal do anything stupid!" came a voice Charlie didn't recognize.

As he stepped up to the driver's door, it was clear that this wasn't Steven Azok. Just who the hell was this guy, and what was going on?

Gordon stepped up and looked in the backseat for another passenger. "They did a switch in Azok's garage. Who the hell are you?"

"Looks like ol' Steve has a younger brother," Charlie said, now that he'd thought about it a few seconds. Then he saw movement out of the corner of his eye—it was Ruth climbing out of the Charger.

"Call Nancy—Sergeant Medina—and tell her that Azok ditched us and his location is unknown. He may have returned to the Back Up office."

Ruth nodded. "Who is this man?"

"Aubrey Azok, lovely lady," the man replied. "Pleased to meet you."

Ruth grimaced, then turned her back and brought out her phone.

Charlie wanted to punch the guy right then, or maybe yank him out of the open window and give him a decent beatdown. Instead he decided on a mad dog stare.

Aubrey, if that was his real name, just smiled. "Is your passenger dating anyone?"

"Can I hit him?" Gordon asked, coming up beside the door.

"Short and baby-faced. You must be the guy Steve roughed up at the hospital the other night."

Both Charlie and Gordon nearly laughed, but there was nothing else they could do. "Where is your brother? Back home, cowering under his bed?" Charlie asked, then realized it was his own anger speaking, not his common sense. They'd been suckered, and it was their fault.

Aubrey shrugged. "No idea. Maybe you should stop by his home—again."

Gordon looked at Charlie, then nodded toward an approaching police car. "Might as well go."

They turned and headed back to their vehicles. "Have a nice day," Azok's brother yelled, followed by laughter.

"Back to the shop?" Gordon asked.

"Yeah, but let's swing back to Azok's place on the way," Charlie said.

When he climbed into the Charger, Ruth was waiting.

"We followed the wrong guy, huh?" she asked.

"Steve had his brother waiting at his house in the Toyota when he returned. Gordon couldn't see into the garage from the angle he was parked, so he assumed that Aubrey was Steve, switching vehicles," Charlie said as he checked traffic, then made a U-turn and headed south again, passing by Aubrey and Gordon, who were still parked on the shoulder.

"Okay. So we don't know where Steve is right now—home, Patricia's house, the business, or on the road," Ruth observed.

"Remind me to make sure he's not headed for the pawn shop, waiting for us to return," Charlie said, checking the mirror to verify that Gordon was now following.

"Nancy sent an officer to watch Back Up, then escort Patricia home to ensure she's not being watched again," Ruth affirmed. "Nancy's going to see if there's any surveillance that may have caught Steve violating the restraining order."

"Good idea. That could get him arrested. Even if he's not the shooter, Steve deserves some justice," Charlie said.

Fifteen minutes later, they approached Azok's house. There was no red pickup visible in the driveway or along the street, so Charlie pulled up beside the curb. "There's a garage window, let me take a look and see if the pickup is still inside."

Ruth unsnapped her seat belt and opened her door. "I've got this," she said, stepping up onto the sidewalk.

"No. If he's inside . . ."

"If he's the one who's killing people, I don't want him to have a reason to shoot you as a window peeper, Charlie. You've got my back, right?" She turned and walked briskly up the driveway.

"Copy," Charlie replied automatically. He already knew how brave and intelligent the lady was, but this was a new side of Ruth he'd never seen before. Beautiful and proactive—that made her even more amazing.

He looked back and forth, checking the windows, doors, and sides of the house, watching for the movement of a curtain, a shadow, anything that might reveal that Steve was watching, or about to react.

Ruth stood on tiptoe and looked inside the side window of the garage, then turned and shook her head. Next, she walked back along the side of the garage and took a quick glance behind the house before heading back toward the car. He leaned over and opened the door as she stepped up on the sidewalk.

She slipped inside gracefully, reaching for her seat belt. "No vehicles at all, not even in the alley behind the house. Here comes Gordon."

Charlie looked in the mirror, seeing his pal's pickup approaching. Gordon pulled up alongside, his passenger window down. "No sign of the red pickup, or any vehicle," Charlie said.

"So, back to the shop?" Gordon asked.

"Might as well," Charlie answered. "Then we can figure out what to do next."

"Okay. You hear from Nancy?"

"No. If I do, I'll give you a call," Charlie replied.

"Copy. See you in twenty," Gordon said, then drove away.

Charlie looked for traffic, then pulled away from the curb and followed Gordon. Then he looked over at Ruth and saw she was texting. "Rene?"

She nodded, checked the display on her phone, then smiled and entered a short message.

"Yes. I've got his teacher's cell phone number and she and I keep in touch. He's doing fine, working with his tablet on a spelling lesson."

"My parents say that their school tablets had a big Indian Chief, in headdress, on the front. And the entry device was a fat pencil," Charlie said.

"Rene began with a pencil and a spiral notebook. He still prefers drawing on paper instead of a screen."

"Colored pencils don't need a battery," he said. "But the good thing is, Rene is able to go to a regular school."

"Right now, I wish he was with us. There's still no news on Lawrence's whereabouts, and he promised to make me pay for sending him to prison."

"He was the one who decided to lie, cheat, and steal from his business contacts—and to hurt you and Rene. All you did was confirm what the FBI already knew."

"A man like Lawrence is a predator with no conscience. The only thing he'd blame himself for is getting caught. I hope he's hiding in some shed in the woods, cold and hungry, with nowhere to go," Ruth said. "How could I have loved a man who's so evil?"

"The heart often controls the brain, instead of the other way around," Charlie replied.

"So, are we stupid, thinking we might have the chance for a future together?" Ruth whispered.

Just the thought of that possibility, and the fact that she'd actually said it, made Charlie's heart pound, and he couldn't think at all for a moment. Finally he reached over and put his hand on hers. It was now or never time. "There's nothing that makes more sense than my feelings toward you, Ruth."

"You have no idea how long I've been waiting to hear that, Charlie."

They held hands until finally Charlie had to let go because of traffic, but he couldn't stop smiling until they entered FOB Pawn. It was past noon now, so Charlie and Ruth walked down to Frank and Linda's to pick up salads and sandwiches for everyone. They all ate in the office, taking turns helping customers who came into the shop.

About 1:00 PM, Charlie's phone rang. "It's Nancy, calling from her downtown desk," he announced to Gordon, who was working with the internet site.

"Detective Medina," Charlie greeted. "What's the news on the Azok brothers?"

"Aubrey, the younger one, has a mostly clean record—just some traffic citations—and works nights at one of the big-box stores in the shipping department. That explains why he was available to his brother, Steven, who is unemployed at the moment. I was able to get a look at elder Azok's rap sheet—all domestic violence arrests—and checked with his listed employer, a medical supply company. He worked part-time—afternoons and evenings—making deliveries of oxygen and medical devices to residences. Steven was apparently fired last week after not showing up for his shift four days in a row."

"Was he off the night of the shooting?" Charlie asked.

"Yes, and also the night you were ambushed," Nancy confirmed. "DuPree wanted to bring him in for an interview, but the officers couldn't get anyone to answer the door at his residence."

"We think he might be in the red pickup, unless he switched back to the Camry his brother was driving this morning."

Nancy sighed. "Explain to me how you came up with that theory."

She wasn't surprised at what had gone down, except for the outcome. "It's probably a good thing, though, not meeting face-to-face with Steven Azok. You're not cops, and he didn't have to talk with you at all. But I do have some good news. If we can track down Azok, he can be hauled before a judge for violating the restraining order."

"An officer saw him stalking her?"

"Not directly, but one of our people managed to find surveillance recordings that show him parked across the street from the Back Up office."

"I didn't notice any cameras."

"They came from the bail bonds office on the next block east. New cameras, apparently, and really good, color images. It was possible to read his vehicle plates from over a hundred yards away. There's a warrant out now for his arrest, so his residence is under random surveillance. There's also an ATL that's been issued county-wide," Nancy affirmed.

"Go get him," Charlie urged. "Can I ask a related/unrelated question?"

"Yes and no. Okay, what is it?" Nancy sighed.

"Have there been any incidents concerning fires since the last threat?" Charlie asked.

"Only a bosque fire across the river from Tingley Beach," she replied, indicating a location southwest of Albuquerque's Old Town. "I heard it was set by some transients who'd walked away from a cooking fire."

"Not exactly a terrorist attack," Charlie said. "Have all the people from the Recognition Park ceremony been notified?"

"Either by email or phone," Nancy replied. "You get anything from the people at Back Up, like their enemies or problems? Issues that could create conflict?"

"Not really, though the bookkeeper said that finances were really tight," Charlie recalled.

"I got the impression that they all wanted to keep the company operating."

"Just how tight are we talking about? Are they broke?"

Charlie explained, the best he could recall, how the money passed through hands in the operation, according to Max and Anna. "It sounded to me that there's a lot of trust involved between the owner and the vets they placed at the various jobs, especially when the vets are paid in cash by their employers. Anna suggested that her boss wasn't very savvy when it came to running a business, at least on the money side."

"We'll see if there were any loans or transactions that might have gone south," Nancy said.

"Maybe a significant number of the vets were underreporting their pay? If the captain found out and said something, that could have created bad blood," Charlie responded.

"Or worse. PTSD added to drinking, drugs, and money

problems is a bad situation. It's worth looking into, if only to rule out. Maybe you can see what Patricia Azok knows about that. She's the new owner, right?" Nancy suggested.

He nodded. "If I'm the one who asks instead of a cop, it doesn't come across as part of the investigation so much?"

"Correct. But ease into it. I doubt anyone would have killed their benefactor over this, but who knows? If the deceased had threatened to press charges it could have backfired on him."

"I was going to talk to some of the vets now working via Back Up anyway," Charlie decided.

"Okay, then. I'll see what I can do without raising any suspicion. If there's nothing else right now, we've got to get to work. Will you call me if there's any news to share?" Nancy asked.

"Of course. One more thing. Any news about Ruth's ex-husband fugitive?" Charlie asked.

"Only that they have no leads on his location since he parted company with those now under arrest. The marshal's service will get that information first, and they should notify Ruth, so let me know when you have something to pass along," Nancy said, then ended the call.

"Copy," Charlie said to the phone a few seconds too late.

The rest of the day was very busy at the pawn shop, mostly catching up on the records and bookkeeping that Jake had been forced to set aside while taking care of customers. Though he offered to stay a little longer, Charlie and Gordon insisted that Jake leave at closing because he'd had such a heavy load. Ruth's sitter had brought Rene by the shop, and the seven-year-old was helping

Gordon sweep floors and dust while Ruth and Charlie finished up in the office.

"Everything is backed up on the hard drives and in the cloud," Ruth said, leaning back in her chair.

"Good. Shutting down my computer," Charlie said, left clicking the mouse on the power-down message. As the monitor image switched to blue screen, something in his peripheral vision moved and he glanced up at the surveillance monitor, which maintained images from the six cameras. Someone was standing in the alley at the north end, holding something in their hand that looked like a big wine bottle.

"Is that a drunk?" he said, pointing to the image just as the person looked up at the camera.

"Wearing a mask and hoodie?" Ruth replied. "I don't think so."

Charlie stood as the person approached the vehicles parked along the back wall, then reached into his jacket pocket and brought out a small object. There was a sudden flash.

"He's got a lighter. Oh, crap!" he yelled, racing for the back door.

Chapter Ten

He opened the back door just as the person cocked his arm, aiming the bottle, which was now flaming at the mouth.

"Stop!" Charlie yelled just as the guy hurled the firebomb right at him.

Charlie yanked the door shut just as the bottle broke against the outside metal. There was a loud whoosh and the instant, acrid scent of burning fuel from the Molotov cocktail. Charlie jumped back and looked to the bottom of the door. Fortunately the flaming liquid didn't penetrate into the hall.

"Firebomb struck the back door," Charlie yelled, grabbing the CO_2 fire extinguisher from the wall hook. "Gordon, we'll have to go out the front and around. Ruth, call 911 and keep Rene hidden below the front counter. Lock the door behind us."

By the time Charlie reached the front door, Gordon already had his keys in the lock. He stepped back, pulling the door open for Charlie, who stepped outside onto the sidewalk, aware that the fire might just be a diversion. He looked for a shooter, but saw nothing more than two cars passing by.

He raced to the corner, then around and down the north side of the building, which faced the side street. In the dark he could make out a figure, running away to the east down the road. Should he attack the fire before it reached the vehicles or chase the arsonist?

He stopped at the alley and looked toward the loading dock. The burning fuel, probably kerosene from the smell, was concentrated on the metal door, the brick walls, and splashed across the raised concrete dock.

Gordon came up beside him and jammed some keys in Charlie's jacket pocket. "I'm going for the punk," he said. "Work on the fire and save the vehicles."

Charlie had encountered fires several times while in the Army, and knew how to put out a fuel fire despite the difference in available suppression equipment. He raced up close enough to see that the burning liquid hadn't splashed back on his car or Gordon's truck, so he could attack the fire first.

He pulled the pin on the handle of the extinguisher, directed the big plastic cone at the base of the flame, and then quickly rotated the dense white cloud of carbon dioxide over the flames. The fire was out almost instantly on the door and wall, and when the cloud descended on the porch, the flames went out as well. The entire process took less than ten seconds.

He stood back, surveying the scene and looking for anything he'd missed. The scent of kerosene and something else, maybe motor oil, was still very strong and he had to watch for any potential reignition from a hot surface. The air was thick with smoke and floating black tendrils, and there was a second, intense odor with a metallic bite to it, probably from the paint that had burned off the heavy sheet-steel door. He discovered a disgusting residue, dark goo on the door, maybe from plastic packing peanuts that had been added to thicken the solution and make the fuel stick to the surface like napalm.

The good news was that the outdoor light fixture above the door was mounted high enough and at the right angle to avoid getting splashed with the fuel mixture.

He looked down the alley, wondering if he should back up Gordon. If this was the same attacker, he might be armed. But then again, Gordon carried a 9mm on his hip, and his pal had serious tactical skills. Hearing a siren in the distance, Charlie decided to move his and Gordon's vehicles. He'd park them down the alley far enough so a fire engine could get in and maybe hose down and cool off the door, walls, and loading dock.

A few minutes later, he hurried around to the front and knocked. "It's me, Charlie," he called out loudly. The sirens were getting close and he wanted to check on Ruth and Rene.

The door came open immediately, and she leaned out and gave him an impulsive kiss on the lips. "You're okay! Where's Gordon?"

"He went after the arsonist. How is Rene?" Charlie asked, looking over her shoulder.

The boy rose up from behind the counter and waved. "A-okay, Charlie."

"Good! You two stay inside, away from the back door. It's gonna be hot, and we want to keep any fumes out of the shop. Right now I've got to check on Gordon."

He reached down and gave her hand a gentle squeeze before closing the door.

Charlie circled back around to the alley and found Gordon standing by his pickup, looking at the damage as he caught his breath. "The bastard got away again," Gordon said, shaking his head. "I lost him in the dark somewhere, and so did our friend."

"Our spook?" Charlie asked, thinking of Russell Turner.

"Yeah. Russell says he was shadowing us today, backed off on our slow-speed pursuit of Azok's brother, then decided to hang out at the far end of the alley and do some laundry at Melissa's at the same time."

"Did he manage to get a look at whoever threw the Molotov?" Charlie asked.

"Just shapes. He'd grabbed his phone to call us when he saw the dude light the top. Once it hit the door and exploded all he saw was the figure head east down the street. Russ decided to try to flank the guy by circling the block. When we met up—nothing. We figured the flamethrower had turned to the north, or hid out somewhere in between. There are several buildings where he could be hiding. Russell suggested I head back here in case there was a second attacker, or the guy planned to take you out with his rifle while you were dealing with the fire."

"Makes sense."

"Sorry I couldn't run the guy down. If I'd have had my M-4 and night-vision optics I could have nailed the bastard."

Charlie shrugged. "Yeah, well, next time we'll be ready."

"Looks like the damage is limited to a smoky wall and the steel door. Are the cameras okay?" Gordon added, pointing to the two mounted up high, close to the roof.

"Don't know," Charlie said. "No matter. We got lucky. The guy threw the bottle at the door, not our vehicles. If one had caught, we might have lost both of them."

"He threw it just when you looked outside, right?" Gordon asked.

Charlie nodded. "If I hadn't shut the door in time, the shop could have been toast."

Gordon thought about it a moment. "And so would have you. Charles, the guy knew the cameras were there, and he was waiting for someone to take a look. He planned to take one of us out in a very painful, agonizing way."

Charlie started to say something, but the siren of the approaching fire truck and the honking air horn made the effort pointless, so he just stood back to give the big vehicle clearance when it came around the corner.

It was close to midnight when Charlie finally pulled up into the driveway of his house. He was alone now. Detective DuPree had one of his officers drive Ruth and Rene to their apartment hours ago. Ruth had insisted she was in much less danger than Charlie, who'd been the clear target of the last two attacks. With no news of her missing ex, the threat to her was still unknown and speculative. Besides, Charlie needed some rest, and her sofa was no substitute for a bed. Still, he had asked that patrols in her neighborhood be increased.

He pulled the Charger into the garage, closed the overhead door with the remote before he got out of the car, and then quickly went into the house. He was weary, but too pumped to sleep at the moment. Grabbing a bottle of water from the fridge, he turned out the light and walked into the darkened living room, finding the couch by memory and the faint streetlight shining through the curtains. Pulling off his boots, he eased into the cushions and leaned back, stretching out his long legs.

The events of the past few hours played over again in his head, keeping him awake. He'd spoken to several federal agents, from FBI to Homeland and another agency he couldn't remember, then with DuPree, Nancy, and two firemen. One of them was an arson investigator, the other some kind of deputy chief. The FBI had taken the physical evidence with them—all the glass they could gather from the broken bottle—plus scrapings of residue from the wall, steps, and asphalt pavement. As a TV crew recorded the action, law enforcement had also hauled away the back door. Now there was just an improvised barrier of plywood, wired shut and blocking the entrance.

After everyone else was gone, they'd flipped a coin. Gordon had lost and was now sleeping just outside their office upon a cot and wool blankets from the for-sale merchandise.

Looking at his watch, Charlie realized that he needed to get up at four and go relieve his pal. One of them had to guard the shop until businesses opened and they could arrange for a new door—and locks. He stood, took a quick look outside through the curtains, and walked into the bedroom. He dropped onto the bed and grabbed a pillow. Sleep came within a few minutes.

Charlie arrived at the shop well before dawn, parking in the alley beside Gordon's pickup. He walked up the sidewalk on the north end of the building and quietly let himself in the front. Quickly he placed the two bags he was carrying on the counter beside the cash register and turned off the alarm, which had a short delay. He relocked the door, then saw Gordon across the room, seated on the cot and buttoning up his shirt.

"You're right on time, Chuck," Gordon said. "Nothing to report. Nobody got inside last night except a cricket, and I was too wiped to hunt the noisy beast down."

"Good. I passed by the truck stop over at University and Candelaria and ordered a couple of their breakfast burritos. Thought you might want to take one with you," Charlie said, holding up the bags.

"Naw, I'm ready to eat right now. You had breakfast?"

"Not yet. Let's eat."

"Sounds like a plan."

The business day started out quickly, with their first calls to warehouse stores in the search for a replacement door, then a locksmith to provide the level of security they required. Fortunately, Jake showed up early, as did Ruth—once she'd taken Rene to school—and that left Charlie and Gordon available to install the door once it was delivered.

They kept getting calls from local news outlets, asking for interviews, and Charlie learned that a local mosque now had a small group of protestors gathered on the sidewalks outside. Clearly news of the firebombing had quickly spread throughout the metro area. Twice, reporters came inside, trolling for sound bites to air on the evening news, but Charlie and Gordon were brief and factual, disappointing the news people, who were obviously hoping for something more sensational.

A few minutes after five, however, Charlie got a call from

Dawud on his cell while finishing up the paperwork on a turquoise and silver bracelet that had just been pawned. He glanced around the room, noting that Gordon was talking to a customer over near the gun safes.

"Greetings, my friend," Dawud began, his tone revealing some hesitation in the words. "I hope your day is progressing well, or at least better than your previous one. I heard that someone tried to burn down your shop last night. Are you all okay?"

"Hello, Dawud. We're safe, there was no damage that can't be fixed, and business is back to normal, maybe even better than normal. Has someone been bothering you or your family? How's Caleb?" Charlie replied, stepping away from the counter as Gordon came over with the customer, a purchase tag in hand.

"There is some hostility at my business, but no one has interfered. My son hasn't mentioned any more problems at school since you spoke to his classmates, but I just received a call from my daughter, Justine. She and Caleb came home from school and there were people waiting outside our home carrying signs and shouting . . . the usual insults."

"Did you call the police?"

"Yes, and they have an officer outside my produce market. There have also been shouts and insults, but nobody has brought their anger inside our shop. This time they are insulting my customers. The police say they are stretched too thin, and can't protect both my business and my home," Dawud explained. "I can't leave my wife here alone. Would you or my friend Gordon stand with my children for a while this afternoon until we can join them? Caleb tells me he will protect Justine. But who will protect him?"

"At least one of us will be there in twenty minutes," Charlie assured. "Let Caleb know we're on our way. I doubt that these pro-testors will do anything stupid."

"They are cowards, they will likely wait until dark, friend. That's when I worry. Thank you very much. My wife and I will close our shop early. We just need some extra help at the moment."

"Give Caleb my cell number. Tell him and his sister to say nothing and remain inside the house, away from the windows. They also need to keep the doors locked. Have them call me if anything looks wrong." Charlie put down his phone and looked over at Gordon, who was loading the gun safe locker onto a dolly.

"Let me help you with that, Gordon. We need to talk," Charlie said, stepping out behind the counter and joining his pal.

Less than twenty minutes later they approached the Koury house, located in a well-maintained lower-middle-class neighbor-hood on Albuquerque's west side. It was only a mile from where they'd rescued Caleb from his tormenters just a few days ago. A television news crew was across the street, filming the activity, and vehicles were parked along both sides of the streets for the entire block. Charlie noted that there was an old black pickup blocking the empty driveway of the Koury house—a small, pueblo-style rental property. The American flag was still flying on a small flag-pole in the yard. A few years ago Charlie and Gordon had been there, helping the Kourys move in. They'd also been invited to an outdoor barbeque the day the entire family received their citizen-ship documents. They'd helped the family raise the flag for the first time.

Currently there were at least twenty people, mostly adults of both sexes, along the sidewalk in front of the house, several of them holding homemade signs or carrying American flags.

"Where we going to park?" Charlie asked, looking down the block.

"Leave that to me," Gordon responded, coming to a stop just behind the black pickup.

He honked the horn loudly, and startled several of those in the small crowd. "Park it, boys, just don't block the street or somebody's gonna bitch!" a husky-looking man in his thirties wearing a camo T-shirt and red ball cap yelled.

"Ah, the self-appointed leader." Charlie smiled.

Gordon leaned out of the window. "Somebody move this crappy pickup before I push it down the street. I'm gonna take over their driveway."

Somebody cheered. "Way to go, pal!" and several people laughed.

"Where the hell am I gonna park?" a tall, slender guy holding a sign yelled.

"Just move that hunk of junk, Ted!" the guy in the camo shirt ordered.

The man named Ted moved his pickup down to the next house, double parking beside another vehicle at the curb, leaving only a narrow lane in the center of the street.

"Told ya," Gordon chuckled as he pulled into the Koury driveway. "These people are sheep. All you have to do is point the Judas goat in the right direction."

Charlie nodded. "Just be aware, Gordon. The goat has a sidearm on his hip."

As they stepped down out of Gordon's truck, Charlie heard a shout from somewhere behind the house.

"That sounded like Caleb," Gordon said. "Let's check it out."

Together the two strode quickly across the xeroscaped front yard, a patterned design consisting of colored gravel and southwestern plants, then hurried alongside the garage side of the house.

As they turned the corner and reached the thin grass of the fenced-in backyard, Charlie discovered a fit-looking man in a red, white, and blue T-shirt crouched on one knee on the lawn. He was aiming a semi-auto pistol at the back of the house, where several inches of a shotgun barrel was poking out the barely opened rear door. The crudely sprayed word, "terrorist," had been sprayed in foot-high letters across the door and wall in black paint. Three more men, one of them a teenager, were crouched down or standing at the far side of the yard, also watching the shotgun barrel, which was sweeping back and forth.

One of the trio was holding an aluminum baseball bat, the teen was carrying a can of spray paint, and the third guy was filming the scene with his cell phone.

The fourth man aiming the handgun didn't bother to look at them. "The rag head punk is just asking for a bullet. He points that barrel at me and he's going down," he added.

Noting that the man didn't have his finger near the trigger, Charlie reached over and grabbed the pistol by the barrel, twisting it down and yanking it from the man's grip.

The man yelled, cursed, and tried to turn and stand at the same time, wobbling off balance.

"Stay down!" Gordon ordered, pushing him just enough to send him falling to the grass onto his knees.

"None of you trespassers move!" Charlie ordered. "Caleb, it's me, Charlie Henry. Gordon is here too. We'll deal with the vandals. Stop waving around that shotgun and close the door!" he yelled.

They heard the voice of a girl inside, and, after a few seconds, the barrel disappeared from sight and the door closed.

"Lock the door, Caleb. You and your sister go into the hall. Stay out of sight until you hear from me again," Charlie said.

The guy on the ground, massaging his injured hand, tried to stand.

"Stay down, pal, we don't want you to make a fool of yourself again," Gordon ordered.

"No problem," the man said, looking at Gordon's waistband, where the model 95 Beretta rested in a holster.

Charlie casually released the magazine on the semi-auto pistol he'd confiscated and let it fall to the lawn, then ejected the round already in the chamber. Sticking the unloaded weapon into his jacket pocket, he walked over to the teenager, who was tall and slender, almost his height but maybe fifty pounds lighter. The person with the cell phone continued to record the events, and Charlie wanted to take advantage of the opportunity.

The man with the bat stood beside the kid and raised it up as Charlie got close. "Stay back or I'm going to clock you, Indian."

Charlie ignored him. "Make sure you get that evidence into your movie," he said to the guy with the cell phone, pointing to the paint.

The kid dropped the aerosol can like it was on fire.

"Lower your slugger, pal, unless you want me to shove it where the sun don't shine," Charlie ordered Bat Man.

"*Now* I know who you are," the guy blurted out, bringing the bat down to waist level. "Sorry, I didn't mean anything personal,

Sergeant Henry. But what the hell are *you* doing here, standing up for this punk Arab? I watch the news. You and your lady could have been killed at the park, shot in the alley, or burned to death just last night. Now you're protecting the kid who's been trying to kill you?"

Charlie heard the sound of approaching sirens, then noticed some activity behind him. There were three more protestors, signs in hand, standing at the corner of the garage, watching. "People, nothing going on here. Let's all meet out front on the sidewalk," Charlie ordered. He looked over at the guy with the cell phone, who was still recording everything.

"What's your name, pal?" he asked the young man, who was probably in his early twenties.

"Andy."

"Okay, Andy. Hang on to that phone and stick with me. The officers might want to take a look at what you've recorded. It'll probably make the news."

Andy smiled.

They all returned to the front yard just as first one, then another black-and-white APD cruiser came up the street. Just a few seconds behind were two SUVs.

Gordon, who'd stopped to pick up the pistol magazine and bullet left behind, joined Charlie just as all four vehicles stopped on the street. "Here come the men in black," he announced.

Someone near him laughed, and Charlie turned back to look at the house. Caleb was looking out through the curtains of the living room window. "*You* didn't call the Feds, did you, Gordon?"

"Hell no, I called Detective Medina. Nancy said they were sending a couple of patrol units."

"Charlie, Gordon. A word," came a familiar voice from the sidewalk. It wasn't Nancy, it was Detective DuPree.

DuPree kept his eyes on the suits climbing out of the black SUVs as he uncharacteristically hurried over to join Charlie and Gordon. "What's the situation here? I need to know before the FBI moves in."

"Moves in for what? Arrest the protestors? That's APD's job, isn't it?" Gordon asked.

"Just be glad they didn't call in SWAT. Tell me. Who's inside the house?" DuPree pressed.

"Just Caleb Koury and his sister, Justine—I think," Charlie replied, wondering what the hell was going on.

"Where did the extra handgun come from?" DuPree noticed the pistol grip sticking out of Charlie's pocket.

"It belongs to the jock over there mad-dogging me," Charlie said, nodding toward the man. "I borrowed it after he started waving the thing around."

"Borrowed?"

"Our kind of borrowing, Detective," Gordon announced with a grin as he held out the loaded magazine. "We'll return it, eventually. Unless you want to check and see if it's stolen or something."

"Might as well," DuPree said, taking the weapon and magazine and sticking them into his jacket pocket.

"So what's the deal?" Charlie asked.

"All I could get was that the Feds want to take the Koury kids in for questioning," DuPree responded, glancing over at the local FBI SAC, special agent in charge, Tyler Jackson. He was a tough, broad-shouldered agent. They'd encountered Jackson before in difficult circumstances when the big black man was working undercover, seemingly part of the other side. "Are the kids armed with anything besides the shotgun? Explosives? What's their demeanor?"

"Pardon the cliché, but why make a federal case out of this?" Gordon asked. "All the kid did was poke the barrel of a shotgun out the back door when a vandal started tagging the house. No shots were fired, nobody that we could see actually had a barrel pointed at them, and when Charlie asked him to lower the weapon, shut the door, and stay quiet, Caleb complied. That was just a few minutes ago."

"Detective Medina told me that Koury placed a trigger lock on that weapon, and their children didn't have the key," DuPree said.

"That's what Dawud agreed to do when we sold it to him," Charlie affirmed. "But if the Feds start waving around *their* weapons, threatening the kids in the house, and Caleb *is* able to fire that shotgun, I don't know what's gonna happen. How about if Gordon and I talk the kids out?"

"I doubt Jackson is going to force a confrontation, he's a smart man. But what if young Koury turns the shotgun on you?"

"Not gonna happen," Charlie said. "The kid isn't a killer, and I think he trusts us. My guess is that he's just protecting his sister and his home. They've been living in a dangerous environment for years, and lately it's been getting worse."

"Charlie's right on this one, Detective," Gordon added. "And why do the Feds want Caleb? We told Nancy about our intervention when Caleb was jumped by those high school punks. Did he commit a crime?"

"Nobody has told me a thing, but both the Bureau and Homeland plan to detain and interview the Koury kids," DuPree said.

"Yeah, well, I guess first thing we need to do is bring out Caleb and Justine." Charlie said, watching as SAC Jackson huddled with three other Feds up on the sidewalk along the street. "Will you tell the suits that we can bring out Caleb—and Justine—without any problems?"

"God's ears," Gordon mumbled.

Five minutes later, Gordon and Charlie walked alongside the Koury teens' sides as they crossed the front lawn. The crowd had been ordered onto the street, held in place by APD cops. Quickly the suits rushed up, placed cuffs on both kids, and one of them, a woman, started to pat down Justine as a male agent did the same to Caleb.

Justine recoiled, embarrassed, and Caleb yelled, twisting away from the Feds. "Hey, get your hands off my sister," Caleb yelled. Immediately SAC Jackson brought the boy to his knees with two powerful arms.

Gordon stepped forward, but DuPree got between him and the Feds. "Not now, Gordon."

Gordon shook off the hand and turned angrily. Then he relaxed. "Sorry, Wayne."

"What are you charging these kids with?" Charlie demanded to the fed standing next to the detective as an APD handler and his dog went into the house. "Explosives? Drugs?"

The agent shook his head.

As Justine and Caleb were manhandled to the awaiting SUVs, the crowd cheered and shouted racist comments.

Tyler Jackson came over and responded to Charlie's question

in a low voice. "They're being detained, that's all at the moment, Charlie. There is newly uncovered evidence that Caleb Koury has been in contact with Middle Eastern individuals or groups via the internet. His school's IT person found some emails on one of the library computers, and Caleb Koury was signed into that device at that time. We may have found a link between him and terrorists. Now all we need to do is locate the rifle—after the house is cleared for explosives."

Chapter Eleven

Gordon and Charlie watched as the Feds drove away with the Koury kids. "I think the apocalypse is near," Gordon said softly, watching the protestors walking to their vehicles along the street.

"From all the fear and violence lately?"

"No. Today Detective DuPree called me Gordon. First time ever."

"That cinches it. Bring on the fire and brimstone. I didn't catch your reply. What did you say when he did that?"

"I thanked him using *his* first name," Gordon replied.

"Hmmm. Do I detect a bromance in the air, bud?"

"Naw, that's just steer manure from the lawn."

"That explains it. Well, people are leaving now since it's dinnertime—so I guess we need to tell Dawud and Jenna what's happening," Charlie said, bringing out his phone.

"Too late, here they are," Gordon replied, pointing to a pickup coming up the street with Dawud and his wife in the cab. On the door of the truck was a sign advertising Koury's American Produce.

"Let's get to them before the demonstrators catch on and come back."

Ten minutes later Charlie, alone in the Koury vehicle, an older model Ford 150, drove across the Alameda Bridge and turned south onto Rio Grande Boulevard. Gordon had gone on ahead with Dawud and his wife, Jenna, to the police station downtown. Gordon's pickup had the extended cab, which provided plenty of room for the three. Dawud hadn't wanted to leave his pickup behind at home or depend on someone to bring them back, so Charlie agreed to follow in the Koury truck. He'd decided to stay off the higher-speed interstate, though, because Dawud's old pickup needed a tune-up and was running rough.

Several miles of the northern end of Rio Grande Boulevard were posted at a 25 mph speed limit, but there was no need to hurry. Experience in dealing with APD, much less the Feds, had taught him that interviews or interrogations could take hours.

He'd waited at the Koury home just until the place had been cleared of explosives—none had been found—then stood back as the K-9 team checked out the pickup as well. An agent had quickly emerged from the home carrying the shotgun—trigger guard still attached—and a laptop. SAC Jackson had the house keys and had offered to lock up the place and have the keys delivered to the Kourys downtown once the crime lab team had completed their search of the Koury home.

It was still hot outside and the sun was an hour prior to setting as Charlie drove slowly down the two-lane street, flanked by low- and high-end homes of every size and shape, surrounded by grassy fields, orchards, and the occasional side street. Trees lined this stretch of the road, some of the old cottonwood limbs extending over the roadway. It was a cool, pleasant drive, with the shade from trees on the west side of the boulevard.

There was some light traffic, with most of the vehicles sticking within 5 mph of the posted 25, but in the rearview mirrors he noticed a gray, mostly primer-coated van coming up quickly from behind. Charlie maintained speed, checking ahead for oncoming traffic. If the guy wanted to pass, it would be better now before they reached some blind curves ahead.

The approaching van was closing fast, so Charlie eased off the gas just a little. He'd let the guy around. Checking the mirror again, he tried to get a look at the driver, but couldn't make out a face in the glare.

The van whipped out around him, passed by quickly, and all Charlie could see was a strange-looking driver wearing a hoodie and ball cap. Suddenly Charlie realized why the driver looked so strange—he was wearing a stocking over his head, like a mask.

Charlie hit the brakes just as the van cut him off, slamming into the front end of the pickup. The pickup shook violently, then skidded toward the shoulder, which gave way to a shallow drainage ditch. He felt the left rear end lifting as the right front left the road and dropped down.

Struggling to maintain control, all Charlie could do was turn into the skid, hanging on as the truck bounced madly over the uneven ground into the narrow, grassy right-of-way.

There was barely time to think, much less react. The pickup barreled through a wire fence, ripping loose the poles, but at least the barrier grabbed the vehicle and helped bring him to a stop after another fifty yards. Two llamas and a donkey far across the pasture started racing back and forth, panicked by the chaotic intrusion.

Charlie didn't know whether to laugh or shout, but at least he was safe and hadn't rolled the pickup. His head hurt, and he guessed that the harsh ride had bounced the top of his skull off the roof.

He opened the door, wondering how much damage had been done to Dawud's pickup, then he remembered he'd just been forced off the road. He turned to look back at the street, reaching at the same time for the Beretta at his hip. That van was coming back down the street, and the driver was leaning out the window with something in his hand.

Gun he nearly said aloud, diving out the door onto the field just as the driver fired a shot. He heard the thud of a bullet somewhere above, striking the truck. Rolling to his right, he grabbed for his Beretta. He rolled one more time, anticipating a follow-up shot. Two more gun blasts told him he'd made the right move.

He brought up his pistol and aimed toward the road, estimating the lead he needed. Then the van passed by an oncoming SUV headed south. More vehicles were approaching, so there was no shot. Jumping to his feet, he waved at the SUV.

The driver, a woman, took a quick look, then sped off. Maybe it had something to do with the gun in his hand. Charlie reached up for the cell phone in his shirt pocket. It was gone. He checked the ground and found it lying there not six inches from some fresh manure. He picked up the phone and called 911, then looked himself over to make sure he hadn't rolled through the stuff. Fortunately, as with the bullets, he was lucky—except for his boots.

The phone rang, and he recognized the number. "Charlie, you injured?" came Russell Turner's voice, showing a trace of his Southern drawl.

If the CIA guy had been trailing him, he'd never noticed. "No,

I'm fine, just a little smelly. Where are you?" Charlie added, looking toward the street. A white sedan had pulled over beside the
gap in the fence line, and he could see a man inside.

"I'm in the car you're looking at, pal. I was leading the way,
watching you in the rearview mirror 'cause I knew your destination. I didn't snap on the van until it forced you off the road. I
tried to intercept, but the guy did a one-eighty and went back in
your direction. I lost sight of it for a while. Did you see it flash by
you?"

"More than that. The driver did a slow-motion drive-by, took
a couple of shots with a hand gun, then hauled ass back north,"
Charlie said.

"Well, I lost track of the van when it went around a curve,
and you were on the ground, so I decided to check on you first,"
Turner replied. "I did get a read at the vehicle tag, however, earlier
when I was watching the action at the Koury residence. I'll message it to you. Call it in while I search the area for the van. Once
you get a name to go with that plate, let me know. I can't use
local sources without identifying myself. There was also a Marine
Corp decal on the left rear window of the van."

"Copy. Thanks for backing me up, but I'd like to ask a favor
right now."

"What do you have in mind?" Turner asked.

Charlie thought about it a second. "If you can't locate the van,
I'd like you to get into a position to protect Dawud and his
family—not me. I've got Gordon and some good APD allies, but
the Koury family is facing some rough days. You saw that yourself
this evening. What do you say?"

"I'll think about it, Charlie. Dawud saved some American

lives, mine included. Meanwhile, I've got to get going. Catch you later." Turner ended the call.

Turner wanted to remain anonymous, Charlie understood. He dialed 911 as the spook drove off north. Rio Grande Boulevard dead-ended at the bosque a few miles to the north, but there was always east and west, or doubling back south. Charlie wanted to alert APD and country deputies ASAP. The van was distinctive, maybe they'd get lucky.

While he was waiting for the Bernalillo County deputies, the law enforcement agency that covered the village, Charlie called Gordon. Looking back at the pickup while he waited for the connection, he saw two bullet holes, one centered in the driver's door, the other just aft of the seat, a few feet above the gas tank. There were probably a hundred feet of wire fencing stretched across the field and wrapped around the front of the truck.

Thinking back at the sensation of his ride, Charlie imagined it was like running into a giant rubber band at twenty miles an hour. Thank God he was going the speed limit already and was slowing down as he was struck by the van. If he'd have gone off the road any faster, he might be lying on his side with a pickup wrapped around him.

Hearing a siren in the distance, he walked over to the pickup and placed his Beretta on the seat cushion. No sense in alarming the law.

Nancy arrived around seven thirty, just after the deputy, despite the fact that she was technically out of her jurisdiction. Charlie had already been told that because of the current terrorist threat, all local agencies would be on call, and for him especially, because of previous attempts on his life. It was uncomfortable being a celebrity for all the wrong reasons, evident when every officer he encountered knew who he was despite having never met.

When Nancy walked up to the scene Charlie had already given BCSD Sergeant Randy Trujillo the essentials on what had gone down, then retrieved his Beretta. Right now, the officer was photographing Koury's damaged pickup and the tire marks in the field.

"You okay, Charlie?" Nancy asked, looking back at him after nodding to the county officer and taking in the mess.

"Yeah, I'm just glad I was creeping along when he cut me off. If I'd have known it wasn't just some crazy out to break the land speed record, I might have been able to prevent this. The van came up fast, I decided to let him come on around, then boom!"

"Shots were fired, I gather. Sure it wasn't just road rage?"

"I can't say for sure, but the driver came back after running me off the road and fired three shots. If I'd have cut *him* off, flipped the finger, or defamed his mother, maybe so. But he was after me all along. I saw a van like this one among the vehicles parked on Koury's street, which means I was followed, then attacked," Charlie said, stretching the truth. He'd probably seen the van, all right, but for the moment, he wanted to leave Turner out of the conversation.

"Again, no description. Good thing you managed to notice and remember *his* plate numbers, though," Nancy said, looking at him skeptically.

"I have a knack for numbers. You have an ID on the owner?" he said.

"Yes, as a matter of fact. The listed owner is a Marine vet, and his apartment isn't too far from here. I'm heading there next."

"Can I go with?" Charlie asked. He was tired of being in the bull's-eye and wanted to take action. "If Sergeant Trujillo says okay." He turned to face the county officer, who'd just come over.

"I've already interviewed Mr. Henry, Serge . . . um, Detective Medina, is it now?" Trujillo said, reaching out and shaking Nancy's hand.

"Good to see you again, Randy," Nancy said, nodding. "How's the wife and daughter?"

"It's the terrible twos with Cindi. She's already developed way too much attitude," Trujillo responded. "Go ahead and take off, people. I've got to wait for CSI," he joked. "When you come back, remind me to show you five hundred photos of my little terror."

Nancy laughed, then put her hand on Charlie's arm. "Let's go before he takes us up on that."

They continued down Rio Grande, with emergency lights on in Nancy's APD unmarked unit, traveling at twice the speed limit. "What else did you get on this Marine?" Charlie asked.

"His name is Benjamin Webster. He served for six years and was discharged at the rank of Lance Corporal. Webster was wounded in Afghanistan, and since leaving the military has changed his residence at least seven times in the last two years," Nancy responded. "No arrests, except two bar fights, charges dropped, both more than a year ago."

"Another vet with issues. I wonder if there's a connection with Back Up?" Charlie asked.

"That could be interesting. When we reach Webster's residence, be on your toes. If he's the shooter, remember that you're the target."

"Maybe you should have some backup."

"Already on the way. If they arrive before we do, the units have been told to keep out of sight," Nancy added.

"I don't think he's the guy that murdered the pilot," Charlie said, "or took the shot in the alley."

"Why not?"

"The shooter has missed me twice. Most Marines could have taken me out with the first shot in the alley."

"Unless he was high on something."

"People high on drugs or booze aren't as careful as the profile suggests. And either the terrorist, or whoever it is, attacked on impulse today, breaking the pattern. Maybe it was someone else, but not the Marine."

"Like a local 'patriot' trying to injure or kill who he thought was Dawud Koury? But you don't look like Koury, and if he was there, the perp in the van probably saw you getting into the truck."

"Okay. Nothing quite fits. I guess we'll have to wait and see."

Twilight was approaching as they drove up the street where Webster supposedly lived. Nancy parked on the street in front of an adjacent apartment building. "There's the van," Charlie pointed out. "In front of what looks like apartment C. The place doesn't look like much," he said, noting the roof of the structure was missing a few shingles, the cinder-block walls needed paint, and the wooden trim around Webster's apartment door was just hanging on.

She grabbed her radio mike and advised her backup officers, setting up approaches to cover her and also to watch the rear in case Webster tried to sneak out a back door or window.

"Stay in the vehicle, Charlie," Nancy ordered. "If he's after you, no sense in giving him an easy target."

"Leave the keys, though. If he runs, you don't want to have your car this far away."

"Okay, but don't move the vehicle without my signal. Just keep an eye on things," she said.

"Be careful, girl."

Nancy smiled. "Always, boy."

As soon as Nancy reached the building, Charlie slipped out onto the sidewalk and watched as Nancy made a tactical approach, backed up by an officer. She knocked, announced she was a cop, then stood back and waited, weapon out but down by her side.

"Police officer, Mr. Webster. Come outside with your hands behind your head," she shouted.

Chapter Twelve

Charlie started walking in that direction, alert to a sudden ambush, his hand resting on the 9mm handgun at his hip. Nancy was a smart cop, but she was also mortal.

Instead of a sudden attack, the door of apartment A, the manager's apartment two doors down, opened. A woman in her early fifties wearing jeans and a loose, sleeveless top stepped out into the common parking area. "What's going on, Officers? Ben's in Phoenix right now."

Charlie continued toward the building, looking around in case the man was hiding beside or behind a house or vehicle. Nearly an hour had passed since he'd been run off the road, so Webster could have returned here with at least thirty minutes to spare. It would be dark soon, and there were plenty of backyards and alleys to hide in. The manager could be lying.

Nancy noticed he was approaching, held up her palm to signal he should halt, then stepped back and gingerly put her hand on the van's hood.

"Maintain position," Nancy ordered the other officers, then, not turning her back to apartment C, responded to the woman. "Are you sure, ma'am? This van was seen several miles from here less than an hour ago. The engine is still warm, too hot for just sunshine."

The lady walked over to where Nancy was standing. "That's not possible. I'm the only one besides Ben with a key, and if it had been . . . oh," she added, looking down at the gravel parking lot.

By then, Charlie had inched closer, and even from twenty feet away he could see two sets of similar tracks in the pea-sized gravel.

The woman noticed Charlie, smiled, and then turned back to Nancy. "Well, it looks like someone had moved his van recently. But it can't be Ben—unless he quit his job and returned without me noticing. He's been gone for two weeks and isn't supposed to be back in the city for several more days. What do the police want with him anyway?"

"You don't have any surveillance cameras, do you Miss . . ." Charlie asked.

"Beverly Larson, handsome," the woman smiled, holding out her hand to shake.

"I'm Charlie, Beverly. About the cameras?" he asked again, looking along the roof trim but not seeing anything.

"Are you kidding? If it wasn't for God, we wouldn't even have air at this dump!" Beverly responded with a grin. "Our slum lord, I mean landlord, cuts corners when it comes to safety and maintenance. When Ben is in town, we all sleep a little better."

Nancy finally spoke. "I'm Detective Medina, ma'am. Did you see anyone near the vehicle within the last hour?"

"No I did not, but I've been catching up on my email. Now,

exactly what could you want with Ben Webster? He's laying off the booze, never causes any trouble, and has managed to find work almost every day since he moved in. He's a vet, I want you to know, and has been through some hard times."

"We appreciate that. Did Mr. Webster leave you a cell phone number? We need to know where he is right now," Charlie asked, then looked over at Nancy and shrugged.

Beverly glanced at Nancy, who nodded. "Make that an official request, ma'am."

The woman shrugged, then reached into the hip pocket of her too-tight jeans and brought out a phone. "Want me to call him for you?"

"Save your minutes, ma'am. Just the number, please," Nancy replied, bringing out a notebook.

The lady read the number off her display, and Nancy wrote it down before her next question. "Ms. Larson. Could you let us into Mr. Webster's apartment just long enough for us to verify that he's not home?"

"Don't trust me, huh?"

"Family and friends of suspects and witnesses to crimes often lie to officers in order to protect someone else," Nancy said softly, now looking back at apartment C with her hand clearly on the butt of her pistol. "I can get a warrant. But why not cooperate and save us all some embarrassment and publicity, and the need to contact your employer?"

"Just what did the driver of that van do, anyway?" Beverly asked.

"Among other things, he tried to kill me," Charlie responded instantly, hoping for impact.

"Oh no! Well, it wasn't Ben, that's for sure. In order to protect him, I'll let you into his apartment. Just don't touch anything, okay?"

"Nothing but a very orderly apartment—and a thin layer of dust," Nancy announced after a few minutes, crouching down low to allow light to enter the apartment from the opened door.

"Smart, checking to see if any fresh boot prints show on a floor with weeks of New Mexico dust," Charlie said, also crouching down for a look.

"If the man has really been out of town, there's no way he used his apartment as a home base for recent events. I'm going to give him a call," Nancy said, turning toward the door where the manager was standing. "We're done here for now, ma'am."

As Nancy walked away, phone to her ear, Charlie had a question for Beverly. "Did Ben happen to get his jobs through a vet's service called Back Up?"

"How'd you know?"

"Just a lucky guess, Beverly. Did he ever say anything about the service, maybe the owner, Nathan Whitaker?"

"You mean the officer killed by the terrorist at that park?" Beverly asked. "No, Ben really respected Captain Whitaker. Said he was a good soldier in spite of being just Army—his words. Wait a minute, aren't you one of the heroes? The Native American who's also been attacked? That's where I saw you, on the news."

"Yes, and that's why I have a personal stake in finding this . . . terrorist. We're doing everything we can to put the animal into a cage."

"Do us all a favor," Beverly declared, her arms across her chest. "Shoot him instead."

"Charlie, let's go," Nancy called. "And thanks, ma'am, for your help. Here's my card, if you think of anything. Officers will remain here until a wrecker comes to transport the van downtown. Our crime scene people are going to search for trace evidence."

"Do you need the key to Ben's van?" Beverly asked.

"That would help," Nancy answered.

"I'll get it then," she said, then walked back toward her apartment.

"How'd the shooter get inside?" Charlie asked Nancy. "A slim jim?"

"No doubt. This is an older model, which makes it easy to gain entry. I also saw fresh scratches on the door. And once inside, it would be easy to hot wire. It's probably been wiped clean, but we need to verify," she replied.

"So the shooter has auto theft skills?" Charlie asked.

"Law enforcement people know how to get inside a vehicle, and so do locksmiths. Or anyone who has access to the internet and the right tools," Nancy replied. "That includes a lot of potential suspects—including lone-wolf terrorists who know how to look up online instructions."

Charlie thought again of Caleb Koury, still unable to believe the kid was a terrorist. "I wonder what kind of conversations Dawud's son had on that computer?"

"The boy's not the shooter, at least for today, that's for sure. Though he may have some idea who that could be," Nancy said just as the woman manager returned with the key.

"What do I tell Ben if he calls?" Beverly asked.

"Tell him to contact me," Nancy answered, taking the key. "I'll try to reach him, but please, ma'am, don't call him yourself, not until we can clear his name. We don't want to point any more suspicion in his direction, do we?"

A short time later Nancy and Charlie were headed west across Albuquerque. Charlie remained silent for a while, noting that the route was taking them toward the north valley and FOB Pawn. "What's next?"

"It's past dinnertime already, and you're going home, I hope. Your car is still parked at the shop, right?"

Charlie nodded. "Did you manage to get Webster on the phone?"

"No, I got the 'not available' message. He may have just turned his phone off to save some minutes. I contacted Max Mitchell, hoping to find out who Webster is working for right now. He gave me a name, I got an answering machine, and left a message. I'm going to have Phoenix PD track down Webster to verify his location."

"Okay, Nancy. But it's no coincidence that the victim and Webster have a connection to Back Up. Why did the shooter, terrorist or not, steal that particular van?"

"Hell if I know. Either way, that individual, or group of individuals, are leading us in a big circle. We have no real motive either, except for that kill the heroes angle."

"I vote we keep one eye on the victim's business and personal life. Azok is still on my list, and just because nobody connected with Back Up has been identified as the potential killer, that doesn't rule them out either," Charlie said.

"I've still got to focus on the terrorist angle, Charlie, but I'll keep after the Webster issue. How about you and Gordon, as vets, start showing a lot more interest in Back Up? Keep digging for those personal motives."

"And Azok?"

"DuPree wants me to run that down, but let's stay in touch. I don't like to see you putting yourself in danger again."

"My plan is to put the shooter in danger," Charlie admitted.

"Yeah, I understand. It means doing things that would get a cop fired. That's the way you work. Still, don't let anything happen to you, or Gordon. Gina would never forgive me."

Charlie nodded. They were only a few blocks from the pawn shop now, and in the back of his mind he was already reminding himself to check his Dodge for a bomb before starting up the ignition.

"Let me off out front, okay?" he asked as they came down the block.

"It's no problem. I can pull into the alley."

"Naw, just out front."

He checked the front door, which was heavy-duty steel, then let himself into the semi-dark front display area, which was illuminated by a couple of well-placed LED lights so any intruder wouldn't bump into things. A few steps away, he entered the security code to deactivate the alarm, then locked the front behind him.

Everything was very quiet, of course, and all he could hear was the faint tick tock of the various clocks that hung on the far wall. The office enclosure was distinguished by the shine from the Plexiglas windows, and only the glow from the red and green lights of the electronics indicated the presence of their computers and office equipment.

Charlie walked across the room and stepped into the office, not bothering to turn on any lights, just the power switch to the surveillance monitor on the wall. He replayed the last few hours of the coverage on the alley beside his Charger at a fast forward, skipping past the images of store owners and employees stepping out for a smoke or disposing of trash in the Dumpsters. Finally he spotted something unusual—a man in a cap and sunglasses strolling closely past the car, seeming to slow for a second just as he passed by the rear end.

Replaying the scene at normal speed, he notice that the person looked down toward the car and his left shoulder dipped slightly. Then Charlie replayed the image one frame at a time. The guy, if it was a man, had been in shadows and there was no facial image at all, despite the light above the small loading dock. The time stamp showed it was well after dark, anyway. All he could learn was that the person was wearing a dark jacket, sunglasses despite the hour, and a black baseball cap with no logo.

It was worth checking the back end of the car before he got inside. Maybe the guy just keyed the trunk lid. Quickly he surveyed the following coverage, all the way to the present time, but the person hadn't returned.

At the moment, the alley looked empty within the range of the camera coverage, so Charlie grabbed a flashlight from a shelf in his office and stepped out onto the loading dock. He held the door open and hugged the wall, looking for snipers or potential danger beyond camera range.

It looked clear, so it was time to get out from under the cone of light. Charlie stepped down from the loading dock and went to the rear of the car, listening for footsteps or vehicle sounds that might precede an ambush or drive-by.

He directed the flashlight beam at the car. At least nobody

had scratched the perfect plum finish with a key or knife. So what
had the guy done as he passed by the vehicle?

If it was a bomb, it would have been tiny. The guy's fist had
been clenched. Aiming the light at the license plate, he noticed a
slight smudge on the edge. He crouched down, and using two fingers, felt behind the plate in the gap. There was a small bump about
the size of a quarter. Dropping to his knees, Charlie pried the object loose, then brought it into the light for a look.

Then he heard a footstep just a few feet away. Charlie dropped
to the asphalt, then rolled to his left, yanking out his Beretta as
he looked up for a target.

"Hang on there, bubba. It's me," Russell Turner exclaimed in
his Southern drawl, stopping short and showing his empty hands.

"I thought that stride of yours looked familiar," Charlie said,
then sighed and placed the pistol back into his holster before sitting up. "This must be your bug."

"Yeah. I've been having a hard time tailing anyone lately, as
you may have noticed. I'm used to working with assets and a team,
and I haven't had enough time in this community to become familiar with the road network," Turner said, reaching out for the
small device. "I keep losing your location, so I decided that a GPS
on your vehicle would make it a little easier. I should have said
something."

Charlie nodded, wondering why Turner hadn't just asked, and
whether Gordon's truck had a similar bug. Domestic CIA operations were unsanctioned, supposedly, but every agency in the world
would break the rules if it was to their advantage. Better to ask
forgiveness than permission, he'd learned the hard way, and clearly
Turner was operating under that philosophy at the moment.

"I'm getting the feeling that your section chief or whatever doesn't know what you're doing," Charlie decided to ask.

Turner smiled. "What I do on my vacations is my own business, Charlie. I'm just trying to look out for my boys, and you and Gordon were the best."

He didn't know what to say, so he said nothing. Charlie didn't like to be reminded of what they'd done in Iraq and, later, Afghanistan. It had taken years to get over the guilt, though the nightmares were now rare and less detailed. Did a man like Turner, or whatever his name really was, have bad dreams too?

"I'm all for saving my own ass, brother, so if you want, put it back on," Charlie said. "I have no real secrets to keep regarding my activities, and you know I'm going to keep after the bastard who's been stalking me."

"You sure?" Turner replied, bending down beside the Dodge, then looking back up at him.

Charlie nodded.

"Where are you going next? Home?"

"Yeah, but tomorrow I'm heading to Back Up. I want to find out who else connected to the operation might be involved."

"Who knew about the van, where it was located, and also knew the owner was out of town so it might not be missed?" Turner said, nodding.

"Exactly. And I have a hard time believing any of the vets have sunken so low as to take on terrorist attacks against their own troops," Charlie admitted.

"It's happened before . . ."

"Yeah, but all the agencies are looking for a lone wolf—an

outsider. I'm thinking this might be the work of an insider," Charlie said.

"I hope you're wrong."

"Me too. Have you thought about keeping an eye on the Koury family? Now that you're able to track my location . . ."

"Yeah, I'm heading over to their home right now. Even if the kid is kept locked up for a while, the rest of them can't just hang around the jail. I'll watch the place, then their shop tomorrow. But if you need me for anything . . ." Turner added.

"I've got your number. And thanks for everything." Charlie yawned. "As for me, I just need to get some sleep."

Turner yawned back. "I'm getting too old for this . . ."

Charlie laughed. "With that well-worn movie cliché, I'm saying good night. Once I reset the alarms and lock up the shop, I'm outta here." He walked up the steps, glanced back, and realized he was alone. The CIA man hadn't lost his skills.

As he stepped back inside to set the alarm again, he wondered if there were any other reasons why Turner had placed that bug on his car.

Chapter Thirteen

It was barely 8:00 AM, already warm in urban Albuquerque. Charlie drove into the only remaining parking place next to the austere Back Up building. To his right was an older model faded gold Chevy sedan with a variety of bumper stickers, most of them from branches of military service, politicians, and gun lobby groups. The other two slots contained an ancient Jeep and a new-looking economy model pickup.

"Looks like everyone's there," he called to Ruth as he hurried around to open her door. Charlie was rested now and needed to learn who might have latched onto Ben Webster's van yesterday. Hopefully the shooter hadn't had time to cover all his tracks.

"Same vehicles as last time, so Anna, Patricia, and Max?" Ruth asked, stepping out of Charlie's Charger.

"I'm guessing that Jeep belongs to Max," Charlie said. "A little rough around the edges but still able to do the job."

"So what's the plan? Do we divide and conquer, or double-team someone?"

"Rene got you watching sports?" Charlie observed with a smile, walking beside her toward the front entrance to Back Up, resisting the urge to take her hand, then giving in.

She smiled and gave his fingers a squeeze, holding on tight. "Of course. But I picked that up in college. Speaking the language helped me fit in and talk to the players, both male and female teams. I made a lot of friends that way," she replied.

"Hmmm."

"Just what does that imply?"

"Never mind," he said. "Why don't we gather as many names of potential suspects from Anna and Max—vets, contacts, or employers who had a beef, or maybe a personality conflict with Nathan?"

"Then we filter through the names to determine who on that list had no obvious alibi? Make some calls?"

"Exactly. And I'd also like you to try and uncover any business-related issues that would fly over my non-MBA head?" Charlie said. "Turning on the recorder now," he added in a whisper, reaching into his light jacket pocket.

"Okay, here goes," Ruth added, letting go of his hand and stepping onto the porch just ahead of him.

As they came into the small outer office, the bookkeeper and Patricia were involved in a heated discussion about something. When they saw they had visitors, the women stopped talking and greeted them.

The attention went immediately to Charlie and his latest encounter. Once it was clear he was uninjured, he declared his reason for the visit. "We came here today searching for the identity of the man who shot at me," he added.

"The same guy who killed Nathan. Is that what you're thinking?" Max asked. "This is all screwed up."

"It was the terrorist. I think he staked out the Afghan family's place, hoping that Charlie would show up at that protest. That what you think?" Anna asked.

Charlie nodded. "Pretty much. The problem is, the van the shooter was driving belongs to Ben Webster, one of your clients."

"No shit," Max responded. "But isn't Ben working that gig in Phoenix?"

"Sure is," Anna replied. "Unless he came back early or skipped out on the job."

"If the vet doesn't show up or has on-the-job problems, don't the employers let you know?" Ruth asked.

"According to what I've been able to learn, Webster has shown up for work on time, every day recently," Charlie said. "We've already ruled him out."

"So what's with his van?" Max asked. "How did the terrorist end up with it?"

"According to his apartment manager, the employer transported their work crew, Webster included, to Phoenix in company vehicles. The van was left at Webster's apartment," Ruth said.

"So Ben was just unlucky. I heard recently that Albuquerque has the highest rate of auto theft in the country," Anna said.

"Except that the van was stolen, used, then returned and parked right back where Ben had left it," Charlie replied, looking from Anna to Max for a reaction.

"That makes no sense at all, unless someone was trying to frame Ben," Patricia said. "This is an odd coincidence," she added.

"Nathan being killed, then Charlie gets attacked by maybe the same terrorist using a van with a connection to Back Up."

"More than a coincidence," Max responded. "That's why you two are here, Charlie. Am I right?"

Charlie nodded. "Who knew Ben was out of town, and that his van would still be parked in front of his apartment? It's an old model that can easily be broken into with a slim jim." Seeing Patricia's raised eyebrows, he explained, "A long, thin strip of metal that can be inserted between the glass and door, raising the lock lever and opening the door."

"*We* knew he was gone—well, not Patricia," Max said, looking over at Anna, who nodded.

"Along with a few of the vets also trying to get that gig, and his other friends, and his neighbors, including that apartment manager, right? Are the police checking with those people?" Anna said.

"Hopefully. But we're wondering if you'd thought of anyone new who might have had an issue with Nathan, or now, Ben Webster?" Charlie added. After what had happened lately, he was more worried about earthly, armed enemies than *chindis*, the evil in a person which remained after their death. He wasn't concerned with speaking names aloud anymore.

Anna and Max exchanged glances, then Anna spoke. "Maybe Todd Colby? He's a hard worker, but he came in more than once complaining to Nathan about the work he'd landed. One time Nathan stood up from his chair while they were arguing and Colby squared off like he was expecting an attack."

"Colby's a whiner and has absolutely no job skills, Anna," Max argued. "The only places Nathan could find work for him involved basic hard labor—digging ditches, loading and unloading construction materials, cleanup and janitorial. He couldn't handle any heavy equipment beyond a wheelbarrow. Once he dumped two loads from a hoist and got fired, remember?"

"Copy that," Anna said. "And his computer skills are limited to video games. He can't even text. We keep trying to place him, but sometimes when an employer gives him a try, they don't call back for more. Todd had a big argument with Nathan about two weeks ago, and Nathan told him to get out. Colby blew up and threw a punch at the door. See that dent in the metal?" she said, pointing to the spot.

"Then what?" Charlie asked.

"Nathan and I made sure Colby left the property. Haven't seen him since," Max added.

"Do you have an address for Mr. Colby?" Ruth asked, looking over at Charlie, who nodded.

"He's no longer represented here, so I guess it's okay. Boss?" Anna looked to Patricia.

Patricia nodded. "If you promise to be careful talking to the man, Charlie. It doesn't take much to set him off."

Anna left the room, heading into her office.

"By the way," Charlie asked, "how did Colby serve?"

"He was in the Army, combat engineers; demolition, if I recall. He was deployed for three tours in Iraq during the Gulf War, and saw his share of the action," Max explained. "My advice is to avoid any confrontations. Colby has PTSD issues, and was drinking heavily when he came here looking for work. First time Nathan smelled it on his breath, he cancelled the job. Colby was annoyed, but promised to quit the booze if he could get another chance. Fortunately, I think he finally quit drinking, or at least cut back."

"Here's the address," Anna said, coming back into the front office with a piece of paper in hand.

Ruth took the handwritten note and put it into her purse. "Thank you so much, we'll keep it confidential."

Charlie glanced over at a dozen clipboards on the wall, all containing what looked like business stationery. "It looks like you have a lot of clients out on jobs today, more than I saw last time. This is good news, right?"

Patricia spoke. "We're hoping to get even more work for our vets. Finances are still tight."

"How exactly does your bookkeeping work?" Ruth asked.

"Some of the employers we work with are still paying our people directly, and that makes accounting more difficult. Right, Anna?" Patricia commented.

"It's a little more work for me, but I don't mind. When our vets get paid directly, they feel a lot better about themselves, even though they're required to pay Back Up a percentage of that salary. They don't like to wait either, often needing the money right away. Most employers, however, insist on sending us the checks, then we pay our clients their share. Having an option was something Nathan always insisted on, leaving the payment methods up to the employers. Sometimes employers prefer dealing in cash, especially when it's one- or two-person businesses who simply require a temp on certain projects, but nothing long-term," Anna replied.

"How can you ensure that the payments made directly to your clients are accurately reported to Back Up?" Charlie asked. "Say, a vet making three hundred dollars on a job, but only reporting two fifty?"

"Anna and I were discussing this problem when you came in," Patricia replied. "I'd like to change over to the less vulnerable system and require that all wages be paid to Back Up directly in order to avoid any potential abuse. Not that I know of anything like that having actually taken place."

"What do you think, Max?" Charlie asked.

"We're hurting for money right now, and I don't want us to lose Back Up. If changing the system will help, I'm all for it," Max admitted.

"If we change over to a private employment agency payout system, complete with contracts, we're going to be telling some of our vets that we don't trust them anymore. That's not good, and that's why I'm against it," Anna replied. "I don't think we're being ripped off, we're just not finding enough work for the vets, and too often the jobs pay just minimum wage."

"Your opinion is noted, Anna," Patricia replied.

"Well, that's a business decision for you people," Charlie said. "All I want to do is talk to some of your clients and see how they feel about Nathan and Back Up in general. Maybe get a hint of who might have been skimming from this office, or had a beef. Someone wanted him dead, and once we rule out all the vets, we'll be able to move on in the search for the killer."

"And whoever has been attacking Charlie," Ruth added.

"So you'd like a list of our vets and their contact information?" Patricia asked. "Please call them first, Charlie. If they don't want to talk to you, I'm asking that you leave them alone."

"Of course."

"Anna, would you mind printing out our active client list?" Patricia asked.

"And maybe those who've moved on within the past year?" Ruth suggested.

Anna glanced at Patricia, who nodded.

"While you're doing that, Anna, may I have a look at your office?" Ruth asked. "I'm interested in seeing your layout. I do a lot of the bookkeeping at FOB Pawn, and we're using a new system ourselves."

"Our software is ancient, but sure," Anna replied, then motioned Ruth into the next room.

"Do you really think one of our vets may be responsible for Nathan's death?" Patricia asked in a whisper.

"Maybe just the attacks on me," Charlie answered.

"Isn't that just a little too coincidental?" Max said.

Charlie shrugged. "That's what's bothering me. I still think the terrorist angle is just a smokescreen to hide the real motives for the attacks. And, maybe, just maybe, I've become a target to promote that theory. That's why I'm taking a different path than most of law enforcement."

"Jealousy, maybe. As with Patricia's ex?" Anna said, just entering the room ahead of Ruth. "Sorry, I couldn't help but overhear."

"Where is Steven, anyway? Has he been located?" Max asked.

"Not that I've heard," Charlie answered. He looked over at Ruth, who held a folder in her hand. She nodded.

"Then I guess it's time to go," Charlie said. "Thanks so much for your help, and, starting with Todd Colby, we'll respect the privacy of your clients." He shook hands with all three of the Back Up staff, then he and Ruth exited.

As they walked back to the car, Charlie had a question. "There was definitely some tension between Anna and Patricia."

"Anna's pretty defensive about her work. I think she's worried about getting some of the blame for the financial situation. I asked about her military service, and she said she was an AP—Air Police—and helped provide security at Air Force bases overseas. She had to deal with a lot of cranky officers, and maybe that's what makes her defensive. Anna said that Nathan was a tough boss, but in a good way. She suggested that part of the reason Back Up is in financial trouble is that Nathan was weak when it came to business practices."

"Maybe that's what got him killed."

"Or maybe he was the one skimming money, not the vet clients," Ruth suggested. "Not that I know of any evidence pointing in that direction. It's just a thought. Money stolen or misspent leads to trouble. Look at what my husband did."

"Okay, but what would be Nathan's motive? Drugs, bad investments, gambling? He had a drinking problem, but had supposedly beaten that years ago."

"Do you kill someone who owes you money?" Ruth questioned.

"I'm still running low on answers, Ruth. Let's keep looking at potential suspects, and maybe that'll lead to the motive."

They were unable to reach Colby by phone, and it turned out that he'd moved from his old address in the town of Bernalillo, north of Albuquerque, to somewhere in Corrales. Fortunately they were able to locate a tenant in the building who could give them the phone number of the apartment manager, and after they'd wasted more than an hour, they approached Colby's supposed forwarding address, a mobile home located in a dead-end street north of the village fire station.

They turned off Corrales Road and drove down the bumpy dirt street, which had been graveled long ago. After passing several old adobe houses and outbuildings, plus a long, narrow alfalfa field, they spotted a mobile home parked to the right of Alfalfa Lane, which dead-ended with a metal barrier. Beyond was the bosque, beginning with a line of trees.

"There's a white Ram pickup." Charlie noted the mud-spattered vehicle parked beside the faded green single-wide.

"We've got reinforcements," Ruth said, looking in the side mirror back toward the highway. "The lights aren't flashing, so I don't think they're after us."

"The State Police," Charlie noted, slowing down, then stopping about fifty feet from the end of the trailer. "It'll be safer for you to stay in the car until I see what's going on. Maybe they're coming to arrest Colby."

He opened his door, then remembered to grab his sunglasses. As he leaned back toward the center console, there was a loud slap and boom. The driver's side window shattered, spraying him with flying glass.

"Down!" Charlie yelled, pushing Ruth toward the floorboards. Three more bullets struck, hitting the windshield and raining cubes of glass down upon them. There was a short pause, then someone behind them started yelling.

"Stay as low as you can, Ruth," Charlie called out. "I'm going after this bastard!"

Charlie threw open the door and rolled out onto the ground, flattening as he yanked out his handgun.

"Anyone hit?" came a familiar voice. It was Detective Du-Pree.

What the hell was he doing here? Charlie wondered, taking a quick look toward the single-wide, then the bosque to the east.

"The shots came from the bosque, the three tallest trees toward the south," called another man, probably the state patrolman.

"Cover me!" Charlie yelled, jumping to his feet and zigzagging to his right toward the far end of the trailer, intending on flanking the shooter. He raced to the corner of the mobile home, took a quick look, then ducked back when he saw a standing figure aiming a rifle from the tree line about fifty yards away. A bullet whizzed by just inches from his face.

DuPree and the other officer opened fire and the rifleman dropped down out of view.

Pistol out now, Charlie slipped around the end of the trailer, jumped across a small drainage ditch, and raced toward the trees, ready to fire if he saw the shooter. He cut left, then right to throw off the aim. If he could reach the bosque and the cover of the flood plain forest, he'd almost be on equal terms with the rifleman. The sunbaked ground of the approach was hard, dotted with clumps of waist-high buffalo grass, but ahead there was taller sagebrush and willows. He now had eyes on the back of the camo-jacketed figure as the man faded into the thicker vegetation, mostly tall willows, shrubs, and trees of all species and ages.

No more return fire had come, and Charlie was already gaining on the shooter, who was slowing. The ground ahead was transitioning from hard-packed clay to river sand, which would explain the gunman's drop in speed. Colby, if that was him, was still fleeing east toward the Rio Grande River, perhaps three hundred or more yards away. The growth was getting denser, and he couldn't see that far ahead. Though it had been a dry year, the area closest to the water table was still green and dense. Charlie knew he could run down almost anyone who wasn't a long-distance athlete. Hopefully, the guy didn't have a vehicle parked on the canal road that lay between here and the river.

Charlie's pace was swift and steady. Long ago, he'd learned how to remain aware of his footing while keeping his sight on the trail ahead. It was evident almost immediately that the shooter had chosen to flee down an animal trail, one used by rabbits and coyotes, based upon the abundance of familiar, yet non-human tracks.

He had to catch up to the shooter, one way or another. The guy had just tried to kill him, and Charlie needed answers. The running man was slipping in and out of view, but hadn't changed direction.

Just then Colby, or whoever it was, cut to the left and disappeared into a thick grove of willows.

The thicket was about a hundred feet in diameter, and appeared to be separated from the surrounding trees, clustered into a big oval. Charlie slowed to a jog, stopped, then stepped softly behind a clump of brush, ducked down, and waited, listening. The thicket was dense, and if that's where the shooter was still hidden, any movement would be obvious as long as he watched the tall, slender tops of the willow branches.

He heard the clump of running footsteps coming up from behind. Charlie turned around as a state policeman appeared in his dark black and gray uniform, moving in a crouch, handgun out. The officer slowed, looked at Charlie and nodded, aiming his handgun toward Charlie's left, covering that flank.

Wary of another ambush, Charlie held his finger to his lips, signaling silence, then pointed to the willow thicket.

The state cop signaled with his hand, indicating that Charlie should hold his position and provide cover fire if needed.

Charlie nodded.

The officer backed into the trees surrounding the stand of willows, then moved from trunk to trunk, circling the thicket, his weapon aimed toward where the shooter was apparently hiding.

"Police officer," the cop called. "You're surrounded," he lied. "Put your weapon down and come out with your hands in the air. Walk toward my voice."

Charlie heard the sound of a vehicle close by, to the east. "Crap!" he yelled. "He's already split."

Charlie jumped up and raced toward the river, looking ahead and spotting the high ground of the conservation road about fifty yards away. It lay atop a levee beside an irrigation canal that ran parallel to the river for miles in either direction.

"Try to get an ID on the vehicle," the cop yelled, following in his footsteps. "I'll call in some units to block off the bosque."

"Copy," Charlie responded, his eyes on the road. All he could see, unfortunately, through the trees and undergrowth, was a blue blur and plenty of dust from the vehicle heading north.

By the time he could get a clear view of the road, it was empty. As the dust cloud dissipated, it was clear that the shooter had turned to the west off the ditch road and fled down some residential street that connected at the end.

He hurried back toward Colby's single-wide, finding a hiker's trail that appeared, from the tracks, to be mostly used by animals. Ruth was back there, hopefully safe with DuPree. Somewhere behind him was the state police officer, but Charlie wasn't waiting.

Finally Charlie reached the last layer of trees and saplings, and emerged into the open. Ahead was Colby's trailer, the Charger, and the state police black-and-white cruiser. Detective DuPree was standing there, pistol down at his side.

Charlie knew Ruth was safe, or DuPree would be with her. Out of the corner of his eye, Charlie heard, then saw the state police officer jogging up from behind.

"Shooter got away, north up the canal road, then probably west onto Corrales Road. Had a blue vehicle—a pickup, I think—parked to the east on the conservancy road," Charlie added. "Where's Ruth?"

"I'm here, Charlie," she said, stepping into view from behind the trailer. "Your car's full of glass right now."

She walked up and gave Charlie a quick hug.

"Better not," Charlie said, backing away after a second. "I'm still full of glitter," he realized, after finally noticing cubes of glass on his sleeves and shoulders.

"Close your eyes, duck down, and shake your head," DuPree suggested.

Charlie did so, then opened his eyes again. "Anything in my hair and on my face?"

"Close your eyes again," Ruth said, then came up and brushed his face gently, including his eyebrows and hairline. "Okay," she concluded. "Better."

"Thanks," he said softly.

"Okay, now that this tender moment is over, I have a few questions," DuPree said. "Did you recognize the shooter? How about a description?"

"All I got was a glance, no ID possible. Shooter was light-skinned, blond or light brown hair, about Ruth's height, wearing jeans and a camo jacket with a hood. No glasses or facial hair noted. I couldn't close within fifty yards and couldn't pick him out of a lineup. Medium to light build, and he knew how to run," Charlie added.

"That doesn't fit Todd Colby," DuPree replied. He turned to the state policeman, who was already on his radio again. The cop nodded, passing along the description.

"Is Colby in the mobile home? He couldn't have missed the gunfire," Charlie said.

"Don't know," DuPree replied. "Can we clear the trailer before you work the scene?" DuPree asked the officer, who was still on the radio. The state cop held up his hand, signaling for them to wait . . .

A moment later the uniformed officer ended his call. "My jurisdiction, Detective, so I'll take the front. Cover the rear. Be careful, Colby worked with explosives."

A minute later the cop yelled, "No response, the door is locked. Check the back, but don't enter. I have a warrant."

"Stand by," DuPree yelled. "Cover me, Charlie?" he asked, then stepped back from the small rear door and reached into his pocket, pulling out a latex glove.

Charlie monitored the door, checking back and forth at the trailer windows in case they were being watched. Then something caught his attention. "You smell that?" he asked.

DuPree looked over at him. "Yeah, smells like . . ."

"Death," Charlie added softly.

Chapter Fourteen

DuPree tried the knob, and the door opened, sending a foul odor reminiscent of a neglected meat locker or a slaughterhouse. Somehow Charlie doubted that Colby had been butchering cattle.

"What is that awful smell?" Ruth asked, coming around the end of the trailer. "Like something died."

DuPree poked his head inside, then stepped back, cursing softly. "Not something, someone. Looks like Todd Colby. Oh, sorry, Charlie."

Charlie shrugged. He walked down the two steps of the small wooden porch, shaking his head. "Well, we can rule him out as today's shooter."

DuPree closed the trailer door, gagging just a little, then yelled to the state police officer, "Body inside. Looks like the resident."

DuPree walked down the steps and joined Charlie and Ruth. "For once, I'm glad this isn't my jurisdiction. I'm leaving this to the state police and the Corrales cops. The guy's been dead at least a day or two. And in this heat . . ."

They walked away from the trailer and stood next to the state police car.

"What brought you here today, Charlie?" DuPree asked. "The Back Up connection?"

"Yeah. According to their office staff, the guy had a beef with the dead man. Well, the other dead man. Is that why you showed up?"

"Pretty much, at least for my interest. But I also found out that the guy inside was being investigated by the State Police for possession and transportation of stolen property. They were sending Sergeant Legler here to interview him, and because I'm interested in finding out if he has an alibi for the previous shootings, I found a way to tag along."

"Stolen what? Guns? Drugs?" Charlie asked.

"No, stolen electronics and computer components that end up at flea markets and internet sales across the state," the state police officer said, walking up to join them. "Inside, along with Colby's body, are cardboard boxes containing everything from laptops and tablets to smartphones and hard drives. There are also what look like industrial explosives and a couple of electrical detonators in a box labeled with the name of a local construction company. But there's something else, and I had to call in my captain. This place is going to get very busy before long."

"What did you find, Sergeant?" DuPree asked.

"Pinned to the east side wall is a poster we've seen before." The sergeant brought out his phone and showed them an image. It was a printout of an ISIS flag, and below it, the message "Another hero sent to hell."

Charlie shook his head slowly. "Looks like our terrorist has changed his tactics."

DuPree swore softly. "How'd he gain entry? I didn't see any marks on the back door suggesting a break-in," DuPree said. "Anything like that in the front?"

Sergeant Legler shook his head. "No open or broken windows either, which means Colby may have let his killer inside."

"Which suggests he knew him," Charlie concluded. "Maybe there was a fight between partners and Colby lost."

Ruth looked back and forth between Charlie and DuPree. "If the shooter is the same man who killed the vet at the ceremony, how did he know we were coming here today?"

Charlie shrugged. "Somehow he knew we'd want to talk to . . . Colby."

"But not when," Ruth argued. "If the terrorist—or maybe the other terrorist—was watching us at the shop or my apartment and he followed us, how did he know to get here first?"

"Because we had the wrong address? Or maybe the terrorist somehow knew about the State Police visit. He shot at us because we were closer or he didn't have a clear shot at the cruiser. Or because he recognized me. There are several possibilities, I guess. Either way, if he wasn't watching me already, then knowing we were coming narrows down the suspect list. Perhaps the shooter is an insider, or there's some very personal motive at stake here."

Charlie immediately thought of Steven Azok, who did fit the description of the man he saw running away. Just how disturbed was the guy, and was he smart enough to pull off such a huge scam?

DuPree nodded. "I see your point. But again, you were the target, and this was way too close. And how did Colby get the explosives, and what did he intend on doing with them? The guy was trained in detonation work in the military, so he had the skills needed to blow things up. We need to get our ducks in a row before the terrorist tries again, Charlie."

"But you're going to be busy here for a while, right?" Charlie asked.

"Undoubtedly a lot longer than I want. I can also expect the Feds currently looking for the terrorist to take over this investigation as well, and they'll want to brush me aside. How about I give you a call when I'm done and we can meet at that little mom-and-pop place down from your shop?" DuPree suggested. "If they're still open."

"Frank and Linda's? Sure. Meanwhile, I think we have better things to do than stand around in this sun," he said, nodding toward Ruth, who'd become very quiet.

"Ready to get back to work?" he asked her.

"How?" Ruth nodded toward Charlie's car, which had both front and rear windshields shattered.

"Forgot about that. The crime scene will be needing my car for a while, right?" Charlie asked.

"Remove any firearms or devices you may have laying around inside, Charlie, then give me your key. I'll find someone to give you two a ride back to the shop," DuPree replied.

Charlie looked down the dirt road. Two Corrales Police cars were parked there, with uniformed officers walking toward the trailer. A State Police car was coming up to join them. "Got my cell phone and the Beretta, but there's one more thing I need. How about you?" he asked Ruth.

"I already have my purse and the folder," she said, holding them up.

Charlie walked over to the rear of the car, removed Turner's bug, and put it into his pocket. Then he returned to where DuPree and Ruth were talking.

"Detective. Will you need me to help locate the shooter's position?" Charlie asked. "There was probably some brass left behind."

"Not necessary. I have a fix on the location. And there'll be metal detectors, if necessary," DuPree replied. "Now go find some shade until I can release someone to give you that ride. Better give me your car key, Charlie."

Charlie handed it to him. "I'm afraid to look, so take good care of her, okay?"

Ruth groaned, grabbing Charlie's arm. "You and that car. Let's go stand under a cottonwood tree and get away from that smell," she added in a whisper, gently brushing a cube of glass off his shoulder with a shaking hand.

Detective Wayne DuPree strolled into Frank and Linda's mom-and-pop grocery and deli at five thirty, just a few minutes behind Charlie and Gordon, who were seated at one of the four lunch counter tables near the deli counter, sipping iced tea. The table gave them a view of the front entrance, so there was no need to wave to the cop; he knew where they'd be.

The interior was long and lean, lined with shelves containing everything from Chinese teas, to Mexican and New Mexican foods for the local residents, half of whom were Hispanic.

Their lunch menu varied, however; everything from green

chile cheeseburgers to Navajo tacos and organic vegetarian salads. Most of the fare originated from local farms and ranches.

"A Navajo taco and an iced tea," DuPree announced to Frank as he approached the deli counter. "You guys already ordered?" he asked Gordon and Charlie.

"Yes, they did, Wayne," replied Frank, a short, barrel-chested man in his late fifties. He placed two plates loaded with burgers and sweet potato fries on the counter. "Here they are, boys."

Frank and Linda had run their small business for two decades, and knew both DuPree and his father, who'd worked this neighborhood as a sheriff's deputy for most of his career.

Charlie stood and retrieved his and Gordon's meals, bringing them to the table as DuPree took a seat. "I've got some very interesting news, guys. I accompanied some State Police officers and a Bureau agent when they interviewed the staff at that vet place, Back Up. Turns out the three who work there had just returned, having shut down their office for a few hours, apparently right after you and Ruth left."

"That's conveniently coincidental," Charlie said. "Where'd they go?"

"According to Patricia Azok, the three had split up to go visit potential employers and search out more temp jobs for the vets they represent. They didn't return until around three, which is about the time we arrived at their office," DuPree explained.

"Which means one of them could have been the sniper who nearly took out Charlie over in Corrales," Gordon responded. "And might even be the killer we're looking for. Any way to check their alibis?"

"That's not going to be easy, Gordon. Some of that time they were in transit. But it might not matter anyway," DuPree said.

"Why the hell not?" Charlie asked. "Except for you and a few state police officers, the only people who knew we were tracking down Colby are those three Back Up people. Unless the shooter was following Ruth and me and somehow got ahead of us. Or, taking the simplest explanation, we just happened to walk into an ambush directed at the State Police. Any idea who might have known about their investigation into Colby? Who sent Sergeant Legler?"

"The state cops are looking into that, but my instincts still point back to that Back Up office," DuPree said.

"So it *does* matter. The shooter, terrorist or not, could be either the ex-wife, Patricia, or Anna Brown, the bookkeeper. They are both about the same size, with similar skin and hair colors. Max is too heavy to have been the sniper I saw. Unless he hired it out. We have already considered that the terrorist might have a partner."

"Ah, but then there's the bug," DuPree responded, shaking his head.

"Bug?" Gordon asked.

"Yes. All three of them immediately denied any connection to Colby's death and the shots fired today, as well as the previous incidents. Colby, as it turns out, worked several days at the company whose name was on the box with the explosives. Max and Anna verified that information. Then the staff began to speculate on ways anyone else could have learned about you and Ruth searching out Colby today, and Anna recalled that Steven Azok had been in the office more than once—before and after Whitaker was shot. She suggested that maybe Azok had bugged the phones to snoop on Patricia. He's been stalking her ever since she threw him out of their place."

DuPree continued, "While the state police officer was on the phone, checking to see if they could get a tech over there to sweep the place, I decided to do a visual. In less than five minutes I found a bug stuck under Max's desk. It was active, according to the tech who arrived a little later. No fingerprints were lifted, so they're trying to trace the device. Apparently it's readily available on Amazon and several mail order suppliers, so unless they can find a name to match with the serial number, it's a dead end."

"I suppose the shooter could be Azok. Still no idea where he's hiding out?" Charlie asked.

"His red pickup was discovered yesterday more than a hundred and sixty miles from here, along the curb on a Farmington street. It's not known how long it had been there. No sign of Azok, however, and his brother Aubrey claims not to know where he might be right now. FPD cops are looking for possible witnesses and checking security cameras in that area of their city," DuPree said.

"What else did they find?" Gordon asked.

"The plates were missing, along with the registration and paperwork. But a set of fingerprints lifted from the interior match Azok's," DuPree said. "And the VIN number matched with the DMV. It's his pickup, all right."

"How about reports of recent stolen cars in that area? Something blue, maybe a pickup," Charlie asked. "Or a recent purchase from a used car lot? Azok's obsessed with Patricia, so he might already be back here. It's only a three hour or so drive from Farmington."

"He's not at his last residence. The ATL is still active, and Patricia Azok has been notified," DuPree said.

"One Navajo taco, Junior," Frank called out, laying the plate on the counter, along with a glass of iced tea.

"Junior?" Gordon said with a smile.

"My dad and I share the same first name," DuPree mumbled, getting up to collect his meal.

"So where do we stand right now?" Charlie asked.

"Caleb Koury has been cleared of any radical activity, and released from jail. His computer emails to and from the Middle East have been between former classmates, not radicalized Muslim extremists," DuPree added. "The list of suspects in the more recent attacks is more clearly defined, but we need to find Azok. This might not have a direct connection to the terrorist shootings, but my gut works against that possibility. Unfortunately, someone is still trying to kill you, Charlie."

"But why, unless it's a terrorist who can't seem to hit the target anymore?" Gordon asked. "Well, except for the guy in the trailer."

Charlie shrugged. "Maybe, from all the pressure, this shooter has been forced to take greater risks."

"That's what I was thinking. A daylight attack, and the increased chance of pursuit and a visual ID," DuPree said. "Waiting in ambush that close to residents was dangerous, especially if he was also the person who killed the guy at the trailer. How long had he been there, waiting within a hundred yards of his last victim?"

"That's why we need to keep up the pressure. I'm going to focus on Azok," Charlie concluded. He'd also call Russell Turner, who'd contacted him a few hours ago, wanting to be brought up to speed on the shooting. The CIA guy was still keeping a protective eye on Dawud Koury, but asked to be contacted when there were any substantial leads.

"Stalkers are obsessed. How about we shadow Patricia Azok and wait for her husband to show up?" Gordon suggested. "I'm in, Charlie. You'll need an extra set of eyes in case Azok turns confrontational instead of running away like last time. And, just in case Westerfield has made it to Albuquerque, we'll ask Stannic— the deputy marshal—to cover Ruth's apartment or provide someone. It's nearly closing now, and she and Jake might be willing to tend the shop. They can run the business with their eyes closed anyway."

DuPree nodded. "Most of our detectives are tied up assisting the Feds, so it's up to you two to do the heavy lifting on alternative theories. The Feds don't believe Azok is a viable suspect, despite not having a clear alibi. They're still reacting to those ISIS notes, concentrating on the lone-wolf theory, trying to guess what might happen now that the guy probably has explosives and detonators."

"How much of that was taken?" Gordon asked.

"There are two sticks of dynamite missing, along with two detonators. ATF is now working on that. I've been instructed to assist in every way possible on the terrorist angle. Just keep in touch. As far as Azok is considered, I'll make sure the APD patrols in the wife's neighborhood know who you are. In order to do that, however, I'll need specifics regarding the vehicles you'll be using," DuPree said.

"Well, my Charger is out of commission at least for a few days, and besides, Azok knows it belongs to me. I have a silver rental sedan right now, a Hyundai," Charlie answered.

"The guy has seen my pickup too," Gordon said. "Maybe Jake would be willing to switch vehicles with me once in a while, which means the patrols need to know about his black SUV. If this goes on for a couple of days, we'll plan to vary our surveillance so it won't spook the guy. One vehicle, two vehicles, like that."

"Okay, guys. Now let's eat. My dinner is getting cold," DuPree said.

"I'm just saying, that if I'd have been with you this morning, we might have caught the bastard," Gordon said, still watching the street west of Patricia Azok's apartment.

"Or you might be in the hospital or dead. Azok would have shot at both of us. You squared off with him at the hospital that night, remember?" Charlie added.

"Yeah, well. I'd have chosen a ride along with Ruth as a companion too. She's much better company than either of us. Speaking of Ruth, how are things going between the two of you?" Gordon asked.

"Much better."

"That's cryptic."

"More than you need to know, Gordon."

"You're in deep this time, Charles."

Charlie looked at his watch. "Speaking of time, you think Azok is really going to come by this late? It's one fifteen."

"Assuming we haven't missed him, he just might make one last drive-by to make sure she's still at home and alone," Gordon responded. "We can wait a few more minutes, then call it."

"Okay. But one of us should probably make a pass by here early tomorrow, or else check to see if Azok might be waiting near Back Up for Patricia's arrival at work," Charlie suggested.

"Now you're talking like a stalker."

"Experience, I suppose. Amazing, the skills you learn after a tour or two out snatching insurgents, day or night," Charlie observed. "Learning habits, profiling."

"Think we'll ever be able to put those days to rest?" Gordon asked.

"All but the memories."

"God's ears, Charlie. Now let's go home before I fall asleep."

Charlie started the engine and took one last glance into the side mirror. "Wait a sec!"

Gordon nodded. "Light on. Now off again. Maybe she had to get up just for a second to grab her cell phone. Or had to use the head."

"Yeah, probably it's nothing. Still, I'm going to circle the block so we can check the alley."

"Good idea. I'm awake again anyway." Gordon sat up in the seat.

They drove quickly down the block, then Charlie turned onto the side street. Nearing the alley, there was the glow of taillights at the opposite end as a vehicle came out into the next street over, turning left.

"No headlights, just the brake lights as he stopped for a second," Gordon exclaimed. "He turned left."

Charlie raced down the street, turning right to locate the vehicle, a pickup, which was continuing broadside south past the next intersection. "I'm following whoever this is. He has no good reason to be creeping down a back alley in a residential neighborhood this time of night."

"Take it slow, Charlie. No need to spook the guy if that's Azok," Gordon warned. "You might wanna go lights out, like him. I'll use the night-vision scope." He reached over onto the center console and brought up the monocular unit, which had been for-sale merchandise earlier in the day at the shop.

"Good thing we brought the scope," Charlie said. "Guide me."

Charlie reached the intersection, passing through instead of immediately pursuing so they could take a quick look without spooking him. "Looks like a Ford 150," Gordon confirmed.

Charlie slowed and quickly turned the small car around in the deserted street, then followed, moving just fast enough to keep the vehicle in sight.

"Glad there aren't many streetlights in this neighborhood," Gordon commented. "I'm trying to read the plate. It's in-state, BMX something."

"You see anyone besides the driver?"

"Yes, but with the headrest, I can't make out anything except for the top of a head. The driver is wearing a ball cap," Gordon announced. "And, the plate numbers are 499."

"Fourth Street coming up, stoplight, and traffic. He'll have to turn on the headlights or get pulled over. The street is well lit, so we'll do the same," Charlie said.

The pickup, a dark blue color, turned left on the arrow, heading north as the driver turned on his lights. Charlie had to run a yellow light to follow, using the delay to also turn on the sedan's headlights to blend it. "I hope we don't end up having to race this guy."

"Hey, at least you'll get better gas mileage."

"Let's ask someone to run that plate and see if we can rule out some innocent who just happens to be cruising around with his date or companion."

"It's gonna have to be Nancy."

"Yeah," Charlie said, following as far away as possible while still being able to make the same traffic lights. He slipped into the right-hand lane, not wanting to be directly behind the pickup on the four-lane street.

It didn't take long for Nancy to answer. As a detective she was usually required to be available. Gordon made the quick request, then ended the call.

He picked up the night scope again, ready in case the pickup turned onto a less-lit side street. "If he keeps this route, we'll be out of the city in another ten minutes," Gordon pointed out.

They continued on, barely keeping the pickup in sight all the way out of north Albuquerque. Once they'd cleared the last large intersection, there were no streetlights ahead on this stretch of El Camino Real, the royal trade route of the Spanish settlers from Mexico to Santa Fe. And here the ancient path narrowed to two lanes.

"He's in no hurry. If this is Azok and he's grabbed Patricia, the guy is at least keeping his cool," Gordon said. "I wish Nancy would get back to us on that license plate."

A few minutes later, Gordon got the call. He listened, gave their location and direction of travel, thanked Nancy, and then said good night.

"Well?" Charlie asked, his eyes on the taillights a quarter mile ahead.

"The plates are stolen, and you wanna guess from where?"

"Farmington?"

"You heard. Well, did you also hear that there's a dark blue F-150 pickup on the FPD hot sheet?" Gordon asked.

"No, but the Four Corners area is pickup heaven. I bet there are a hundred missing Ford pickups in San Juan County. I grew up in Shiprock, remember, and even my dad had his truck stolen once," Charlie admitted. "But does the most recent theft fit within our time frame?"

"Sure does, and APD dispatch is notifying the Bernalillo cops and the State Police to pull him over once he gets within their city limits. Nancy wants to make sure we keep the vehicle in sight until then."

Charlie nodded. "So the worst we can do tonight is help catch a pickup thief." We're good at that, he recalled, from a series of incidents last year.

"Crap," Gordon muttered, bringing the night scope to his eye. "They're pulling off the road."

"Is there a . . . ?"

"Yeah, a side road that leads beneath the railroad tracks," Gordon completed the sentence. "But he's coming to a stop."

Charlie slowed. "Suppose he spotted us?"

"Now he's taking off again," Gordon said. "Raising dust."

Charlie accelerated. "He's making a run for it!"

"Wait!"

"Wait why?"

"He left someone by the road. Or else met them there," Gordon replied. "I can't make out who it is. But we'd better stop and see."

"Yeah. If it's his wife, we have to pick her up. The cops ahead should be able to stop him."

Charlie slowed again, seeing someone standing beside the road, waving their arms.

"It's a woman, I think. She's wearing a hoodie."

They pulled off the highway and the woman was clearly visible at the edge of the headlight cones. "It's Patricia!" Charlie exclaimed, braking to a stop.

Gordon already had the window down. "Are you okay? Was that your . . . husband?"

"I'm fine, Gordon. Just a little scared," she answered, her arms wrapped around her chest tightly. "And yes, that was Steven."

Gordon jumped out and held the door open for her. "You're safe now. Get in."

"I can ride in the back."

"No. We need to get moving," he said, motioning her toward the seat.

Patricia slipped into the front, tears in her eyes. "Hi, Charlie. Thank you, guys, for looking out for me. After Steven realized we were being followed he freaked out. I didn't know what was going to happen next."

"Let's roll," Gordon said, climbing into the back and reaching for his seat belt.

"There will be officers ahead, planning to pull him over. Is there anything you should tell them, like, is Steven armed? You said he freaked out," Charlie asked as he pulled out onto the highway again, looking ahead for Azok's taillights.

"He thought you were the police in an unmarked car. Steven

said he couldn't be caught with me—he'd end up in jail. He said he just wanted to talk me into taking him back."

"What will he do when he sees the police cars ahead?" Gordon asked, bringing out his cell phone.

"I . . . I don't know. He has a gun," Patricia said in a whisper. "Some kind of pistol."

"I'd better call 911 and get the message relayed ASAP."

A vehicle approached, with high beams on, and Charlie blinked his own lights, warning the driver. "Crap, just what we need, some drunk or moron," he grumbled, avoiding the glare as much as possible.

"He's coming over into our lane!" Patricia cried out.

"Hang on!" Charlie yelled, swerving toward the shoulder and hitting the brakes.

The brakes pulsed, preventing a skid, but Charlie had only inches of road to his right as the vehicle, a pickup, flashed by. Like walking along the edge of a cliff, Charlie managed to keep the car just inside the safety margin. If one tire left the pavement into the dirt, it could cause a slide, or worse, a roll.

"Who was that?" Charlie managed, slowing to a crawl as he eased back into the center of his lane.

"Azok, in that damned pickup," Gordon answered. "Bastard forced us off the road."

"Call it in," Charlie said as he came to a quick stop. Not seeing any oncoming traffic, he did a quick three-point turn and accelerated back south.

"He was flying. We'll have a hard time catching up," Gordon said.

"Yeah," Charlie answered. "But let's try and get close. We can call in his location, then leave this to the cops. You think?" he asked the woman beside him.

She nodded. "He's scared and on the run."

Charlie drove as fast as the narrow road allowed. He didn't see any sign of taillights ahead. "Did Steven say anything about the shootings, the attacks, and the hidden microphone?"

Patricia shook her head. "The only thing he insisted on was that he didn't kill Nathan. Steven just kept asking for me to forgive him."

"When did he discover we were following him?"

"When we were turning off onto the old highway at the end of Fourth Street, that's when he started cussing and looking in the rearview mirror. Finally he pulled over and told me to get out. Thank God," she whispered.

A few minutes later, approaching the long curve where three roads came together at the end of Fourth Street, Charlie pulled over to allow a racing State Police cruiser with emergency lights flashing to pass. He glanced over and saw Patricia was crying. "We need to meet with the police now, Patricia."

She nodded.

Chapter Fifteen

Charlie and Gordon remained with Patricia at APD headquarters in downtown Albuquerque for two additional hours, providing all the information they could regarding the evening's events. Jackson, the FBI special agent in charge, also had questions because Patricia hadn't gone with her husband willingly. According to her, Steven had hinted that he might kill her and himself if she didn't cooperate.

After escorting Patricia to her apartment, Charlie and Gordon walked back to the rental car. A brilliant but cool sunrise was approaching over the Sandia Mountains to the east. There wasn't a cloud in the clear, blue sky.

"Well, that was an interesting evening," Gordon commented with a yawn, standing by the passenger-side door as Charlie searched his jacket for the key, his thoughts on the surrounding homes and apartment buildings.

He paused, glancing at a large, fifties-era, wooden two-story home across the street. "Hey, Gordon, are those surveillance cameras underneath the porch eaves on that white house, the one with the Taos blue trim?"

Gordon turned for a look. "Are you thinking what I'm thinking?"

"If Steven Azok was stalking his wife the night the helicopter pilot was killed—and we know she was here—then, like he said, he couldn't have been the shooter," Charlie said. "Maybe one of those cameras might have recorded his presence here at that time."

"Yeah, it's worth checking out," Gordon responded. "How about we come back here in an hour or two and see if there's anything the owner can provide?"

"First of all, though, let's grab some breakfast and go clean up."

"Truck stop or fast food?" Gordon asked.

"Truck stop. How about one of those over by University and Menaul?"

"Deal. Let me write down the house number so we can pass the address along to Nancy or Wayne. Just in case we can't get the owner to cooperate with us civilians," Gordon suggested.

At seven in the morning, still on coffee highs after a sleepless night, Charlie pulled up at the curb outside the house with the cameras. They'd only been parked there a few minutes, discussing their approach, when a white-haired man in his sixties, wearing a robe and slippers, came out to retrieve his newspaper off the small lawn. He was wearing a blue ball cap with the name USS NEWPORT NEWS—CA-148 on the front, plus numerous patriotic pins and patches.

"Good morning, sir, can we talk to you a few minutes concerning your neighbor across the street? She was kidnapped last night," Gordon added, stepping out of the car. Charlie did the same.

The man stood up straight, his eyes wide open now. "Patricia? What happened? Was it that low-life husband? He's been stalking her."

"Yes. Yes, the story is probably in your newspaper, sir. But Mrs. Azok is safely back home now," Charlie added. "We'd like to talk to you about Steven Azok and see if you managed to capture anything on your surveillance cameras that the police could use to make a case."

The man came closer, staring as Charlie walked around the front of the car and joined Gordon on the sidewalk. "You're that Indian soldier who has been driving the local terrorist nuts. The Army hero. Your picture was in the paper. Charlie something."

"Charlie Henry, Mr. . . ."

"Foster, Donald Foster. Let me shake your hand, soldier. You're one lucky SOB."

"Got that right. Glad to meet you, sir." Charlie gave the man a firm handshake. "This is my friend and fellow vet, Gordon Sweeney. We served a few tours together."

Five minutes later, sipping some good, strong coffee, Gordon and Charlie stood behind Foster, a Navy vet who'd served during the war in Vietnam. The retired electronic countermeasures technician was seated with his laptop at the kitchen table as he displayed what his cameras had captured. They were quality images and covered the past two weeks. What they were seeing came from the cameras directed toward the front street and nearby yards.

"I save the images for two months at a time onto a flash drive, and then copy over them unless something shows up that looks bogus," Foster said, flipping through the displays with the touch and skill of a sixteen-year-old hacker. "I especially keep an eye on those apartments. Sometimes they get a renter who raises hell and it ends up spilling out into the street."

Within a few minutes, Foster brought up the images of the day of the ceremony, then slowed the fast forward down so they could scroll through the images for the afternoon and evening. Patricia's car pulled into her parking slot at 4:25 PM, she got out, checked her mail, and then went inside her apartment. Less than five minutes later a familiar-looking red pickup passed slowly by the building, then disappeared. A minute later, the same pickup stopped down the street, parking against the curb.

"That looks like Azok in the truck, the one he used to drive. He can see her car from his position, but she can't see him without coming outside, I don't think," Charlie said. "Her windows all face west, or into what appears to be an interior courtyard."

"That's him," Foster said. "I remember when the police came and arrested Azok about a month ago. I made a copy onto a DVD just in case Patricia needed it in court."

"Can we scan the images just slow enough to spot him if he turns toward the cameras?" Gordon asked.

It didn't take long. "That's the guy, all right. And the time is . . . 7:15 PM," Charlie said, looking at the numbers in white at the bottom of the image. "Can you freeze it?"

"Of course," Foster answered. "You want me to print an image?"

"Really?" Gordon asked.

"Done, and done," Foster responded with a grin and a click of the mouse. There was a short delay, then Foster stood. "I'll grab the images from my office printer." The man crossed the living room and went down the hall.

"The pilot was killed around that time, wasn't he?" Gordon asked.

"Yes, between 7:15 and 7:18, based upon the reports and cell phone images from the guests and first responders at the ceremony. It's clear that Azok was not the person who shot Captain Whitaker," Charlie admitted, "though I suppose he could have hired it out."

"Interesting that Azok chose that particular moment to look directly into the camera," Gordon observed.

Charlie felt a chill go down his back, then turned, hearing footsteps.

"Here you go, boys," Foster said, walking back into the kitchen. "I printed two copies, one for you and one, maybe, for the police. And I'll archive the file."

"Great. Can we look at the rest of the coverage for that evening?" Charlie asked.

A short time later, with a copy of the surveillance coverage on a borrowed flash drive, Gordon and Charlie drove back to FOB Pawn, hoping to arrive before Jake opened up for the day.

"Once we pass this information along to Detective DuPree, what's next, Charlie?" asked Gordon, who was starting to yawn again.

Charlie couldn't help but yawn back before he could answer, trying to focus on the early commuter traffic and workmen off to their first client of the day. "Anna Brown? She's still the only viable suspect so far that we can check up on without getting in the way of the professional law enforcement agencies. Based on the Corrales ambush, if it wasn't someone working in that office, then the information on the pending law enforcement visit had to come from someone inside the State Police. Or an informant."

"Unless it was Azok, or someone working with him."

"Assuming he also placed the bug, Gordon. Anyone who's ever been in that office had the opportunity."

"Well, we've got to start somewhere. I'm wondering if Anna was really out trolling for Back Up employers the other day. Suppose we can get a list of the people she claims to have contacted without letting her know we're checking her alibi?" Charlie said.

"If they made contact lists, Patricia should have them. And I have the feeling she'll turn it over after last night," Gordon said.

"Okay, Charlie, we've got the list of contacts from the day of the most recent shooting. Crap, I hate saying it that way. Too much like an AAR—after action review," Gordon clarified to Ruth as he approached the two, who were standing beside the front register.

"You're talking about the employers that Max, Anna, and Patricia supposedly contacted later that morning?" Ruth asked. "I know you have to do this, guys, but I still have a hard time thinking that Anna Brown might have killed her boss, then blamed it on terrorists."

"Well, if we can rule her out, that's a beginning, even if it leads to a dead end. According to Nancy, Anna and Max are vets who served honorably and have clean records. Homeland Security vetted them as well," Charlie said. "I wonder if the Feds will be able to connect that listening device to any individual."

"Well, let's get started then, Charlie," Gordon said, holding up two copies of a list of names, addresses, and numbers. "Do we call these people up, or do we drop by their businesses?"

"I've got a time-saving idea, boys," Ruth said.

"We're listening," Charlie nodded.

"How about I call, thanking them for meeting with the Back Up staff? A follow-up courtesy call, like after an interview. It's a common business practice," she added. "I can identify myself as Ruth, who works in the office, without saying which office? I can use my cell phone."

Charlie nodded, looking over to Gordon, who was nodding and smiling. "I like it," Charlie said. "It'll save a lot of time, and you only have to contact the individuals on Anna's list."

"And we can look after the shop, for a change," Gordon added.

Less than ten minutes went by before Ruth came out of the office and waved to Charlie, who was helping a young couple with some jewelry. He nodded, then went back to serving the clients.

A short time later he walked into the office, where Ruth was talking to Gordon, leaving Jake to tend the customers. "That didn't take long," Charlie commented. "Or did I misread your signal?"

"I got confirmation that Anna Brown was up in the northeast heights at three different warehouses during the time of the shootings across the river in Corrales, Charlie," she said, looking down at her notes.

"There were less than fifteen minutes between consecutive meetings, pal, and there was no way a round trip could be made during that time interval," Gordon affirmed. "Anna couldn't have been the shooter unless she beamed over."

"I even made a few calls to Patricia's contacts as well. She was exactly where she said she was during the critical times," Ruth added.

"So, we're running out of suspects. Maybe there really is a terrorist, and for some reason he's been expanding his list of targets," Charlie said.

"The known targets still have one thing in common; they're all vets, especially you," Ruth said softly, reaching out and touching him gently on the shoulder.

Charlie wanted to pull her into his chest right then, but they had a problem to solve, and his tenuous love life would just have to wait.

"So now what?" Gordon asked. "Check on the vets who've worked for Back Up?"

"I suppose. Let's start with those who quit coming to the service within the past few months, maybe with a grievance toward Nathan that wasn't known to the staff," Charlie suggested.

"That would include anyone who's landed a job on their own without any motive for revenge," Ruth pointed out. "But it's a start."

"Cold call their last listed number to see if they're still in the area?" Gordon asked. "Then ask if we can meet?"

"You guys with vet cred better handle that," Ruth said. "I'll go out there with Jake and help with the customers."

"Vet cred, huh?" Gordon said. "I like that."

"Flip a coin for who starts?" Charlie asked.

"Naw, rock, paper, scissors."

"How old are you boys, anyway?" Ruth asked with a wide smile.

"Yeah, well," Charlie replied. "What do you suggest, drawing straws?"

"Casting lots?" Gordon said. "Whatever that is."

"Never mind," Ruth said. "Charlie, you go first."

"Can't argue with that," Charlie said. "Where's the list?"

"Green folder in the misc basket—the one that says 'Back Up clients,'" Ruth said with a hint of sarcasm, pointing at the folder. "I'm leaving now," she added, stepping out of the office.

"We'll trade off in an hour," Gordon announced, looking up at the clock.

Charlie nodded, reaching for the folder.

It was nearly three o'clock when Charlie and Gordon drove up to the Rio Rancho work site. An upscale pueblo-style home was under construction about a mile west of Highway 528 in an area of small hills, arroyos, and plenty of juniper, sage, and buffalo grass. To the east was the entire Rio Grande Valley, the village of Corrales, and the Sandia Mountains on the horizon. As Gordon pulled up beside another two pickups, a jackrabbit with long, black-tipped ears slipped into hiding, then crept away.

"Haven't seen a jackrabbit in years," Charlie commented, climbing down out of the big truck. He took a quick look at the photo of the man they were looking for, a short Marine vet in his late twenties who was just a few inches taller than Gordon.

"Schroeder says he's taping and texturing drywall today, so he's probably inside," Gordon said, stepping toward the open front door, which had been hung but was still missing the hardware. The exterior walls had just been given their scratch coat of stucco and the moist, distinct scent filled the air.

"You the guys I spoke to a couple of hours ago?" A slender man matching the photo and wearing a drywall-flecked gray work shirt with a company logo above the pocket stepped up to the entrance.

Immediately he came outside onto the sagging square of plywood now serving as a porch. He had a gray, soft cap atop his sweat-covered hair, the bill facing backwards, and his brow was wet from perspiration.

Gordon quickly reached out his hand to shake, introducing himself and Charlie, who also shook hands.

"So you two are trying to track down whoever killed Nathan Whitaker. Taking it personal, I suppose. I read that the guy's been gunning for you, Mr. Henry."

"Got that right, Marine," Charlie said. "And call me Charlie. Mr. Henry is my dad."

"There are maybe a hundred members of law enforcement around here searching for the terrorist, or terrorists, but we're still trying to rule out a more personal motive for killing the captain," Gordon said.

"Personal? Then why does the killer keep taking potshots at you, Charlie? Or trying to, what, set you on fire?" Schroeder asked.

"That's the part that doesn't really make much sense, which is why we're going in a different direction. Nobody we've talked to seems to have had any particular beef with the victim, but can you add anything to that? Anyone connected to Back Up, staff or clients, who would have wanted Whitaker dead?"

"According to the papers, there's that guy who's married to Nathan's ex-wife. Jealousy is a strong motive. But as far as Back Up is concerned, Nathan never doubted any of us. Of course, I heard a rumor that some of the vets that were being paid in cash by their employer didn't report all of their income to Anna Brown. We were supposed to pay a percentage of our wages in return for Nathan finding us work. That's what keeps Back Up running."

"You suggesting that Nathan found out and got pissed?" Charlie asked.

"Who knows? Maybe? He was big on integrity. If he'd have found out, though, he would have shown them the door."

"Do you personally know of any people that might have ripped off Back Up?" Gordon asked.

"Not by name. Besides, I heard that most of the guys were paid by checks sent directly to Back Up. Anna handled the checks, figured out the percentages, and issued the vets their share via checks or cash. I never heard any complaints, and Anna was quick and efficient. It usually took a couple of days for the turnaround, just long enough for the employer checks to clear," Schroeder said.

Charlie nodded, having already heard a description of that process.

"So why did you stop using Back Up for placement?" Charlie asked. "Was it that ten percent fee?"

"Not at all. On my own I landed a full-time, regular job, and didn't need Back Up anymore. They're doing a great service to vets who need the money and can't find jobs, but I finally developed the skills needed to advance beyond the basic day-to-day labor market and bump up my pay grade. Nathan wrote me a great recommendation, by the way. His loss hurts all the vets," the man added.

"Know any guys who left Back Up with a bad attitude in general?" Gordon asked. "Not necessarily toward the staff."

The man thought about it for several seconds, then finally shook his head. "I didn't really meet or deal with the other vets unless we got the same gigs. When I wasn't working I was out hustling for any job that could keep me off the streets. Most of the guys, and a few lady vets, didn't show up at Back Up in the first place if they weren't really desperate for work. Any job beats begging on the streets and sleeping at the shelters. Of course, there were some that couldn't get placed no matter what, either because they failed to show, did a crappy job, or came to work high. But Max and Nathan didn't share any of their names with the rest of us. It was none of our business, and I respected that."

Charlie looked at Gordon, who nodded. "Well, thanks for the help, and if you think of anything that might help us track down the shooter, terrorist or not, please give us a call." Charlie handed his business card to the man.

Schroeder looked at the card carefully. "FOB Pawn. Yeah, fits a vet-run business. Ooh-rah." He shook both their hands, then stepped back. "I've gotta get back to work. You soldiers stay safe."

Chapter Sixteen

Charlie was in the FOB office logging in some recently available merchandise to the website when the business phone rang. "FOB Pawn, Charlie speaking. How may I help you?" he answered automatically.

"I need your help, Henry. Don't say a word to anyone until you hear me out," came a hurried but distinctive masculine voice Charlie instantly recognized.

"Not unless you're ready to turn yourself in to the cops, Azok," Charlie responded, standing to look through the office glass, hoping to catch Gordon's attention. Unfortunately, his pal was working on a display and his gaze was focused elsewhere.

"And don't put me on speaker either," Azok added.

"Okay. What do you want?"

"I want to turn myself in to the APD cops—not the Feds—and I want you to pick me up and take me there," Azok said.

"Why me?"

"You're not a cop, and you have a stake in all this. I know you've been trying to track me down. Trust me, you'll want to hear my side of it."

"Where do we meet?" Charlie asked, still trying, unsuccessfully, to flag down Gordon. Just then Ruth, at the front counter, turned and looked his way curiously. Charlie held his finger to his lips, then pointed toward Gordon.

Ruth caught on immediately, walking over toward Gordon.

"Be in the parking lot of the Home Depot off Coors Bypass in twenty minutes. Come alone. Once you're there, call this number. It shows on your phone, right?"

Charlie nodded, looking toward Ruth, who was with Gordon now. Both were looking his way.

"You got the number?" Azok insisted.

"Yeah, sorry. But it might take more than twenty minutes getting across the bridge this time of day," Charlie responded. It was the truth.

"Then you'll have to hurry, won't you?" Azok said. The line went dead.

Gordon entered the office just then, noting that Charlie had set down the receiver.

"What's up?"

"Grab your weapon, Gordon. We're going to meet with Steven Azok and hopefully turn him in to the cops."

"You think we might need something besides our pistols?" Gordon replied, nodding toward the locked-up storeroom.

"Yeah. But we'll have to hurry."

•   •   •

They took Gordon's truck, with him driving, while Charlie called Nancy to get her up to speed. After a minute or two of arguing, Charlie ended the call.

"She think it's a trap?" Gordon asked, not taking his eyes off the road as they approached the Corrales Bridge across the Rio. Traffic was moderate but typically there was a bottleneck just across the river at a major intersection, so they needed to keep up the pace.

"Of course, and I have my doubts as well. But this is mid-afternoon, not the time the terrorist usually strikes," Charlie said.

"Except for the bosque thing and the van shooter," Gordon reminded. "Which is why we decided to wear the vests."

"Not the latest technology, but they should stop pistol rounds."

"Except the terrorist uses a .223 rifle most of the time," Gordon reminded.

"Azok has an alibi for the first attack."

"So he's a part-time terrorist?"

Charlie shrugged, trying to plan ahead as they crossed the river. "Only a few minutes away now. Nancy said there should be a unit in the area, parked in the Walmart lot a few hundred yards to the north. Meanwhile, she's on her way across the city."

Gordon looked at the dash clock. "We're going to be a few minutes early. Wanna park out in the open, or get in close beside other vehicles?"

"The latter," Charlie said, checking the Beretta again before slipping it back into the holster at his waist.

"Yeah. Any possible sniper will have to get in close for a clear shot."

A short time later Gordon parked the big pickup between two other vehicles, close to the center entrance to Home Depot. They both looked around, trying to see if anyone was sitting inside their vehicle, but although they noticed a few workmen or retirees coming and going, they couldn't locate Azok.

Charlie made the call, on speaker, and Azok answered immediately. "Get on 528 and drive north through Rio Rancho. Continue driving until I give you the next location. I'll be texting from now on."

"Why text?" Charlie asked, but the line was dead.

Gordon looked over. "Yeah. For some reason that worries me."

"And once we leave Albuquerque, APD loses jurisdiction."

"Chances are Azok is in Rio Rancho or beyond by now. Call Nancy and let APD figure out who's going to shadow us," Gordon replied, pulling out of the parking slot. "Still, you might want to keep an eye out for a tail."

"Or a drive-by," Charlie added. "Just in case he's closer than we think."

Less than ten minutes later, as they were approaching the northern terminus of Highway 528 where it intersected Highway 550, Charlie got a text. He looked down at the device.

"Now what? We've got to go west, or east into downtown Bernalillo?" Gordon asked, glancing over. "Please, don't say we have to turn around."

Charlie chuckled. "Go west on 550 until I text you again, it says."

"Out into the boonies and pretty open terrain. If it's an ambush there can't be any close backup," Gordon pointed out.

"He's not stupid. This way Azok can make sure I'm, well, we, are alone."

"It's still daylight. He'll have an easy shot."

"So will we," Charlie said, pointing down at the scoped M-15 resting against his leg. "I'll update Nancy and see if she can get us direct contact with that State Police officer sitting tight in Bernalillo. He can get ahead of us before we turn west and stay close by."

Another text came within ten minutes. Charlie read it aloud. "Left hand turn onto the first dirt road south once past SA pueblo. Locate white trash bag on the fence. Look for the blue pickup. Stop beside black trash bag. Exit vehicle, no guns. Wait."

"The guy is really paranoid. I don't like it, Charlie."

"One of us can get out at the highway and flank the blue pickup," Charlie suggested.

"Meaning me." Gordon said. "Good. I'm a better shot than you."

"In your dreams."

"Hey, I'm good enough. And I'm nearly invisible out in the brush . . ."

Charlie nodded, not adding *because you're a little guy*, which tended to feed further comments. "I'll notify Officer Willie, but ask him not to contact the tribal authorities. If someone unexpected shows up, that might cause too many problems."

"Santa Ana is the first pueblo ahead, right?"

"Yeah, the second one west is Zuni."

Traffic was light at mid-afternoon and before long they passed the exit that led to the pueblo. It was less than a mile before Gordon saw the dirt side road leading through a gap in the fence, across a cattle guard. The white trash bag was tied to a fence post. As soon as they were inside the fence, Charlie stopped the pickup.

They put on Bluetooth ear pieces, needing to keep their hands free now that they were vulnerable.

"I don't see any sign of a blue pickup, but the junipers and sagebrush here are pretty thick. There's a low ridge ahead. The pickup might be just beyond, out of view from the road," Charlie observed. "Want to go a little farther?"

Gordon shook his head. "No, once we see the pickup, Azok will see us too and know you're not alone. I'll circle to the right, around the west side of that ridge, and hope I don't have to hoof it very far. Give me five minutes before you continue down the road, and maybe I'll be able to spot the pickup and let you know where I am," Gordon added, climbing down out of the truck.

Charlie handed him the assault rifle. "Be careful. I'll call you as soon as I get a visual on the pickup or Azok."

Gordon fed a round into the chamber of the M-15. "Same here."

Charlie slid over to the driver's side as Gordon crossed the dirt road and moved into the brush. He looked down at his watch. Gordon was already out of view. He hated to wait while someone else was moving into danger, so he checked his pistol one more time, slipping off the safety before putting it back into the holster. Then he waited.

The dirt track was at least solid enough from last month's rains to avoid getting stuck, despite there being at least three new sets of tracks. One of those came from a pickup, judging from the width of the tracks, which made sense. The road turned to the left, east, angling along the side of the low ridge, away from where Gordon was moving, so Charlie slowed down even further to give him more time to locate the blue pickup.

Less than a quarter mile from the highway, the pickup tire tracks led around the ridge covered with junipers and clusters of head-high piñon trees, then turned back to the west, on higher ground. Ahead, up a gentle slope, Charlie could see a tall juniper beside vehicle tracks. A big black trash bag was attached to a branch with blue plastic ties. He inched forward, trying to locate the blue pickup.

He got a call and switched on the phone. It was Gordon.

"The pickup is uphill, about fifty meters south of the juniper with the black bag," Gordon said softly. "Someone is inside the cab, looking toward the highway, I think. It looks like Azok through the scope, but there's some glare on the rear window and I can't be sure."

"I'm going to drive up to the bag and see what he does," Charlie said. "But I'm not getting out into the open until the guy calls me."

"But, if he shows a gun . . ." Gordon said.

"Only if he points it in my direction," Charlie said.

"You sure?"

"Yeah. The guy is probably not the killer," Charlie replied.

"He could have done Colby," Gordon reminded.

"Hold back anyway," Charlie decided. "But stay on the line."

"Copy," Gordon answered.

Charlie drove up the hill slowly, and finally saw the blue pickup as he pulled up almost even with the plastic trash bag, which was flapping in the light breeze. The whole set-up was just a little too planned for a quick surrender, so Charlie wasn't about to present a clear, open target. He leaned back in the seat, using the front doorframe as protection as he looked for Azok.

The guy was sitting there, wearing a baseball cap, leaning against the driver's-side door and looking straight ahead, not toward Gordon's truck. Charlie reached into the glove compartment and brought out the small but powerful binoculars they'd brought along with them.

Through the binoculars Charlie could confirm that the man was Steven Azok, but his head was dropped down, his chin on his chest. Azok's eyes were closed and his mouth open, as if he was asleep.

"It looks like he's dozing, Gordon," Charlie said. "I'm getting out now."

"Copy."

Charlie slid across the seat and exited through the passenger side, placing the truck between him and Azok. Once he was out, he waited, looking across the hood toward the blue pickup with the binoculars. Azok still hadn't moved, but there was something odd about the situation. "His windows are up, and it's probably ninety degrees right now," Charlie observed, feeling the heat immediately.

"Maybe he's running the AC," Gordon commented.

"I don't hear any engine noise."

"Maybe he's passed out. Let's move in slowly and keep watch. If he wakes up and sees us closing in, he's liable to freak."

"Right. Stay put and I'll call his number," Charlie said, staying out of view to make the call. He heard the ringtone, but Azok didn't pick up.

"No response," Charlie reported, now looking at Azok through the binoculars. "You in a position to cover me?"

Gordon waved, and finally Charlie spotted his pal, down on

one knee behind a juniper to his right. They were about equal distance from the blue truck now.

Charlie stepped out into the open, walking up beside the pickup tire tracks. He stopped fifty feet from Azok's truck and brought up his binoculars. "Azok still hasn't moved an inch."

"I'm going to wake him up," Charlie said. He put the binoculars into his pocket, brought up his Beretta, then reached down and picked up a rock about the size of a golf ball. "Ready?"

"He's filling the scope. Go for it."

Charlie threw the rock, which thudded against the side of the pickup.

"Nothing." Gordon reported.

"Something is definitely not right," Charlie observed. "Keep your sights on him while I look around."

Charlie turned slowly, checking each juniper and stand of brush for a second perp. From this point he could even see the highway, maybe a quarter mile away. A faded gold or yellow sedan was parked there, not the State Police unit, and someone was standing by the car, watching them.

He brought up his binoculars for a look, then was rocked by a massive pressure wave and an enormous boom. Searing heat flashed him and something struck him in the back, knocking the wind out of him and throwing him to the ground.

"Gordon!" he tried to yell, but it came out more like a croak. Rolling onto his side, he tried to spot his pal.

"Yeah? You okay?"

Charlie muttered a quick prayer of thanks his dad had taught him as a child. "Think so," he managed. "You?"

"Concussion rattled me, and I have some cuts and picked up some shrapnel. Frigging Azok set us up," Gordon said.

Charlie managed to stand, then looked at the burning shell of the pickup. The upper half of the cab was gone, along with the back and both doors. He thought he could see two legs—at least the lower halves—then decided to look away. The rest of Azok was probably all over the place, and he didn't want to see any more.

"I don't think so, Gordo. I think he was probably dead already, propped up so we'd come in close and get caught in the blast. I saw someone standing over at the highway, watching. When I raised my binocs for a look, that's when the bomb went off."

Charlie glanced back in that direction. "The car is gone now—a gold something . . ."

"Hey, check this out," Gordon called.

Charlie turned and saw what Gordon was pointing at. There were shreds and pieces of posters, fluttering around in the air. He recognized the images—slogans and ISIS flags like the ones they'd seen recently. "Terrorist confetti?"

"Maybe the guy did blow himself up. That martyr tactic is usually part of their end game," Gordon said. "But he set it off too soon to take us out."

"Still don't think he triggered the blast, Gordon. My money is on the person watching us from the highway. When we started getting text messages instead of live conversations, I think Azok was already dead. He was the lure," Charlie added. "At least we now know what happened to the rest of the explosives found in Colby's trailer."

"You're probably right," Gordon said, walking over toward him, a limp in his stride. "Whoops, can't trip over that," he mumbled, sidestepping what looked like blast debris on the ground.

"What?"

"Azok. Well, most of his upper half," Gordon answered.

Charlie ran his hands over his aching head, brushing off bloody dust and something moist and chunky, hoping it didn't belong to him. "I still have most of my skull and ears, but for sure I lost my Bluetooth."

"Found mine. Want me to call it in—if my phone still works?"

"Go for it. Meanwhile, let's step away from this mess and check out our body parts. The vests saved our lives, but let's make sure we're not losing any blood."

Charlie and Gordon were being treated by EMTs out of Bernalillo when SAC Jackson came up carrying a battered, hard plastic rifle case.

"Let me guess. It's a Ruger carbine in .223 caliber," Charlie said.

Jackson opened the case for them, verifying Charlie's guess. "I'm hoping it's the weapon that killed Nathan Whitaker, Charlie," the agent answered. "You still think that the bomb was set off by the driver of that gold sedan?"

Charlie nodded. "How did the rifle survive the blast in almost perfect condition? That plastic case isn't exactly bombproof."

Jackson looked from Charlie to Gordon. "The techs think it was placed in the truck bed, not with the driver. And, something odd, the tailgate was down. The blast blew the rifle away from the truck. It was found, still in the case, wedged in the branches of a juniper tree thirty feet away. Why would the dead perp drive down this god-awful track with the weapon lying on the pickup bed where it could slide right out onto the ground?"

"Because it was placed there *after* the pickup arrived at this location. The gun was supposed to survive the blast intact so it could be tested by the ballistics people," Gordon suggested.

"So we'd think Azok was the terrorist?" Jackson nodded. "Makes sense. But the story is all wrong. According to APD, the surveillance recorded outside his estranged wife's home places Steven Azok ten miles away during the attack at the park."

"Maybe whoever is trying to frame Azok doesn't know about the cameras," Charlie said.

"The guy in the gold car," Gordon said with a nod.

"Who's maybe the original shooter," Jackson concluded. "We've discovered a set of bootprints leading to vehicle tracks that don't match those of the truck. There were two vehicles out here, and Azok had this other person with him for a while."

"Looks like the terrorist was using Azok as a throwaway partner," Charlie said. "He managed to set up Azok to lead us here today, even providing him with a script. Then Azok was killed. The texts came from the gold car guy later on."

"Either Anna, Max, or Patricia," Gordon offered. "Or someone manipulating one of them. A person we haven't seen yet."

"Good point. I'm not a hundred percent sure Patricia didn't have a hand in this. At this point she might have done anything to get Steven out of her life," Charlie suggested. "He would have come to meet her here if she'd played it right."

"Cap him, then set us up to die? I don't think Patricia is really that cold. Let's concentrate on Anna, Max, and maybe one of the

Back Up clients we haven't met yet," Gordon argued. "Anna drives a gold sedan, and that puts her toward the top of the list. But maybe someone stole *her* car, like with Webster."

Jackson shook his head. "I'm a little out of the loop here, guys, with the Bureau's focus on some still unidentified person or persons. Fill me in on what you know. I want to make the arrest when it goes down."

Chapter Seventeen

After refusing the advice of EMTs to go to an emergency room for further examination, Charlie and Gordon gave their official statements to the FBI agent and the State Police, and were able to head back to Albuquerque about seven in the evening.

"I wonder what Jackson is going to find, looking deeper into Anna Brown and Max Mitchell's backgrounds," Gordon said as they reached the street leading to FOB Pawn, and Charlie's rental. "Supposedly, Back Up was closed today with all the current clients scheduled for temp jobs. I think Max is in the clear, but not Anna. And, maybe not Patricia. She inherited all of Nathan's estate."

"They're vets, Anna in the Air Force, and Max in the Army. They were apparently his first and only employees, but besides what they apparently do for Back Up, we never really checked up on them. All we know about Patricia is some personal stuff concerning Azok and her ex. She's never served, if I recall," Charlie said.

"Two out of three had weapons training, especially with Max. Patricia may have gone to the range with either of her husbands. A lot of people who serve make sure their family members are also familiar with firearms. Safety issues, spouse and family protection while they're deployed, stuff like that," Gordon pointed out.

"Let's go straight to the source, then, starting with Max. See what he can tell us about the ladies?"

"Works for me. Let's call him tonight and see when, and if, he'll be available. Maybe join him for a few beers. I've met a few soldiers who are willing to talk once they've discovered someone else is buying," Gordon said.

"First, let's clean up at your place, then grab some dinner. I haven't eaten since, well, that nutritious spinach salad at lunch," Charlie said. "Ruth insists it's healthy."

"Hey, it works for her."

"No substitute for man food, however."

"Amen to that. How about we order pizza? The place on Fourth. Once we get sanitary again," Gordon said. "Those disinfecting wipes back there just weren't enough to clear away whatever landed on me," Gordon said.

Charlie felt the back of his head, recalling the blast. It would take a long, hot shower before he'd consider resting on a pillow again. Ruth and Rene were still being covered by Deputy Marshal Stannic and his people from WITSEC, so he was going to limit his time with her to a phone call instead of a night on the couch. Hopefully tonight the dreams that had haunted him for years, enhanced by the gore of today, wouldn't be paying *him* a visit. He'd go to sleep thinking of Ruth, of course—after a Navajo prayer giving thanks for being able to live another day.

Max told them that he was on the wagon now, but he agreed to meet at an old family restaurant on Fourth Street for pie and coffee. When they walked into the small establishment, they immediately spotted the Vietnam vet sitting at a booth across the room with a view of the entrance. Just as a waitress approached, Max stood and waved them over.

"We're meeting a friend," Gordon told the woman with a smile. "Can we start out with coffee for all of us?"

Max greeted them with handshakes and a weak smile. "I managed to catch the evening news. Glad you boys escaped with nothing more than scratches and the mother of all headaches. It's sad to hear about Steven's death, though. Nobody should have to die like that. On the plus side, it might take a lot of pressure off of Patricia. Is it true that the Feds think Azok killed himself, and that he was one of the terrorists?"

"They asked us not to discuss the details," Charlie replied, taking a seat and sliding down to make room for Gordon. "But there are some conflicting theories," he added, stopping as the waitress came up with a carafe and two big mugs. Max already had his own coffee.

After they'd ordered, and the waitress was out of earshot, Charlie continued. "We don't know for sure what else Azok was doing besides stalking, then kidnapping Patricia, but we do know he couldn't have been the sniper who killed your boss."

"The Feds are concentrating on finding that individual. As for us, we're still checking out the possibility that the shooter at the heroes ceremony may have had a personal motive for killing Whitaker," Gordon said.

"And Colby, and for trying to take you, well, both of you out,"

Max concluded. "If it wasn't a terrorist, just what the hell kind of motive are we talking about? What's behind the three murders—so far?"

"Hate, revenge, jealousy, greed, mental illness? Who knows? Whatever the reason, we'd like to get deeper into Nathan's life, not just concerning his relationships with Back Up clients, or his ex-wife," Charlie said.

"We've been told that Nathan was trying to get back together with Patricia and that enraged Steven Azok, but what else can you tell us about Whitaker's personal life?" Gordon asked. "From the time you met him, at least. Any old friends, enemies, bar fights, road-rage incidents, girlfriends, anything like that," he added.

"Well, I'd put this out of my mind until just now, but when Nathan started up the company, he was hooking up with someone. And, please, don't say where you got the information. I respect the woman, and I have to work with her," Max added.

Charlie and Gordon looked at each other. "Anna Brown?"

"Yes, but there wasn't anything going on when they were at work, though it wasn't exactly a secret. There were a lot of smiles and frequent glances, much more than friendly gestures. That went on for some months, then stopped all of a sudden. For a while their conversations were strained, they stopped looking at each other, and it was strictly business. There was never any fighting or insults that I saw or heard. They'd just turned cold, and that was strange."

"Any idea what caused the breakup?" Gordon asked.

"I was smart enough not to ask, but I have an idea. Not long before the split, Patricia came into Back Up. She was really upset and told Nathan that she was going to divorce Azok. Steven was being abusive and that marrying him had been a big mistake," Max said.

"How'd Nathan take that?" Charlie asked.

"He wanted to go beat the crap out of the guy, and I volunteered to help," Max said. "But Patricia said she didn't want anyone to get into trouble. That she'd already kicked the guy out and had filed a restraining order. She said she could handle it."

"Any idea why she brought that news to Nathan?" Gordon asked. "They'd been divorced for a while, right?"

Max nodded. "Maybe Patricia was looking for sympathy, a shoulder to cry on, or even reconciliation. Something."

"Anna overheard Patricia's story?" Charlie asked.

Max nodded. "In the following days, Nathan began talking to Patricia on the phone in the office, sometimes for fifteen minutes or more. I could see how jealous and hurt Anna was whenever I went into her office. I asked what was wrong, and she said it was personal and to butt out. I backed off, and after a few weeks everything was better," Max explained.

"On the surface," Gordon said.

"Yeah, pretty much," Max said. "Eventually the strain went away and we were all friends again, or, well, office friendly."

"How much interacting is necessary for operations at Back Up? Didn't Nathan and Anna still have to work together on expenses, budgets, taxes, and wages?" Charlie brought up.

Max shrugged. "Nathan and I handled almost all the contacts with clients and employers, and Anna took care of the books. We're not even networked except in sharing WiFi and a common printer. We have our own laptops or a desktop, and share files using flash drives if we need. The financial part of it Anna handles on her own, with software she's configured to fit our business model. You already know how the vets get paid."

"And that Patricia is trying to change all that now," Gordon said. "Is Anna still against the move?"

"Yeah, and she's been dragging her feet, complaining that we have to remain flexible in order to get jobs for small operations and employers who just want to hire someone on a particular project. Like a homeowner who needs someone to help put up some gutters or lay down some tile, but wants to pay in cash," Max said.

"You mentioned that everyone works with their own computer," Gordon said. "Didn't I hear someone mention a few days ago that Anna also has Nathan's laptop?"

Max nodded.

"Do you use them for personal emails as well?" Charlie asked, alert to the direction his pal was taking.

"I do, and I think Nathan did as well," Max confirmed. "As for Anna, she has a desktop in her office, so I'm rarely looking over her shoulder."

"Have any law enforcement officers asked to look at Nathan's laptop or the contents of his desk, just in case either of them might provide a lead?" Charlie asked.

"No, but Detective DuPree asked us to keep everything secure and available, and not to delete any computer files or emails in case they are ever subpoenaed by a prosecutor."

"How about if we make the suggestion to SAC Jackson to take a closer look, or maybe just keep it local with DuPree?" Gordon asked. "I think we'll get further if we stick with APD."

"I don't think the law will even need a warrant. Patricia has a big stake in finding Nathan's killer, and I'm positive she'll cooperate. She's already received the paperwork from county and is now, legally, the owner of Back Up," Max suggested. "It's her call."

"Good idea," Charlie said. "I'll pass that along to my contacts, and ask Ruth to come along tomorrow. I can use her business expertise."

Gordon just smiled.

Charlie pulled into a parking slot beside the small Back Up office, noting the three vehicles belonging to the regular staff were already there. As he walked around to join Ruth, who had just climbed out of the rental, Detective Medina pulled up into the remaining slot in her unmarked sedan and nodded to them.

"Hi, guys. Gordon not coming?" Nancy said as she got out of the car.

"He needed to catch up with the online business this morning, and Ruth already has established some rapport with Patricia," Charlie said. "Besides, Gordon's charm doesn't seem to work on Anna, who, we think, might not be that happy being asked to turn over Nathan's laptop. She's already fighting Patricia over the bookkeeping methods."

"DuPree still wants our computer forensic expert to examine the laptop for anything that might help with the investigation—well, investigations—into each attack that seems to be directed toward Nathan and those individuals with a connection to him and Back Up," Nancy said. "He also wants me to box up any physical evidence, papers, and so forth, then bring the contents in. Until now, there hadn't seemed to have been any urgent need to look inwardly for other possible motives for all the crimes committed so far."

They walked up the steps and Nancy, in the lead, knocked as she turned the knob on the door to Back Up. Inside the outer office, Patricia and Max were seated at their desks, and Anna stood in the doorway to her own area, her face flushed and her eyes shooting daggers. Max relaxed slightly, obviously glad to see them. Patricia stood and walked around to greet them.

"Welcome, Detective Medina, Charlie, and Ruth. We were just working on some issues concerning Nathan's computer." Patricia motioned to a silver and black laptop on her desk. "Is it possible for us to make a backup of all the files before you take the computer?"

"I'm still against this, people," Anna declared immediately. "It's not right turning over the personal files of our clients. The private information of all these vets shouldn't be seen by some shop owner who has no legal authority whatsoever to examine these records."

"This shop owner has been the target of at least four attempts on his life since Captain Whitaker was killed, Ms. Brown," Ruth called out, her voice ice cold. "I was there in several of those incidents, and was seated next to Captain Whitaker when your boss was killed. His blood was on my clothes. Where were you, and why do you want to impede Charlie's efforts to track down the person who's been trying to kill him? If he doesn't have the right to search out the killer, then who does?"

Anna's face turned even redder than before and she clenched her fists so tightly her knuckles turned white.

"Charlie won't be permitted to see anything on that computer directly, we're already clear on that, Ms. Brown," Nancy declared. "Mr. Henry will be briefed with any information needed to protect him from further attempts on his life. He seems to have a knack for ferreting out the truth, and if he happens to discover the identity of the persons or people responsible for recent events, that will serve us all. Isn't that what we want?"

"Well, Patricia has the last word on this, unless you have a warrant," Anna said, her anger fading, resigned to the reality of the situation. "But I still need a copy of the text and data files. I need to be able to access client information in order to continue to serve our function here."

"You don't back up your files?" Ruth asked.

"I have a separate hard drive for the business records and software, and Max and Nathan backed up their own files on flash drives," Anna said, now assuming a less confrontational tone.

"Nathan kept his in there," Max said, pointing to the drawer at the desk where Patricia was sitting.

Patricia brought out a cigar box. Inside were three flash drives. "He actually used two, the red and blue ones. The white drive is mine," she said, handing the first two to Nancy.

"I've only used Nathan's computer as a source of information. I haven't changed any files or deleted a word," Anna said. She reached into her jacket pocket and pulled out a flash drive that was still in the bubble pack. "This is brand new, hopefully with enough capacity to copy all the text and data files on the system, including his emails, correspondence, attachments, zip files, and pdfs. The works."

"Then go ahead," Nancy replied, looking over to Patricia, who nodded.

The process took several minutes, and during that time Patricia took out all the papers and folders from Nathan's former desk and a file cabinet drawer, handing them to Nancy, who placed them in two cardboard storage boxes that she had brought with her. When the files were backed up onto the flash drive, Anna removed the device, shut down the computer, and then stepped back.

Patricia handed the laptop to Nancy, who put it into one of the boxes. Then Max wrote something down on a memo pad. "Here is the user name and password needed to access the computer," he said, handing her the paper. "We all knew each other's passwords, in case one of us was sick or needed to take the day off."

"They were left here at night?" Charlie asked.

"The laptops were always locked in Anna's office," Patricia said. "There's an old gun safe in there that was donated by the family of one of our deceased vets."

"You have your own personal computers at home?" Ruth asked, looking from person to person. They all nodded.

"And Nathan?" Nancy inquired.

Patricia shrugged. "I've only stopped by his apartment to pick up essential paperwork and empty the refrigerator," she said softly. "I saw an old desktop computer, but if he has another, I didn't notice. I don't like being there, though I know, sooner or later, I'm going to have to deal with his stuff."

Nancy nodded. "I'll talk to my superiors, and they may want to have a look through his apartment. We can obtain a search warrant for that, if you like."

"That might be a good idea, to avoid any hint of privacy issues," Patricia said, looking to Anna for a few seconds. "But I'd like to be there during the search."

"That will probably have to wait until tomorrow," Nancy said.

"The process usually takes several hours. You've got the only set of keys, right?"

Charlie noticed that Nancy started to look back to Anna, then managed to cover the move by glancing up at the clock on the wall. He'd already told Nancy about Nathan and Anna's old relationship, and knew that Nancy was probably wondering if Nathan had ever given Anna a key.

"I've got to get that search warrant request into the system, but first I'll give you a receipt for all this," Nancy said, changing the topic. "I don't know how long it'll take to examine the computer and papers, but at least it's not going to hurt your work here—except for the temporary loss of the laptop, of course."

"One more thing I just remembered," Max announced. "I think Nathan may have stored some files on the cloud."

"That's news to me," Anna said. "I don't recall any expenditure like that in the expense account. When did he set it up?"

"About a month ago, I think," Max replied. "He'd asked me if I thought files were secure in some distant, unknown server, and we talked about it for a while. The next day he said he'd decided to set one up."

"That might be important, especially if the content is personal," Nancy said. "Any idea where his user name and password might be?"

"No clue. Maybe he wrote them down in his papers somewhere, or at home, or in his wallet," Max suggested.

"I haven't seen anything I thought might be a password among his stuff, and he never mentioned any of his accounts to me," Patricia said. "We didn't exchange emails either. How about you, Anna?"

The bookkeeper shook her head. "No personal emails. We were strictly business," Anna replied through tight lips.

She paused, clearing her throat. "But if we can discover the vendor of the cloud network, we might be able to get online and try to guess his user name and password. A lot of times people use the same passwords for more than one account."

"That's true. I'll make sure the forensics people look for anything resembling a password or user name on the laptop and in his papers," Nancy said. "Now let me write out a receipt for what I'm taking. I've really got to go."

A few minutes later, Charlie helped Nancy carry the boxes to her squad car while Patricia walked Ruth to Charlie's rental car. Charlie said good-bye to Nancy, then walked over to join Ruth and Patricia, who were still talking.

"Ruth now has a key to Nathan's apartment, Charlie," Patricia said softly. "I was hoping you might go over there tonight and look around. But wear gloves and don't leave any sign that you were there, please?"

"Is there something else I should know about?" Charlie asked.

Ruth looked up at him. "Patricia says that Anna and Nathan were—dating—when Back Up first opened. That relationship ended after several months, though, and there were hard feelings."

Patricia nodded. "It's something that happened when Nathan and I were apart, so I just learned to deal with it and I've kept it a secret. But now I want to make sure there aren't any letters or photos or items that might prove embarrassing, not only to Anna, but to Back Up."

Patricia's face had turned red. "And if you happen to come across anything that'll help track down Nathan's killer, great.

I know Detective Medina will do what she can to speed up the police search, but every night the killer is out there, someone, especially you, could be in danger."

"So, if I find something that concerns Nathan and Anna's relationship, you want me to bring it to you or destroy it? I can't do that." Charlie explained.

"I know. Take photos if it'll help, but leave anything you find in place. Just let me know if it might cause a problem. I don't think Anna realizes I'm aware of her affair with Nathan, but, like I said, I need her right now. Anna is essential in keeping Back Up running," Patricia said.

"I don't think the police will have the need to tell anyone about the relationship unless it leads to a suspect. Don't worry, Nancy is discreet, and so is Detective DuPree," Ruth mentioned.

"Well, maybe there's no need for Charlie to go into the apartment at all. But we still want to find out how to access that cloud. One more thing is bothering me. Why would Nathan need to put files, photos, or whatever where only he could access them? Was he up to something that may have put him in danger, and ended up getting himself killed?" Patricia asked. "Or was he just looking for a new way of protecting Back Up files?"

Charlie shrugged. "There's only one way to find out."

Chapter Eighteen

Charlie parked the pickup in the parking slot that had belonged to Nathan Whitaker. It was actually Whitaker's vehicle, loaned by Patricia, and though he felt strange driving the vehicle of a dead man, it was something he'd done before during some of his more rebellious years away from home.

Traditional Navajos, however, would have avoided the personal property of the dead, vehicles included. He thought of the "dead" hogans he'd seen sometimes on the Rez while growing up. They'd been abandoned, of course, because the evil in a dead person was said to remain close to the site of their passing. The unfortunate survivors of that family were forced to find new lodging, often with close relatives.

"Good tactic, us representing the executors of his estate," Gordon mentioned as they stepped out of the vehicle. He adjusted his tie, but kept the light suit jacket unbuttoned. It was a hot afternoon. "Considering the fact that it's still broad daylight and we can expect to be seen by renters coming home from work."

"Nancy and DuPree are still waiting for the paperwork to do the search, so now's the only time we have. Nancy said they hope to be approved by midmorning tomorrow," Charlie said, locking the pickup with a touch of the key fob.

He stopped and took a look at the apartment doors on the ground floor of the four-story brick structure. "Room 108 is over here." He pointed to the west side of the structure, then led the way down the sidewalk that bordered the lawn, which encompassed the grounds on the east and west sides of the building. It quickly became clear that Whitaker's apartment was the last one on this side.

They remained quiet as they walked, nodding to a man in a suit just opening the door of apartment 107 as they approached. The man turned to face them.

"You relatives or cops?" the man asked. "I knew Nathan, and everyone here is sorry for his loss. I hope the guy who blew himself up yesterday was the killer."

Gordon stepped up immediately, extending his hand. "I'm James Stinchcomb and this is my associate Nabor Malka. We represent the Whitaker estate, and are here to photograph the belongings of the deceased." He brought out an expensive camera taken from the shop inventory.

The man shook both their hands. "I'm Greg, and I really appreciate all the work Nathan was able to do for our vets at Back Up. One of my cousins is a vet and a client. He's on a job right now in Phoenix. Tell the Whitaker family that I keep recommending Back Up to every vet I meet. Spread the word, as Nathan always said."

"We'll do that. Have a good evening, Greg," Charlie said, turning back toward apartment 108 as the man went inside.

Glancing through the curtains of the single west-facing window, they couldn't make out any objects except for what appeared to be the backside of a sofa. Ahead, attached to the brass doorknob by a rubber band, was some kind of flier.

Charlie inserted the key, then turned the knob and opened the door. There was a low, very distinctive sound, ending with a click, as he stepped inside.

"Was that a door closing?" Gordon, right behind him, whispered.

Charlie scanned the room quickly. There was a kitchen area to the east behind a waist-high partition, but no outside door. The sound came from the short hall, where there were three more doors. The closest one, on the west side, had to be a closet judging from the distance to the outside wall. The south door was open slightly, revealing a tile floor and obvious bathroom.

Charlie pointed to the closed door on his left, the bedroom, then brought out his backup pistol from his pocket, shifting to his right to cover the closed door from the corner. Again he heard a noise—this time clearly coming from the bedroom.

"Police officer!" Gordon lied, bringing out his own weapon. "Come out slowly with your hands up."

There was a pause, the sound of papers, then Charlie smelled something familiar. "Smoke!" he called out. "He's lit a fire!"

Gordon, having inched up against the living area wall, peeked around the corner. Smoke drifted out from under the closed door. There was the sound of a sliding window and a sudden gust of smoke.

"He's bailing!" Charlie realized, turning and heading for the outside door. "Kick down the door and put out the fire!"

Charlie ran outside and reached the building corner just as a figure in sweats and a hoodie went over the cinder block wall at the back of the apartment property. He raced across the lawn toward the wall, shoving the pistol back into his pocket. In the background, he heard the sudden, nerve-grating screech of a smoke alarm.

The wall was about six feet high, no problem for Charlie to clear, but he could hear the tear of his dress pants and feel the burn of his knees scraping against the stone-hard blocks as he came over the top. He landed in the hard ground of a dry utility easement and saw the burglar nearing the street at the end of the block. This guy could sprint, Charlie realized, as he took off after the running figure, but he'd been a distance runner back in school. Charlie knew he'd be able to catch up to the guy, despite the suit and street shoes, unless the guy had parked his vehicle within a block. At least it wasn't the bosque this time.

Not wanting to slow down by pulling out his cell phone, Charlie concentrated on his stride. The packed dirt made running easy, unlike the sand along the river or the rock-littered ground he'd experienced in Afghanistan. The gray hoodie guy took a hard left at the street, disappearing from view due to the cedar fence at the end, but Charlie had already cut the guy's lead in half.

Reaching the end of the alley, Charlie cut left and saw the guy running down the sidewalk to the east. Ahead was a street full of traffic in the afternoon rush hour, and the guy would have to cut to the right or circle the block.

Charlie had narrowed the gap to maybe a hundred feet now, slowing just a bit in anticipation of a sudden left or right. Instead, the guy ran right out into traffic.

Cars braked, tires screeched, and drivers swerved, but the guy made it across the street without a scratch. Charlie thought about making the run, stepped out into the street, and had to jump back onto the sidewalk as a driver in a commercial van changing lanes nearly ran him down. Shaking at the near miss, Charlie had to laugh as the driver slowed just long enough to give him the one-finger salute.

Then he saw an opening. Charlie dashed out to the center, waited for a car to pass by in the far lane, then hurried to the side-walk, ignoring the honks and shouts of another stressed-out driver as he looked for the burglar.

The guy had disappeared into the crowded Smith's grocery parking lot, so Charlie had to come up with a quick strategy. His target was likely headed for a vehicle in the lot, not being stupid enough to go inside the grocery, where cameras could record his passage. The burglar might be able to hunker down in a vehicle, or just drive away.

He'd concentrate on checking out the cars and vehicles several slots back from the street but still at a distance from outside store cameras. Charlie brought out his smartphone, ready to record a video if he saw someone that fit the description of the burglar. He walked down the rows just to the left of center, alert to anyone in a vehicle, ignoring people with shopping carts or a companion.

An old gold Chevy sedan pulled out several vehicles down, having backed into the slot, and he started filming with the camera immediately. The driver was a blond woman wearing a baseball cap, and she looked familiar. She didn't look his way, so all he got was a profile as she turned and headed toward the entrance.

Charlie picked up the pace, jogging to keep the vehicle as close as possible. She turned sharply at the end of the row, forcing a man carrying groceries to jump back, then raced out of the parking lot onto a side street. He stopped recording; there were too many objects between him and the vehicle.

He moved out of the way of a passing car, then headed toward the end of the block, where there was a stoplight. Recalling that there had been a fire in Whitaker's apartment when he left, he hustled across the street at the pedestrian walk, then, once across, jogged back at a reasonable pace. The lack of sirens suggested that Gordon had managed to extinguish the fire, so he slowed down to a brisk walk. He didn't see smoke anywhere, and recalled having seen a fire extinguisher in the apartment over by the kitchen. Not that he'd need one—Gordon was smart and capable of dealing with anything.

He decided to try and contact Gordon. His pal answered immediately.

"Charlie, where are you? Any luck catching the burglar?" came Gordon's voice.

"The bastard—or more likely the bitch—got away. I'm headed back," Charlie answered. "What about the fire?"

"It's out. Just a paper fire in a metal wastebasket to divert our attention. I'm venting the apartment now. I also called Nancy. She's on her way and sounds pissed. What's this about 'the bitch'?"

"It's just a guess, but I think the burglar was a woman, maybe even Anna Brown. She drives a gold Chevy. Call Nancy and tell her that the perp disappeared into the parking lot of the Smith's over at Fourth and Orchard. Slender, about five foot eight, dark blue sweatpants, gray hoodie, and white running shoes. Also brown

gloves, leather, I think. I didn't get a face-on look, just enough of
a profile to verify that the person looked like Anna. Facial color-
ation and blond, shoulder-length hair all fit her, however. If this
was the burglar, and I think it was, she'd shed the hoodie and put
on a red cap."

"Did you see the license plate?" Gordon asked.

Charlie stopped on the sidewalk. "Let me check my cell and
see if I caught that."

"You got her on camera? Good man."

"Yeah, but I don't know how clear it is." Charlie ended the call,
then played back several seconds of video. He froze the image and
saw the plate number and letters immediately. There were also several military bumper stickers visible.

He called Gordon again. "Hey, bro, it's NHE-440, and I'm
almost a hundred percent it's Anna Brown's car. Pass that along,
okay?"

"Right. Okay. See you when." Gordon ended the call.

By the time Charlie returned, there was an APD squad car at
the street and several residents were out on the lawn or standing
in their doors, wondering what was going on. As Charlie approached Gordon, an APD officer, and the guy next door, Greg,
Charlie also noticed a metal trash can on the grass. Next to it was
an oven mitt, a small fire extinguisher, and what looked like an
old-school hardcover business ledger. The ledger had a black oval
in the middle.

"So you put out the fire by the book," Charlie joked, pointing
to the ledger.

"Yeah. Smothered the burning paper. Found the fire extinguisher later and brought it along just in case," Gordon responded,

looking down at the tear in the knees of Charlie's suit pants. "You take a dive, bro?"

"Naw. I just couldn't leap over that block wall in a single bound. Skinned my knees, I guess," Charlie admitted sheepishly. "Probably frightened some shoppers over at Smith's as well. Running around, looking into cars like a deranged businessman."

"But at least you have an ID on the burglar. Nancy's going to go by Anna Brown's apartment first, but she wants us to stick around."

"Hang on," Charlie said. Several seconds went by. "Okay, done. Wanna take a look?"

"Why not just talk to Anna personally? I think that's her," Gordon said, pointing to a gold Chevy pulling up at the curb behind the police car.

Anna Brown, wearing the dark sweats, white shoes, and a gray hoodie but minus the red cap, climbed out of the car and walked toward them. "Charlie, are you okay? I need to apologize for the mess I made, and for running away like that. I just panicked. The papers I burned in the wastebasket were personal, and I was embarrassed that someone would find them. I hope nothing else was damaged. I'm so sorry," she added, wiping tears from her eyes as she looked at the items on the grass.

The uniformed police officer came out of the apartment just then, looked at Anna, then to Charlie, who nodded.

"This is the woman you want to talk to, Officer Roseberg," Gordon said.

"The woman you say fled the apartment, the person you chased, Mr. Henry?" Roseberg asked. "Miss. . . . ?"

"Brown, sir," Anna said, reaching out to shake the hesitant officer's hand. "Anna Brown. I confess to setting the fire in the trash can, but only to destroy some embarrassing personal mail. I didn't intend on hurting anyone, or damaging someone else's property."

"How about breaking and entering?" Gordon suggested softly.

Anna's face turned red. "I still have the apartment key Nathan gave me. I guess it's time I confess to withholding information. Nathan and I had a relationship for a while when I first began working at Back Up, and I spent some nights here. But that was many months ago, and after all this trouble surrounding his murder, I was afraid someone would find out. I don't want to lose my job. You understand how Patricia might take this news."

"This is getting complicated," Officer Roseberg said. "Let's take this one step at a time, okay?"

Charlie saw flashing lights in the street. "Here comes Detective Medina. Maybe she can help unravel what's going on."

"Am I going to be arrested?" Anna whispered, looking from Charlie, to Gordon, and then to Officer Roseberg. The cop looked back toward the apartment, then just shrugged.

"So despite the presence of some charred paper copies of possible emails between the two of them, did you believe Anna's story that she came here ahead of us *just* to destroy evidence of her affair with Nathan?" Gordon asked Nancy as they searched through Whitaker's apartment.

Charlie looked up from the kitchen cabinet he was looking through. "What he said."

"Not really, but it's hard to read minds some days, Gordon,"

Nancy replied, sorting through the scorched ledger and other papers piled on the dining table. "She'll still have to pay a fine for setting the fire, and if Charlie had been a cop, she'd be up on other charges. My guess is that she was looking for the same thing you came for—the user name and password on Nathan's cloud account. That suggests there's something more than just love letters that she'd been wanting to get rid of today."

"Just how serious was their relationship, at least in her eyes? Could she have killed him out of jealousy, then planted those terrorist fliers just to cover her ass?" Charlie asked. "These days, any shooting like that gets a lot of attention."

"After all that time?" Gordon said, searching through the hall closet. "Jealously is all about emotion, and if she'd have wanted to kill him after the breakup, why wait for months?"

"Ah, but recently Patricia and Nathan started seeing each other more seriously, and Patricia had kicked Steve to the curb and filed for divorce," Charlie pointed out. "That meant Anna no longer had a shot at winning him back."

"It's just that Anna didn't come across as an obsessive woman, at least not today. Not a stalker or hysterical person," Nancy said. "Even our interview was calm and controlled."

"I think it's just an act. You suppose she would have confessed to being here if Charlie hadn't gotten close enough to ID her?" Gordon asked. "She just got caught and is winging it, trying to stay cool. I think that love letter stuff is a pile of crap."

Charlie looked over to Nancy, and she nodded.

"So we have to find that cloud username and password," Gordon said.

"Maybe Anna found them first and is keeping that from us.

Or Nathan just had them memorized, or kept the password on him, like in his wallet?" Charlie asked.

"Hopefully there's a written record still out there," Nancy said. "My understanding is that his personal effects, whatever he had on him, like wallet, watch, and any jewelry, were returned to whoever is handling his estate."

"Patricia?" Gordon asked.

"Correct. I'll call and ask to see everything he had in his pockets, and his jewelry, at the time of his death," Nancy said.

"Aren't his clothes still stored as evidence? Isn't that the way it's handled?" Gordon asked.

"Yes," Nancy answered.

"Including his belt and shoes?" Charlie asked.

"You thinking of the old spy craft hollow heel trick?" Gordon asked, bringing out a labeled, sealed plastic bag from the closet. "And here they are, I think, along with his belt."

"Patricia must have brought them here once she was given a set of keys," Nancy said. "Let's take a look."

"Let's handle them with gloves, okay?" Charlie suggested. "I remember seeing some in a drawer," he added, going through a drawer and bringing out some blue latex throw-away cleaning gloves.

"That *chindi* thing sticks with you, huh?" Gordon asked.

"Ah, the Navajo evil spirit," Nancy said. "Gina told me about that."

"We're not supposed to discuss these things," Charlie replied softly, handing each of them a pair of gloves. "I'll check the belt, you guys each take a shoe."

Gordon handed the bag to Nancy, and she opened the plastic

strip and handed Gordon a shoe, and Charlie the belt, which was stained with blood around the buckle.

He turned the belt to check the inside. There was something scratched into the leather. "I may have something here," he said, holding the belt up close. "Write this down, somebody," he added. "Capital I, then lower case pa, number 2, lower case tfot, upper case US, lower case o, upper case A," he added.

"I get it," Gordon said immediately. "I pledge allegiance to the flag of the United States of America. Easy to remember, harder to decrypt."

"Sounds like a good password," Charlie admitted. "But we still need a user name."

"Belt? Size forty-two?" Nancy said, looking at the stamped size in the belt leather.

"Keep looking," Gordon advised, examining the left shoe. "Nothing here."

"Not this one," Nancy said. "Unless the shoe size or manufacturer is the answer."

"My guess is that it's not any of these. It's more likely a name, or a tie-in with the information he uploaded into the cloud," Charlie suggested. "It could be something in his wallet, or wait, he had to pay for the cloud storage service, right?"

"And probably by credit card. You're right, Charlie. And once we—well, I—get a look at his bank and credit card records, that might help," Nancy said. "If we can find the vendor, maybe we can discover his user name as well, even if it requires a warrant. The forensics people are working on his computer. I'll have to ask them to list any purchases he made. "

"Meanwhile, let's see if there are any receipts here. We haven't checked that accordion file yet." Gordon pointed to the table. "Patricia gave us permission to go through his stuff, but we should probably call her about what happened this evening. She's going to find out anyway."

"Hello, people," Patricia said, opening the apartment door, which had been propped open about a foot to help vent out any remaining smoke. "It doesn't smell so bad. Thanks for saving Nathan's stuff."

Nancy stood and offered her a chair at the dining table, which was almost clear now except for some bank statements in a shoe box. Gordon and Charlie were drinking Cokes they'd purchased from a machine in the apartment building's recreation room.

"I saw the charred trash can outside on the grass. How did the fire get started anyway? Either one of you guys smoke?" Patricia asked the men, who'd stood when she entered.

"That's one of the reasons I wanted to speak to you face-to-face, Patricia," Nancy said.

"Charlie and Gordon caught someone in here going through the folders kept in the desk, and she climbed out through the window after setting some letters on fire."

"Charlie ran after her while I put out the flames," Gordon announced, "but she got away. As for the fire, there was some smoke, but only the metal wastebasket suffered any damage."

"You said she, not he. By any chance was it Anna Brown?" Patricia asked. "I saw her car when I drove up."

Nancy nodded. "She came back about fifteen minutes later and admitted going through his papers and setting the fire. She said she wanted to remove any embarrassing letters or items Nathan may have kept."

"So she admitted to the affair? Well, technically, the relationship, I guess," Patricia said, shaking her head. "Do you think she was really after any information that Nathan might have stored in the cloud?"

"I do," Charlie said.

"We all do," Nancy said. "But she had a key to this place, which I insisted she turn over. All I could do was have her arrested for trespassing and misdemeanor vandalism. An officer took her to the substation on Second Street. She probably won't spend any time in jail."

"She even asked me to drive her car over there so she'd have a ride home," Gordon said.

"Anna apologized to me twice for causing so much trouble. She offered to replace the suit pants I tore chasing after her," Charlie said.

"Is she worried about losing her job, or does she have more secrets she doesn't want us to know about?" Patricia asked.

"Both?" Charlie suggested. "It's hard to tell. She's mixing cockiness with sincerity, at least in my opinion."

"So, people, should I fire Anna, or let her try to set things right again? Can she be trusted?" Patricia asked.

"From a strictly business standpoint, she probably should be fired," Gordon suggested. "But . . ."

"If she's no longer around, it's harder to keep an eye on her," Charlie pointed out.

"But if she's guilty of committing some of the crimes we're already investigating, she'll be in a good position to do even more damage," Nancy said.

"I say we keep her around, at least until we find out what

Nathan was hiding. If she's innocent, there shouldn't be any more problems, at least coming from her," Charlie said.

"Keep your enemies closer?" Patricia asked.

"Beginning with a much closer look at Anna. Where she's been, where she goes, what weapons she owns, what her skill sets are. Can we do that?" Gordon asked, looking at Nancy.

"I think we have to," Nancy said. "If you decide to keep her on staff, Patricia, just be very careful. And clue Max in on the situation."

"If she does show up for work, I'm going to force her to switch over to the new system, where all wages paid to our vets come directly to the office via checks or bank transfers. That'll keep her busy, and will be a test to see how badly she wants to stay with Back Up. I'll make it a condition of her employment," Patricia said.

"And we'll continue searching for the missing link needed to access that cloud," Nancy reminded. "But let's make sure not to discuss that around Anna."

Fifteen minutes later, Charlie looked around the apartment, then at his watch. "We done here now? Gordon and I still have to drop Anna's car by the police substation, and it's getting late. If we encounter her, we'll play dumb regarding her job," he added, looking at Patricia.

She nodded. "And I'll make sure she finds out the name of the vendor of that cloud storage site—as soon as I do. With that, Anna will know we're getting closer every moment to, hopefully, discover what she's been up to. That should put her on edge."

"Her apartment will be watched in the meantime," Nancy said.

"Let's go, Gordon. We have to drop off Anna's car," Charlie said, standing. Leaving Patricia and Nancy to close up the apartment, Charlie and Gordon walked back to the parking area.

"You up to something, Charlie? I caught that look in your eye when you suddenly went off Indian time," Gordon joked, recalling the notion that Indians were less concerned with schedules and timetables in their daily activities.

"Yeah. There's something in the glove compartment of my rental that I thought I might want to give to Anna."

"Ah, Big Brother strikes again."

"Appropriate trivia, guy. Isn't it amazing how your high school reading list can come back to haunt you at the strangest times? Let's hurry and get that done before the ladies come out. Nancy might not approve," Charlie said.

"Looks like Jake beat us to work this morning," Charlie said as he stepped out of the rental car. He'd pulled in the parking slot beside FOB Pawn's loading dock just after Gordon parked, and his pal had waited for him at the door.

"As usual. We need to lighten the load for him and Ruth. They've really been holding down the fort these days. Is it okay to say 'fort,' Charlie?"

"As long as you don't mention cavalry, John Wayne, or old westerns in the same sentence, pal," Charlie reminded. "We Navajos have long memories."

"How about if I'm referring to Fort Knox?"

"Gold is okay, and speaking of gold, we'd better get to work before our meager supply runs out," Charlie joked, standing back as Gordon entered the keypad code that unlocked the heavy steel door.

They'd just stepped inside when Jake called out, "Guys, good news! The Feds think they've caught the terrorist!"

Chapter Nineteen

"Seriously?" Gordon replied, leading the way into the small office, where the small television was broadcasting a news bulletin.

"Anyone we heard of?" Charlie asked, standing beside Jake and Gordon as they watched the screen.

"No name given yet," Jake responded. Without asking, he brewed three cups of coffee from their pod machine and handed Charlie and Gordon filled mugs.

Some Fed Charlie didn't recognize was busy thanking local law enforcement and other agencies, but Charlie noted SAC Tyler Jackson was standing beside the speaker.

Their eyes were glued on the screen throughout the five-minute bulletin, then, when the programming switched back to one of the prerecorded national morning shows, they sat down together.

"So is that the guy?" Jake asked Charlie.

"I wish I could say that he's the one who shot Whitaker, but he's not the person who killed Colby. This guy is an Iraqi, dark-haired and husky, and doesn't fit the person I chased into the bosque," Charlie pointed out.

"Well, we'd already taken on the theory that there were at least two people involved," Gordon said. "And if he's the person who blew up Steven Azok and planted the Whitaker murder weapon for us to find, then he gave up that rifle, which explains the need for another long weapon."

"This guy has apparently been on the Fed radar for a while. Nailing him trying to buy an M-15 clone out of an undercover officer's trunk was good work," Gordon added. "And he did have a pistol in his car. Maybe he was the guy watching Dawud's house, the guy in the gray van who shot at you on Rio Grande."

Charlie shrugged. "Maybe."

"I wonder what they'll find on his laptop," Jake said.

Charlie's phone rang and he brought it out of his pocket. "It's Nancy on her APD phone."

"Put it on speaker," Gordon whispered.

"Charlie, you hear the news?" Nancy said.

"Just now. Can I put you on speaker for Gordon and Jake?"

"Go ahead. This affects us all."

"Done. Now, do you really think they've arrested Whitaker's killer?" he asked.

"I'm withholding my opinion until there's more concrete evidence. The suspect was set up. He'd been told by an undercover officer that he could make a private purchase of a semi-auto assault rifle and a hundred rounds of ammunition from a guy in a parking lot. That's still perfectly legal, even for people on the No-Fly List. The Feds had profiled the man as a potential radical. He has a history of arrests for DWI, abusing his girlfriend, shoplifting, and recently lost his low-paying job. There are a lot of losers who turn to terrorism these days."

"Besides fitting the profile, what actual evidence do they have?" Charlie asked.

"Turns out the man is a former Iraqi soldier who's been the subject of harassment, which cost him his construction gig. Former coworkers say he threatened to kill them in their sleep if they didn't leave him alone. The man has given no alibi for the night Captain Whitaker was shot. Oh, and he resisted arrest during the sting and tried to grab Agent Jackson's weapon."

"That explains the broken arm," Charlie commented. "But how about connections to radical groups?"

"Can't say, don't know. The Feds apparently have his computer, and scuttlebutt is that he's been in contact with online sites being monitored by the authorities. Until there's more, the Feds aren't releasing anything else. We've been told to stay alert in case there's a third perp out there."

"So they're also convinced that Steven Azok was involved in the attacks?" Gordon suggested.

"Yes," Nancy said. "And DuPree and I have been assigned to search for possible links between Azok and the Iraqi suspect."

"What about the rifle Azok had in the pickup?" Charlie asked. "It was damaged in the blast, right?"

"But easily repaired without jeopardizing the forensics. Techs were able to fire a round for comparison," Nancy explained.

"Was it a match for the slug recovered from Whitaker's body?" Gordon asked.

"Yes, and also with the ejection marks on the recovered brass at the park. What we need to know now is how Azok ended up with the murder weapon. Based upon the images from the neighbor across the street from Patricia's apartment, we can confirm that Azok couldn't have been that shooter."

"Hence the Iraqi being the sniper suspect," Charlie said. "But there are a lot of unanswered questions. I still believe that somehow the Back Up staff or one of their clients are involved. Maybe both, especially Todd Colby."

"Yeah, and you guys opened the door to that angle and have gained Patricia Azok's confidence. I've got some help checking out Anna Brown's background, but I can use an extra set of eyes. Will you guys keep investigating in that direction as well, keeping Anna in the dark if at all possible? Low-key, of course," Nancy said.

"Low-key? Us?" Gordon said.

"Sometimes I forget who I'm talking to, Gordon," Nancy said.

"I'll keep him in line, girl," Charlie replied, rolling his eyes.

"Whatever. Meanwhile everyone remain vigilant. It's possible the Feds have grabbed the wrong man—not that he didn't have the potential to strike out in the future."

"You'll keep us informed if there's something else we need to know?" Charlie asked.

"Count on it. Stay safe, I've gotta go now." Nancy ended the call.

Jake grinned, then looked down at their mugs. "Celebrate the positive news with a refill?"

Ruth came in fifteen minutes later with a big smile on her face, and a pleasant hug for all of them, especially Charlie. Stepping back from him, her eyebrows furrowed and a frown appeared. "What's wrong? They caught the killer, didn't they?"

Charlie reached out, taking both her hands. "I hope so, Ruth, but we need to wait and see if the evidence is really there. I'd like to believe it's all over now, but there are still some details that don't fit."

"Crap! And you're usually right about these things. How about you, Gordon?" she added, turning toward him.

"These terrorist attacks, or whatever they are, always seem to bring people out of the woodwork and lead to more confrontations. Hatred, racism, accusations, retaliations, and the hardening of both sides. Was the guy they arrested looking to replace the weapon he used to kill Whitaker, to add to the damage caused by the first attacker, or just to defend himself from those who assume he's their enemy?" Gordon said.

"So we all have to watch our backs until this is settled, Ruth. You included," Jake said. "Let's talk about it over a cup of coffee, or maybe tea?"

Ruth squeezed Charlie's hands, then let go with a smile and reached for her mug. "But stay positive, right? How about one of those French roast brews for me? But first, guys, you'll have to tell me what you were up to yesterday afternoon," Ruth said, sitting down into the chair Charlie positioned for her beside his own.

After a few minutes listening to Charlie and Gordon's description of the events at Nathan's apartment, Ruth spoke again. "So even if Anna didn't kill Nathan—who she apparently loved at one time—she's got secrets. I keep coming back to the fact that she's been the one handling the money at Back Up, that she's against changing the system, and that a supposedly very successful operation is in financial trouble. That cash reporting system, to me, is a real red flag, and it's obvious that this would be the easiest way to skim the business. Any idea what her personal financial situation is? Large purchases, big debts, stuff like that?" Ruth asked.

"Her vehicle, at least the one we've seen, is an older model mid-range sedan. I don't know about her apartment; however, it may be laden with big-ticket items," Gordon said.

"Excuse the old-school input, people," Jake interjected. "But wouldn't it have been easier to skim some of the incoming cash and just put it under her mattress? The only real record of cash coming in is the actual bills themselves, and she keeps the books. Why flash your crime with an extravagant lifestyle?"

"Well, now that her romance with Nathan is out in the open, I guess we'll see how she behaves," Charlie said.

"You mean she's at work today? Patricia is going along with that?" Ruth asked.

Charlie quickly explained the conditions Patricia was going to implement, and Ruth nodded. "I'd have terminated her," Ruth said. "There's no way of knowing what might be missing from Whitaker's apartment or how many times Anna has been there since his death."

Jake looked up at the clock. "I agree with Ruth, but time waits for no man—or woman. I need to get set up out on the floor before our customers start showing up."

Gordon stood. "No, you and Ruth take care of the office today, Charlie and I will handle the customers, right, Chuck?"

"Good. Ruth was going to show me how to work the website anyway," Jake replied. "Later I'll check to see what items can be priced and put out on display."

Except for a few reporters who came by in the morning asking for a comment from him regarding the arrest of the suspected terrorist, business at FOB Pawn was typical, and that was just fine with Charlie. The high point of the day was taking Ruth to lunch at Frank and Linda's while Gordon and Jake tended to customers. Charlie and Ruth had a great conversation, mostly about Rene, who was coming to the shop next Saturday. Then they walked up the alley to the shop, holding hands.

"We're back," Charlie announced as they came in through the rear entrance. "Anything new?"

"Does that include us?" came the voice of Detective Wayne DuPree, who stood when they came in. Nancy was there as well, in the office.

"Bearers of more good news, I hope?" Ruth said, stepping forward to give DuPree a hug. He stood there a second before returning the gesture, somehow barely touching her. His face turned red.

Ruth laughed, then gave Nancy a much more appreciated embrace. "Charlie and I are finally having a really good day. Please tell us more."

Gordon came up quickly to the office door. "Go ahead, guys. You're gonna want to hear this. Jake and I've got things handled out here," he added, nodding to a customer who'd just approached the front register.

Nancy glanced over at Ruth, who'd quickly taken a seat, then gave Charlie a mischievous wink. Everyone was picking up on the fact that Charlie and Ruth were finally becoming a pair.

Charlie sat at his desk, noticing a folder there with DuPree's name on it. "Can I take a look?"

He opened the folder and discovered Anna Brown's military records inside. A quick glance confirmed what he'd already been thinking.

"So Anna was AP, Air Police, and spent much of her time working base security. She was trained in detecting and handling explosives—like with car bombs—and in gaining quick entry into and out of vehicles. She barely qualified with her handgun, but shot expert with a rifle. I see she received a commendation for rescuing a child in a hot car using a slim jim. Not a bad record at all."

"You haven't seen the last two pages, Charlie," Nancy said.

He read the report, which contained several redacted names, then looked up at Nancy, who nodded. "Yeah, I get it. She was accused of stalking an airman, even attacking his new girlfriend. She avoided a disciplinary hearing by leaving the service. Honorable discharge, even."

"So maybe she also had problems with Nathan, if she has a history of being unable to let go," Ruth observed.

"That's certainly possible, but as for killing him, that's still unclear. Ms. Brown might have an alibi for that night," DuPree said, looking over at Nancy. "Detective?"

Nancy nodded. "We always start with the obvious—where were the people who knew him best? I interviewed Anna and Max Mitchell the morning after the attack. Anna claimed to be at her apartment and Max was at a local café. I was able to verify Max's alibi. Patricia Azok was at her place, with Steven Azok watching her front door, as we already know."

Charlie thought about it for a moment. "How do we know for certain that Anna was at home? Are there parking lot cameras at her building, as with Patricia's?"

DuPree looked at Nancy, who nodded. "Let me follow up on that."

"You might want to see if there's a back window to her apartment. Anna knows how to make a quick exit," Charlie suggested.

"Well, if we can't arrest her for shooting Nathan, we still have a good shot—pardon the expression—with Todd Colby's murder," DuPree said with a grim smile.

Nancy held up a second folder, with a New Mexico State Police emblem on the outside. "I can't show you this, but I can tell you that the state crime lab found Anna Brown's prints in Colby's apartment—on the back of the ISIS poster, no less. Plus a few blond hairs in the hall beside his bed that apparently belong to a woman. If we get a sample of Anna's DNA, we might find a match."

"Aren't her fingerprints enough?" Ruth asked.

"More is better. A defense attorney might argue that the fingerprints on the poster only prove she handled it, maybe before it was placed in Colby's trailer. Still incriminating, but less so," Dupree pointed out.

"I see," Ruth replied.

"So circumstantial evidence suggests that Anna may have had a motive to kill Nathan—extreme jealousy—and that she was involved with Colby in some way. Maybe they also had a relationship that . . . went south," Charlie said.

"Or she used him to get the explosives, then created the bomb that blew Azok's body apart, at the same time framing him for Nathan's murder," Nancy suggested.

"But she didn't know Azok had a clear alibi for that shooting, did she?" Charlie asked.

"This is getting complicated," Ruth said, shaking her head.

"How will you put all this together to charge her with . . . whatever crimes she's actually committed?"

"That's the problem. We have all this circumstantial evidence, but nothing solid—not yet, anyway," DuPree said.

"But Anna's starting to make mistakes now, like getting caught in Nathan's apartment," Charlie concluded. "So if we can increase the pressure a little more, maybe she'll crack."

"But what about the terrorist guy the FBI arrested?" Ruth asked. "Does he know Anna? Could he be working with her?"

"Consensus among our department is that the guy is a nutcase who's too stupid to have done the deed, and he may have even been out of state when Whitaker was shot. The witness who came forward with that information isn't quite sure, unfortunately. The Feds are trying to clarify the issue," DuPree said.

Nancy nodded. "So Charlie, would you be willing to give the Back Up staff some face time, maybe putting more pressure on Anna? We're trying to get a judge to force the cloud vendor to give up Nathan's user name. We're hoping that whatever Nathan was saving in those files may provide enough evidence to charge Anna, or at least clarify a motive. Unfortunately, the opportunity to access that information hasn't come through yet."

"Can the state attorney general call the vendor and ask for an immediate response? Or maybe the governor, or one of our two senators?" Ruth suggested. "Terrorism is a big concern."

"Good idea," DuPree agreed. "I'll pass that along to our legal people."

"If Anna discovers just how close she is to being arrested, there will be problems," Charlie suggested. "I'm guessing she already has an escape plan."

"We're having her apartment watched, beginning this eve-ning, and we're hoping you might want to go over to Back Up for a little undercover work. Stir the pot," Nancy suggested.

"Neither of us can do this, she'd behave perfectly. But you might be able to get her angry. You're good at that, Charlie," DuPree said.

"You mean I can be really annoying," Charlie said with a smile.

"Not nearly as much as Gordon, but you have a greater stake in all this," DuPree pointed out.

"Isn't that dangerous, if Anna really is a killer—the killer?" Ruth asked. "Has she been the one taking shots at him? What about the firebomb?"

"Charlie will be armed," Nancy said. "She's more likely to flee than risk a close-quarter shootout."

"I'll carry my Beretta," Charlie said. "And my backup knife."

"And you'll also be wired," DuPree added, placing the small device on the desk.

"Finally, we're getting to the real reason you guys came here today," Charlie said, rolling his eyes.

DuPree nodded. "We spent the morning planning all this."

"Just be safe, Charlie. We'll be listening in," Nancy assured. "But there's something else you might want to know . . ."

Chapter Twenty

Charlie arrived at the Back Up office a little after one thirty, having made a quick call to Patricia. She welcomed his visit and the offer to search for the potential user name necessary to access Nathan's mysterious account.

Pulling into the parking slot beside Max's old Jeep, he noted that both Patricia and Anna's vehicles were in their usual slots. Of course he knew Anna's vehicle would be there, since he'd been tracking it from his cell phone ever since Russell had emailed him the app and codes for the GPS bug Charlie had placed the other night. Gordon had the codes as well.

Quickly Charlie adjusted the small audio bug DuPree had required. It was attached to him near the groin and tended to shift. "Can you hear me now?" he joked, then climbed out of the rental car. A vehicle horn from somewhere around the corner verified that Nancy and Gordon were in position to listen, but not be seen. Now all he had to do was carry out the plan.

Five minutes later, he was quietly looking around the outer office, searching behind posters and wall photos while Patricia and Max were working at their desks. Currently they were taking turns calling employers who were part of the program, trying to get work assignments for vet clients. Anna had greeted him with cold politeness, then quickly left the room.

Not finding anything written onto what he was checking, he took notes on the subjects of the images instead. The photographs included a Huey slick rising from a Vietnamese fire base, a Navy Intruder aircraft launching from a carrier, an Abrams in Baghdad, a Hummer in 'Stan, and so forth. He noted anything that might serve as a user name, wanting to look busy for Anna's sake.

After that, he examined the file cabinet in the front office, looking at the names or words on folders, jotting down a few that were written in a different color ink. Several minutes later he abandoned the pretense and stepped through the doorway into Anna's office. She'd been standing, apparently watching, but sat down in her desk chair after he entered.

"I'll try to keep out of your way, Anna, but this is the only place I haven't checked. Patricia and Max have already gone over their work areas, and I assume you've done the same."

"Of course. Go ahead and look around, but I've got a lot of work to catch up on."

"That new system Patricia wanted?"

She nodded.

"How many clients were paid in cash since Back Up began operations? Any idea?" he asked, approaching her desk.

She shrugged. "More when we began than now. Still, I keep reminding Patricia that many homeowners prefer to pay in cash.

Those jobs were often just one or two days long, and the amounts rarely exceed a few hundred dollars."

He nodded. "But every dollar helped the vets still looking for permanent work. I spoke to some of them on the list Patricia provided, and there were a few that admitted underreporting their income. You knew about that?"

"It's not my place to ask. I'm the bookkeeper, and my job has always been to hold back ten percent of what they declared. I never questioned their honesty. Those men and women need every dollar," she said.

"So you don't think Back Up deserves an honest and fair commission for tracking down those jobs and placing the vets? Money that makes all this possible."

"That's not what I said."

"Did Nathan know how much skimming was going on?"

"I have no idea what Nathan was thinking," she replied.

"But you got to know him so very well. Intimately, right?"

Her face lit up. "Just do what you came here for, and get your ass out of my office!"

"But didn't you notice that some of the vets payed in cash weren't reporting amounts that matched their agreed-upon work hours and salaries? You had to know what the employer was paying them, since the Back Up staff set up the jobs and settled on the terms," Charlie argued.

Anna didn't comment, but Charlie could see her face turning red. Her fists were clenched, and her eyes were narrowed. Several seconds went by, then she relaxed, at least on the inside, and resumed working at her keyboard.

He felt his own face reddening as well. His father had taught him from childhood to respect women, and he couldn't recall if he'd ever deliberately antagonized a lady. Thinking back, all he could recall was that time with Rose Davis, in the fourth grade. She'd deliberately tripped him in the lunch line, and he'd retaliated by dumping his food tray over her head. He'd ended up in the principal's office, but it had been worth it.

This time, though, there was more than embarrassment at stake. It was time to play his trump card. He wandered over to the wall opposite her desk to view the photo of soldiers being greeted at an airport by relatives and other passengers with handshakes and welcome home signs. He wrote down some of the messages on the signs in his notebook, then moved down to the four-drawer file cabinet in the corner, just a few feet from the entrance to the front office.

Charlie looked at the cabinet itself, opened the file drawers one at a time, taking notes on the contents, before examining the calendar that was fastened to the metal side with magnets. The photo above the dates was of White Sands. He took off the magnets, looked through the previous months, and then put the calendar in place. Again he took notes.

"Hey, what is this?" he said, looking along the gap where the back of the file cabinet was nearly touching the wall.

Hoping he had her attention, he pulled out the cabinet a few inches, then put his pen and the notebook in his jacket pocket. He reached into the gap and brought out a blue Post-it note, which had been in his pocket until just now.

"This was attached to the wall behind the cabinet with some poster putty," he announced. "You hide it there, Anna?"

She stood. "What does it say?"

Charlie looked down at the writing. "Anna at Brown, and some gibberish. Capital I, then lower case pa, number 2, lower case tfot, upper case US, lower case o, then an upper case A. That gibberish sounds like a password, doesn't it? And that's your user name, right?"

"Not even close. My user name here is abrown at backup dot org. You planted that, didn't you?" Anna asked. "Trying to get me fired."

"Nice try," he replied. "But since you insist this isn't yours, I know you won't mind checking it out," he said, stepping toward her desk and handing her the paper.

"Like hell I will. You're playing some sick game and it ends right now." She pointed toward the door. "Out!"

"Okay," Charlie replied, turning on his heels and walking back into the outer office. Behind him, Anna slammed the door and he heard the faint click of a lock. Patricia and Max looked up, clearly surprised.

"I think I may have annoyed your bookkeeper," Charlie said softly, his hands out, palms up. "Sorry for interrupting your work."

"What did you say to her anyway?" Max asked, rising to his feet, his face flushed. "Anna is part of our team and she deserves respect."

"It's okay, Max. There are some additional things I need to tell you about our bookkeeper," Patricia said softly, rolling her chair closer to his desk.

Charlie nodded, standing to one side, his eyes on the door to Anna's office. He had to be patient if this was going to work. Hopefully it wouldn't take long.

Less than three minutes went by, then he heard a click and

Anna's door opened about a foot. She looked out into the office. "I'm sorry and I want to apologize, Charlie. You were just looking for anything that might help us solve Nathan's murder. Let's see if this can get us to that cloud we've all been curious about," she added.

Charlie was surprised, but tried not to show it. The plan wasn't working. Were they wrong about Anna?

Then she stepped into the room, pointing a revolver right at him. "Nobody move until I say so," she ordered coldly. "And you, Charlie, remove the pistol from your belt with two fingers of your left hand and set it on that chair." She nodded toward a wooden chair positioned against the wall beside her office entrance.

"So you accessed the site and looked at the file. Didn't like what you saw, huh?"

"You set me up. Now get rid of your gun, slowly. I'm not going to deliberately miss this time," Anna said.

Charlie complied, seeing the anger in Anna's eyes and hoping her survival instincts would keep her from exploding completely. He would never be able to clear his weapon in time, and she was too far away for him to grab the revolver. Dropping to the floor without cover was a bad move as well, and any shots fired could hit Patricia or Max. He'd stupidly followed his hopes instead of his instincts. The good news was there was backup outside, hearing every word.

"Lock the door, Max," Anna ordered, nodding toward the main entrance to Back Up. "And if you make the wrong move, I'll shoot your new office help," she added, nodding toward Patricia.

"Sure, Anna. But why are you doing this? Did you kill Nathan?" Max said.

She didn't respond, her pistol still directed at Charlie as Max locked the door. "Now sit back down, Max. And you, Charlie, remove your cell phone and toss it into the wastebasket between the desks. Activate anything and I'll shoot Patricia," she added, shifting her aim back and forth between him and the shocked woman still seated at her desk.

He did as she asked, then waited patiently as Patricia and Max were required to do the same with their phones.

"What are you going to do, Anna? We don't know anything that could hurt you, not . . ." Patricia pleaded.

"Until now, sweetie? Just stay calm and don't do anything stupid and you'll be just fine. All you have to do is make sure Charlie and I can get out of here with a minimum of interference. First thing, disconnect the office phone cords and use one of them to tie Max's ankles together. Do it tightly, with the knots in the back, by his heels."

Soon Patricia and Max were on the floor, her tying his legs together at the ankles. Within a few minutes, she was done. "Now sit back down, Patricia. And you, Max, scoot your flabby butt against the wall and sit there. Don't move, or you know what will happen next."

Anna turned to face Charlie, who she'd kept well out of reach. "Okay, Indian scout, take off your jacket and shirt."

"Seriously? I didn't think you liked me," Charlie replied.

"I'm immune to your muscles," Anna replied. "Trust me, you aren't that hot."

He slowly started to remove his jacket. "But I'm a little hot, right?"

"God. Hurry up. Okay, now the shirt."

Charlie did as she asked. "Okay, now it's your turn, Anna."

"I'm so tempted to shoot you and really mess up that six-pack," Anna said. "Turn around slowly. If I find out you're wired . . ."

"You're making me blush."

"How can you tell?" Anna asked.

"Notice my native-born tan? I'm always blushing," Charlie said, hoping to stall as long as possible. Gordon and Nancy already had plenty of time to get into position.

"Just shut up. Now, Patricia, check and see if the duct tape we use for packages is still in your bottom drawer. Good, now take that over to Max and sit down in front of him. He's going to tape *your* feet together, then you'll tape his hands together at the wrists. Charlie will tape your hands after that. Got it, everyone?"

A few minutes later, Patricia and Max were sitting against the wall.

"Okay, Charlie, put on your shirt."

"Disappointed?" Charlie said, slowly going through the motions, but not wanting to piss her off by showing a deliberate stall.

A minute later, she looked out the small window into the parking area. "Looks clear. Now you and I are going outside to my car, Charlie. Here are my keys," she said. "If you do anything stupid I'll shoot you, then come back and get rid of these witnesses as well. If anyone is outside waiting to jump or shoot me, I'll put a bullet in the back of your head. Understand?"

Charlie drove slowly through the older residential neighborhood just east of the remodeled Winrock Shopping Center, glancing in the rearview mirror. Anna was seated in back on the opposite side, where she could see and shoot him through the gap in the seats.

He'd avoided looking in the side mirrors for Gordon and Nancy, hoping that they wouldn't tip their hand too early.

"Where are we going, anyway? If you're planning to leave the city, we're heading in the wrong direction. North or south is quicker."

"Pull into the driveway of that white house on the left, 1013," Anna said, ignoring his comment. She'd calmed down once they were mobile, and he no longer felt like he was in danger of being shot. Anna just wanted to get away.

"A two-car garage, in this neighborhood? Buy this with the money you skimmed from Back Up?" He looked in the rearview mirror and saw she was holding a garage door remote.

"It's not my house, stupid," she muttered, this time with a hint of a grin. The garage door opened, revealing a white, full-sized Ford sedan parked in the right side of the garage. "Pull into the garage, and be careful not to bump into anything. I'll have the pistol barrel in your back, and any sudden jerk and my finger will squeeze the trigger. You've made it this far, Charlie, and if you play your cards right, you'll survive to annoy some other unfortunate woman."

They sat there in the garage for several seconds, the lights on, then she climbed out of the passenger side, never taking her aim away from him. His own Beretta was in her jacket pocket, well out of reach, and from the angle, seated behind the steering wheel, his chances of making a move were limited.

"Stay!" she ordered, walking around the back of the car, then coming up behind him on the driver's side. "Now, get out, slowly."

Charlie sat there, hoping to stall a little longer, looking around and noting that Sheetrock had been attached to the inside wall of the garage, but only halfway up. The job hadn't been finished. On the right side, away from the house, the wallboard was only four feet high. In the rear of the garage was a counter that ran along the wall, and above, several empty shelves. He was searching for any kind of tools that might serve as a weapon. "What about the keys? Won't you need them?"

"You're so thoughtful, Charlie, nice-looking too, and smart. We could have made a good couple, if you'd only been a little more . . . dishonest. You're not the love them and leave them type. I've seen the way you look at Ruth. Just be careful, though, for the next few minutes, if you ever want to see her—or anything—again."

"You killed Nathan because he dumped you, is that it? Stealing from him wasn't enough?" he said, then immediately realized that was a stupid thing to bring up this late in the game. If he was shot, she might also discover the wire he was wearing.

"Keep pushing and I'll change my mind about letting you live," she uttered, cocking the hammer on her revolver.

"Sorry. Remember, no noise. A gunshot will gather way too much attention," he urged. "Don't blow your getaway by blowing me away.'

"Just get out, asshole, and stand over in that corner, facing the wall." She nodded toward the left corner of the garage in front of the car. It was just a few steps from the door leading into the house. "That door is locked, so forget about ducking inside. If you turn around and look at me, your tight ass is going to be hamburger and your voice will go up a whole octave."

"Damn. A minute ago, I thought you were finally starting to appreciate me," Charlie said, making sure he followed her instructions to the letter. So far, so good. He'd never been afraid during actual combat, only before and after, but this time he wanted to live more than ever. He was looking ahead to a future with Ruth, and now was no time to take unnecessary risks.

"Stay still, don't get killed," Anna said, walking away. He listened carefully, then heard what sounded like keys. More footsteps headed to his right, then he heard a loud snap, a paper or cardboard crunch. His memory bank of early construction projects suggested she was tearing away some of the Sheetrock.

The money she's skimmed, he realized. She was gathering up her stash.

"You're going to hear me getting into the car, Charlie, but the window is down and I'll have my revolver aimed at your back. Just stay put. Once I back out, I'll lower the door. Then we'll both be on our own."

Chapter Twenty-one

He stayed put. As the noise of the motor raising the garage door started up, Charlie heard a faint thump overhead. Somebody was on the roof. He held his breath, hoping Anna hadn't noticed.

Anna started the Ford's engine, and when the door mechanism stopped, he heard the crunch of tires on the concrete garage floor as she backed out of the garage.

"Stop the car and lower the weapon!" Nancy yelled from somewhere close by.

Charlie spun around and dove to his left, out of Anna's view.

"Do it!" Gordon yelled from above.

Charlie rose to his knees, eyeing the gap on his side of the garage beyond Anna's gold sedan. He thought about it a second before realizing that running outside now could get him shot by a jumpy cop.

Tires squealed and he saw an APD cruiser pulling into the driveway, blocking Anna's escape car. A uniformed officer raced up to the passenger side, riot gun aimed through the open window.

The cop glanced over and saw Charlie, who held up his hands to show he was unarmed. The cop nodded, his weapon still aimed at Anna.

Charlie remained low as Nancy came up, handgun ready, and took Anna's revolver. "Now turn off the engine and step out. Keep your hands where I can see them," Nancy added.

Anna turned off the engine.

"She has my Beretta somewhere," Charlie said, standing up and stepping out of the garage.

"It's on the passenger seat," the officer with the shotgun said.

"Don't shoot," Anna said, lifting her hands off the steering wheel, palms up. "I'm going to open the door."

Once Anna climbed out, she turned, hands behind her back, as Nancy put on the cuffs.

"You okay, pal?" Gordon asked.

Charlie turned around and looked up at his friend, who was crouched, pistol in hand, on the garage roof.

"Yeah," Charlie answered. "Thought it might be you up there, light on your feet. My new guardian angel."

"Float like a butterfly, sting like a bee," Gordon joked, holstering his handgun. "Now I've got to find an easy way back down. That peach tree I climbed was scratchy."

Charlie looked into the garage. "There's a ladder in here. I'll bring it out."

"That'll do."

As Charlie moved the ladder against the side of the garage, he turned his head and saw Anna being placed in the cop car.

"Any idea what's in the dusty gym bag, Charlie?" Nancy called out, looking into the interior of Anna's Ford. "Money? An escape kit?"

"Probably some of the cash she skimmed from Back Up." He turned and pointed into the garage. "It was hidden behind that busted Sheetrock. I wasn't looking, but I heard her break it loose."

Nancy nodded, then came over and gave him a handshake that turned into a hug. "You did a great job, Charlie, and I'm glad you kept it together. I'm sure she killed Nathan, and I was afraid you were next," she added, stepping back. "She almost lost it for a moment."

"Yeah, accusing her of killing Nathan was a dumb thing to say at the time. Oh, is the bug still on?" He glanced down at his crotch. "This thing itches like hell."

"Yeah, thanks for reminding me. While you were stalling we had to get into position," Nancy said. She reached into her jacket pocket, brought out a smartphone, and touched the screen. Several seconds later, she looked up and put the device back into her pocket. "A copy has been delivered to the station's server."

Gordon, off the roof now, stepped up and gave Charlie a hug and a handshake. "You done good! For a moment there, in the Back Up office, Nancy thought we might need to crash the party, especially when Anna started checking you for the wire."

"I'm glad she was in a hurry and didn't order me to 'drop trou.' By then I believed she just wanted to get away clean. Nathan had enough evidence hidden up in those cloud files to send her to prison. His mistake was confronting her first without telling anyone," Charlie said.

"I think Nathan wanted to save Back Up's reputation," Gordon concluded.

"I wonder. Did she kill him to cover up her thefts, or did she finally lose it when she knew that Patricia had won him back?" Charlie asked Nancy.

"Jealousy was always part of the picture," Nancy suggested. "That had to burn."

"And Anna couldn't kill the ex-wife because that wouldn't solve the theft issue," Gordon pointed out.

Nancy looked down the street, noting the arrival of more vehicles, including the crime scene van. "Guys, I've got more work to do, but stay close. On the way over here, I got in touch with DuPree, but I haven't had the time to get him up to speed. He's going to have a lot of questions," she added.

"I'm hoping this is the last of all this. Whoever it turns out to be, I think Captain Whitaker's killer is finally in custody. I'm going to call Ruth at the shop and see how things are going," Charlie said, then noticed both Nancy and Gordon smiling. "What?"

Several minutes later, while the guys were seated on the lawn in the shade, a neighbor man who'd been watching from his porch came up to the yellow crime scene tape and motioned to Charlie. "What's going on with the cops, buddy? Somebody break into Azok's place? Poor guy's suffered enough. I heard he blew himself up the other day. "

Gordon and Charlie exchanged glances, then they both stood and walked over to the stranger. "You're talking about Steven Azok, right?" Charlie prodded. "How long had he been living here?"

"Just about a month, I recall," the man said. "We shared a couple beers on my porch and Steve told me he and his wife were going to be getting back together again. He was thinking about buying this place and fixing it up. I've been wondering why the police never came here after he died."

"He had an apartment as well, so maybe they didn't know about this place. Unfortunately for him, I heard his attempt at reconciliation fell apart," Gordon said.

"Small wonder. Steve had this blond gal coming over at odd hours. Decent-looking too, but not at all friendly. Wouldn't even look at me. Hey, that's her car in the garage," he said. "I remember the bumper stickers."

"Yeah, that's right, bud. By the way, I'm Charlie and this is Gordon."

"Pat Reed," the man said, shaking their hands. "You guys narcs?"

"Can't say," Charlie said. "But you'd better stick around. The detectives are going to want to interview you. Maybe you can help seal the conviction of that terrorist."

"What does that have to do with Azok?" Reed asked.

Just then Charlie heard the door leading from the house into the garage open, and out came Detective DuPree.

"Hey, guys, you'll never guess who's been renting this house," DuPree said.

"Wanna bet?" Gordon replied with a smile. "Detective, you're gonna want to talk to Mr. Reed here. He's got some very interesting information to share about Mr. Azok and a certain lady bookkeeper."

"I hope it helps with the homicide cases. The Arab guy the Feds nailed the other day has an airtight alibi for the Whitaker shooting. All they have on him now is failure to love America," DuPree commented dryly. "They had to let him go."

"It looks like most of the danger has passed, then, from the terrorist angle. Any word from the marshal's service regarding Lawrence Westerfield's status?" Charlie asked.

"According to Stannic, the men captured in New Jersey have been positively identified as participants in his escape. They've already told the Feds that Westerfield claimed to be heading for Canada with another of their crew. They couldn't give any description of that guy, however; he's always worn a mask, even around them. All they said was that the guy acted ex-military, or law enforcement, and had a Southern accent," DuPree added. "Deputy Marshal Stannic has already given Ruth the updates. He's going to make sure Ruth and Rene make it home safely."

"You going to spend the night there?" Gordon asked.

"Probably a good idea," Charlie said, looking forward to seeing her and Rene again, after what could have been his last day in this world.

Gordon and Charlie didn't make it back to the shop before Ruth left to pick up Rene from school, so the guys sent Jake home, then stayed until closing. Charlie called Ruth to check on her, and right away she asked him to come over for dinner and spend the night at her apartment—on the sofa. He agreed, eager to spend whatever time he could with Ruth. They still had a first date to make up and, besides, he could look after her at the same time.

Almost nervous now as he locked the back door, Charlie turned and waved as Gordon drove off, a silly grin on his pal's face. Tomorrow, hopefully, they would be back to close to normal, or as normal as could be in his life. He also knew that his own car would be available again and he could pick it up at impound. The rental was fine, but it wasn't a Charger.

The drive to her apartment building was routine, but Charlie found himself shaking just a little as he pulled up into the covered parking lot for residents. There was an open slot next to Ruth's small sedan. Luck was certainly on his side at the moment. It had been a long day. He was feeling weary and worn-out and what kept his head up was knowing he'd be seeing Ruth. Any time with her was the bright spot in his day.

Charlie glanced around, noting that most of the parking spaces were in use. This building catered to an older clientele, mostly retired couples, and Ruth and Rene were as safe here as anyplace in the city. Stepping out of the car, he thumbed the key fob to lock up and walked toward the main entrance. A tall, older woman with silver hair and a long print dress had her back to him, reaching into the backseat of a car for a bag of groceries.

"Hi, Charlie!" came a distinctive male voice as the woman turned to face him.

He instantly recognized Ruth's ex-husband, Lawrence, who was disguised as a woman. Charlie reached down for his Beretta. Suddenly his body was wracked with agonizing pain. He turned his head as he fell to the asphalt, realizing he'd just been tased. A man wearing a camo mask and ball cap was standing there.

"Don't fight it," the guy ordered in a Southern drawl. He lowered the Taser device in his left hand, but raised a pistol in his right.

There was a small plop, and Charlie looked down through watery eyes at a tranquilizer dart stuck in his gut. As he fumbled for his pistol, Charlie felt a massive impact at the back of his head and everything went dark.

Charlie woke up on his back upon a cold, hard-metal, uneven surface. He was covered by some kind of cheap tarp, judging from the strong, plastic smell of the material. His head was throbbing and his hands were tied behind his back with what felt like rope. He tried to roll over to relieve the cramp in his arms, then realized his hands were also connected to some unyielding surface.

As his thoughts cleared, he discovered he was tied to the bed of a pickup and not a van, based upon the roar of the road and the rush of wind across the open bed that caused the tarp to flap up and down. The tarp was tied down as well, but at least he could breathe, and he wasn't wounded, and hopefully not dead and in limbo. He'd suffered the blow to the head and the obvious scrape and scratches incurred when he was thrashing about from being tased, but he knew he'd be capable of fighting back when the opportunity came.

He extended his legs, probing the bed of the pickup and restoring circulation at the same time. Charlie was grateful that he was the only person back here. On the down side, Gordon was probably at home, and Turner was watching over Dawud Koury and his family, which meant he'd be elsewhere. He could use some help right now.

With no idea where he was, or where Ruth's ex and his masked companion were taking him, Charlie knew that his captors had kept him alive only because killing him outside the apartment would gather way too much attention and leave a mess. There was no doubt in his mind, once Westerfield had shown himself, that this was intended to be a one-way trip, and not to Canada. He and

Gordon had destroyed Westerfield's attempt to kidnap Ruth and their son a few years ago, and this had led to the man's arrest by the FBI. If they wanted him to dig his own grave, at least he could deny them that final indignity. Someone besides him was going to be hurt tonight. There was no way Charlie was going down on his knees and submit to a shot in the back of his head.

Not knowing how much time he had, though, Charlie assessed his options. He was still wearing his boots and belt, and didn't have any way of knowing what was still in his pockets. Naturally his weapon and cell phone were gone. The phone itself had no doubt been disabled or trashed. What he needed most, right now, was figuring out how to free his hands.

Charlie tugged to the left, then right, confirming that he'd been anchored to opposite sides of the pickup bed with ropes attached to the screw eyes often used to tie down loads. He was able to sit up a little, but it strained his arms and back, so he lay back. All he could do at the moment was try and loosen the knots around his wrists—if he could reach with just his fingers. He could also listen and guess if and when they slowed down going through a village or town. Maybe he could yell and gather some attention, or pass by a big truck and get spotted by the driver. Unfortunately, that might get an innocent citizen shot. He'd have to decide instantly if the opportunity arose, weighing the risks.

The pickup continued at highway speeds for an estimated half hour or more, then the truck slowed. The occasional passing vehicle told him they were most likely on a two-lane road. If they'd left Albuquerque on the interstate, they would've taken an exit before he had regained consciousness. The pickup turned off onto bumpy, uneven ground. The driver geared down and they fishtailed slightly. That suggested sandy ground, which didn't rule out many locations in New Mexico. He sat up the best he could to avoid smashing his head against metal with every bump.

There was the vague scent of pine, or juniper, which suggested they'd left the highway in the vicinity of the Sandia or Manzano Mountains. That's where the forests lay, at least considering the time period he estimated. Until he got a glimpse of the horizon again, however, it was only a guess. He could also be in the Jemez Mountains farther to the northwest.

He was bounced around for several minutes and at one point it sounded like they were stuck in the sand or mud. The tires had spun and whipped back and forth, and he'd smelled hot exhaust. Finally, just about when he was wondering how much more he could remain in a slanted, seated position, they came to a halt, though the motor was still running. Charlie lay back down, trying to recharge his muscles and be ready when the time came.

It was very dark, with just a crescent moon high in the sky. Someone untied the tarp and threw it up and off of him. "Get your side, Larry," he heard Westerfield's partner order from the driver's side of the pickup bed.

Westerfield cleared his throat. "Shine your light on Charlie first, Porter. He's a troublesome bastard and he might have untied a rope. I'm not reaching in there until I know both his hands are secure."

"No lights, Larry," Porter ordered. "Even here, there might be some idiot hanging out, jacking deer, who'll spot us."

"But they wouldn't hear the truck? Just do it. That's what I'm paying you for," Westerfield snapped.

"Okay, but it's your sorry ass too. I'm not the one who's going back to jail for life."

Charlie closed his eyes once he heard the flashlight click on, not wanting to ruin his night vision.

"Afraid of the dark, Charlie?" Westerfield said.

Charlie coughed.

"Hope you're not coming down with something," Ruth's ex said with a chuckle. "Okay, it's loose, Porter," he added, pulling the tarp off the truck bed onto the ground.

Charlie felt a tug on his arms and then the release of pressure. Westerfield had also unfastened the rope that anchored his left arm to that side of the truck bed. It was still too early to make a move. He needed to be out of the pickup first.

Instead of rolling over onto his side, he waited until the second rope was loose. Once that was done, he sat up slowly and looked to his right, where he'd heard Porter's voice. There was enough light to see that the man was still wearing that camo mask, the kind bow hunters used to hide in blinds and ambush deer. In a warped way, that gave Charlie some hope.

"Stay still, it might keep you from being shot," Westerfield ordered as he walked slowly around to the tailgate, aiming what looked like Charlie's Beretta. The masked man remained at the other end of the pickup bed beside the driver's door, his light on Charlie.

"Now scoot toward me," Westerfield ordered.

"Okay, Larry," Charlie said, eager to put some motion to his muscles and ease the cramps and aches.

"That's Mr. Westerfield to you, Indian."

"Whatever you say, Pale Face," Charlie replied.

Porter laughed.

Charlie continued inching along the pickup bed toward the tailgate, pulling himself with his legs, one at a time. He was sweating now, and the ropes around his wrists seemed a little looser, but not enough to slip them off. The needle-sharp pain of restoring circulation required him to focus on the immediate problem—survival.

When Charlie's feet reached the tailgate, Larry stepped back, taking the flashlight from his companion. Porter came up beside Charlie, aiming a revolver with his gloved right hand. In his left hand, also gloved, was a large machete.

"Okay, Charlie, slide off the tailgate onto your feet," Larry ordered. "Don't even think of making a run for it."

Charlie complied, now certain he knew Larry's plan. He had to keep him talking, because every second was important. Any lie would help. "So you were responsible for the shootings and threats, Larry. You want my death to look like the work of a terrorist. But why kill Nathan Whitaker? You or your sniper missed me by three feet."

"That wasn't us, Mr. Henry. We didn't arrive in Albuquerque until three days after it started," Porter protested.

"I should have been so lucky, having some Arab nutjob killing you first. It would have saved me the trouble and I could have gone straight to Central America a happy camper," Larry replied. "I'm an opportunist, though, and with the money I'd kept stashed in a few places—minus Mr. Porter's fee—I'll be able to live the rest of my life elsewhere. For you, however, it's the end of the road. Or trail of the Great Spirit, I guess."

"What about the woman you abused for so long? Your son?"

Charlie asked, then turned to face the masked man. "Don't take part in hurting a mother and child for this perv's gratification, Mr. Porter," he added.

Westerfield chuckled. "Don't worry, Charlie. I'd considered punishing her, but this terrorist opportunity provides me with such a gift. There's no way I can be blamed for taking you out now. It's a perfect setup. I've even printed up a message announcing the latest ISIS victory against the American dogs—you. Copied right off a local news website. It'll be found on your decapitated body, of course."

"So you don't know they've already caught the killer. It was actually a woman, not a man," Charlie responded, hoping to stall a little longer.

"Nice try, Charlie. It's time now, Porter," Larry added.

"Step away from the tailgate, Mr. Henry. Slowly," the masked man ordered, motioning with his revolver barrel.

Charlie took a reluctant step, his eyes on the mask. "Make Larry do his own dirty work, Mr. Porter. He's a gutless, child-abusing, wife beater who stole millions from people like you and me. Don't be his patsy."

"Shoot the bastard, Porter. That's what I'm paying you for," Westerfield ordered, aiming the flashlight at Porter.

Porter pulled the hammer back on the revolver. Charlie tensed, watching his trigger finger.

Charlie dove beneath the tailgate. Porter fired, and there was a gasp. Charlie looked up and saw Lawrence's hand at his bloody face. Lawrence dropped to the sand, thrashed around for a few seconds, and then remained still.

Porter stepped over, grabbed the Beretta off the ground, and turned toward Charlie. "Come on out, soldier, but stay on your knees. I won't shoot unless you grab for a weapon."

"What just happened?" Charlie asked.

"When I found out who you really were, I wasn't about to kill one of my own, not unless I had to. I was paid a shitload of money to get Westerfield here, then take you out. He's a sick, sorry bastard that needed to die. I'm going to be leaving in a few minutes, so don't screw around and get yourself hurt. You good with that?"

"I'm good."

Charlie watched as Porter, which was clearly not his real name, tossed the machete into the bushes, then crouched down beside the body and removed the contents of the dead man's pockets. Porter took the wallet and cell phone, then stood and faced Charlie as he put the items into his jacket pocket.

"I want you to walk maybe twenty feet over there, Charlie, then set your butt on the ground." Porter pointed, then waited until Charlie had complied. Charlie found it a bit awkward to sit down with his hands still bound behind his back.

"Here's your wallet and keys, soldier," Porter announced, dropping them on the ground. "I'm taking your cash, but I'll leave the credit cards and ID. By the time you hike out to the road it'll be close to dawn and I'll be long gone. A final warning, though. Learn something from this and don't let yourself get kidnapped again. It was too damned easy."

As the pickup drove away, lights on, Charlie looked at the license plate codes despite knowing that the tags had probably been stolen. Then he scrambled to his feet and walked over to search in the bushes for the machete. It had landed in a cluster of scrawny-looking sagebrush, nestled on some branches about a foot off the ground, positioned almost horizontally. He balanced on one foot, raising the other to push and lift the long blade out from the bush. It took a few tries, but within seconds the machete was on the ground. He pushed it a little farther away from the brush to give himself room to sit down beside the blade.

A few minutes later enough of the rope had been cut for him to slip off the rest. Charlie's hands and arms ached, but at least he was free, and he hadn't cut himself except for a few scrapes and scratches. This time he stood easily, then looked around, gathering his keys and wallet, which, as Porter had said, was only missing the cash.

Lawrence was still dead, and the thought of going through his pockets was disgusting, but maybe there was something that had been missed. He established quickly that Porter had been very thorough. All he found was a pack of Tic Tacs, a small spiral notebook, and a pen.

He kept those, but decided to leave the machete behind. Carrying an eighteen-inch-long blade would send the wrong kind of message to any potential driver willing to stop once he made it back to the highway.

If Gordon or law enforcement was looking for him, and he was certain that was already a fact, there was little chance they'd find him outright. He had to make his location known, and the first step to getting help was reaching the main road.

Charlie took off at a fast jog, following the pickup tire tracks, hoping it was only a few miles, not ten, before he reached a road and any kind of traffic. The route he was taking right now was north, and in the near horizon was the vague outline of a mountain range that he knew was either the Manzanos or the Sandias.

Both were west of his location. Once he reached either North or South 10, the highway which paralleled the mountains, he could catch a ride back, or at least have someone make a call.

His head still ached, but that was something aspirin would hopefully cure once he was back to civilization. He regulated his breathing and picked up the pace. Charlie had grown up running long distances on sand and dry earth, and this mountain dirt was hard and rocky in places, easier to traverse as long as he didn't trip over a boulder or twist his ankle. Sunrise was probably hours away, so he'd have to do the best he could with only stars and the trace of the moon to light the way.

His watch had been taken off to make room for his rope hand-cuffs, but Charlie had a good sense for time. It only took about an hour-long run for him to see the highway in the distance. Another fifteen minutes and he was on the pavement, now walking and cooling off after the run through the forest. He'd violated one of the Navajo taboos, taking from the dead, but those Tic Tacs had helped keep his mouth moist.

Passing a mile post along the road, he wondered, for the first time, was that the distance from the last community, or the distance to the next? He suspected, from his current position relative to the mountains, that the next community he'd be reaching was Tijeras, on the south end of the mountain pass. There lay the twin highways of I-40 and old Route 66.

Just as he was trying to estimate the remaining distance, he saw approaching headlights as a vehicle came around a curve in the steep side-canyon road. Charlie stepped a few feet out into the oncoming lane and held up his hands, waving. The vehicle was some kind of van or pickup, and as it closed the distance Charlie stepped back, still in the headlights, and beckoned for the person to stop.

The pale green pickup came to a stop about fifty feet away, and Charlie realized it was a forest service truck, complete with emergency running lights atop the cab. His day was looking up.

Chapter Twenty-two

The sun was high in the sky and there were over a dozen people standing in the lobby at the downtown Albuquerque police station when New Mexico State Police Officer Leon Nez escorted Charlie into the building through the law-enforcement-only entrance. Charlie was dragging, having spent hours traveling and telling his story at the spot down the forest road where Lawrence Westerfield had taken the dirt nap.

The first person he saw was Ruth, who smiled widely as their eyes met. She came forward in a rush, giving him such a welcoming hug that it almost made up for last night. He felt her tears on his cheek, and he would have kissed her if it hadn't been for the news cameras and reporters.

"You know about Lawrence?" Charlie whispered, lowering his head so a lip reader couldn't pick up his words. There were two cameras directed at them now.

"All I care about is that you're safe, Charlie. Is it over now?"

she whispered, stepping back, placing her palms against his chest as she stared into his eyes.

"I think so," he answered, unable to suppress a smile.

Hearing footsteps, they turned as Gordon, Nancy, and Detective DuPree walked over to join them.

Charlie got hugs from Nancy and Gordon. DuPree shook Charlie's hand and even smiled.

"Sorry we didn't catch up to you," Gordon apologized. "There was video of the attack and the Chevy they dumped you inside, but we ran into a hitch when the car was found just a few blocks away in a parking lot, along with the smashed remains of your dearly departed cell phone. That's where they must have transferred you to that pickup."

"We've got an ATL out of the truck with the plates you provided, but no luck so far," DuPree cut in. "Medina here thinks that Mr. Porter may have already switched vehicles. We don't know what to look for now. Wish we could put a face to him."

"The man may have left some trace DNA in that vehicle," Nancy said, "but he's got several hours' head start. He could be out of state by now. Or in Juarez."

Charlie nodded. "That would be my guess. I think the guy was a vet, so fingerprints should be on file. Maybe, at some point, he wasn't wearing gloves."

"Excuse me, people, but I need to break up this party and interview Mr. Henry one more time," SAC Jackson stated, walking over to join them. "You're invited to attend, Detectives," he noted to Nancy and DuPree. "Ready, Charlie?"

"Just a minute, Agent Jackson." Charlie turned to Gordon.

"Jake might need some help at the shop. You and Ruth don't have any reason to stick around, and I have a friend keeping an eye on the Koury family." Charlie nodded to Gordon, knowing he'd get the message. "I'll catch a ride to work from here." He was still holding Ruth's hand, and gave it a squeeze.

"You might want to get some sleep first, Charlie," Gordon suggested. "My place, maybe?"

"I'll see how alert I am once I'm done here."

"He didn't take your keys?" Gordon asked.

"Miraculously, no."

"Porter must have liked you, pal. Getting new keys, changing locks, canceling credit cards, that'd be a hassle," Gordon said.

"Somewhere in there was a conscience. He's killed before, though. It didn't seem to bother him at all, taking out . . ." Charlie looked down at Ruth. "Sorry. I don't mean to sound cold."

"I understand," she replied. "But you'd better get started here with the FBI," she added. "The sooner you're done, the sooner you'll be back with us."

Back with us. Charlie liked the sweet sound of that, or maybe it was just Ruth's slightly deeper voice, a beautiful sound he'd only heard when they were alone. He gave her hand a final squeeze, ignored Gordon's smug smile, and then nodded to the SAC. "Let's do this."